Welcome to the No. 1 Ladies' Detective Agency

The story so far ...

At a local wedding, Mma Ramotswe met a handful of old acquaintances. The first was a long-lost friend, Calviniah, who confided in Mma Ramotswe that her daughter had inexplicably become estranged from the family. The other was a woman who had simultaneously lost all her money and found solace in a mysterious, self-styled reverend. Having little work on at the agency, Precious and Grace decided to investigate these curious situations.

Meanwhile, part-time detective Charlie was preoccupied with matters of the heart. His beloved Queenie-Queenie was determined to set a date for their marriage, but with little money to pay for a dowry, Charlie was forced to consider a very dubious business opportunity.

By Alexander McCall Smith

How to Raise an Elephant

an Elephant

ALEXANDER McCALL SMITH

ABACUS

First published in Great Britain in 2020 by Little, Brown
This paperback edition published in 2021 by Abacus

1 3 5 7 9 10 8 6 4 2

A CIP catalogue record for this book is available from the British Library.

ISBN: 978-0-349-14410-8

Typeset in Galliard by M Rules
Printed and bound in Great Britain by Clays Ltd, Elcograf S.p.A

Papers used by Abacus are from well-managed forests
and other responsible sources.

Abacus
An imprint of
Little, Brown Book Group
Carmelite House
50 Victoria Embankment
London EC4Y 0DZ

An Hachette UK Company
www.hachette.co.uk

www.littlebrown.co.uk

This book is for Mats and Cecilia Ögren Wanger,
Swedish friends of Botswana.

Chapter One

No Double Bed

Precious Ramotswe, owner and only begetter of the No. 1 Ladies' Detective Agency – established to deal with the problems of ladies, and others – looked across her office towards the desk occupied by Grace Makutsi, former secretary and distinguished graduate – with ninety-seven per cent in the final examinations – of the Botswana Secretarial College. The sun was streaming through the high window behind Mma Ramotswe's desk, sending a narrow butter-yellow beam to illuminate small particles of floating dust, just perceptible, feather-light, moving up and down, sometimes sliding sideways in obedience to the invisible currents in the room. But for the most part the air was still – it being that sort of day, sluggish and non-committal. The sort of day on which something might happen, but was more likely not to.

It was not unusual for Mma Ramotswe to look up and see Mma

Makutsi staring back at her; and the same thing might be said for Mma Makutsi, who would suddenly lift her gaze from the papers in front of her and notice Mma Ramotswe watching her thoughtfully. Neither minded this – indeed, both were used to it, and when either of them was out of the office for whatever reason, the other would find that she missed seeing her colleague there at her desk when she looked up. This was particularly true for Mma Makutsi, for whom Mma Ramotswe was a reassuring presence every bit as significant, every bit as reassuring, as the great rock dome of Kgale Hill on the outskirts of town, or the deep waters of the Limpopo River, just a few hours off to the east, or the sandhills of the Kalahari over to the west. These were all geographical facts, just as Mma Ramotswe herself seemed to be a geographical fact. She was simply there – as predictable and as constant as any of these things. And her voice was as familiar and as loved as the voice of the doves inhabiting the acacia tree behind Tlokweng Road Speedy Motors; indeed, she would not have been surprised had Mma Ramotswe suddenly started to coo, just as those doves did. Mma Makutsi could not imagine Botswana without those doves, and she could not imagine it without Mma Ramotswe; if she were not there, then it would be just any other country; with her it was something special – it was Mma Ramotswe's place, a place bathed in the warmth of her presence as effectively as the sun blesses the land each morning with its warming rays.

Now Mma Ramotswe looked across the office and noticed that Mma Makutsi was looking back at her. There was something different about Mma Makutsi, she thought, and it took Mma Ramotswe a little while to work out what it was. It was not what she was wearing: she had on the green dress that for some reason she liked to wear on Fridays – Mma Makutsi was a creature of habit. No, it was something else, and when Mma Ramotswe realised what it was she reproached herself for not noticing it at once. Mma Makutsi's glasses, normally large and round, like outsize swimming goggles, had shrunk. They were still round, but the lenses were considerably smaller – tiny discs, by comparison, no bigger than the coins to be found in a pocket of small change. Any detective worth her salt would have spotted the change immediately, thought Mma Ramotswe. She had always prided herself on her powers of observation, but it was hardly very observant to miss a detail such as this. Of course, she had the excuse of the familiar: the eye is lulled into complacency when contemplating those things and people we see every day.

'Your glasses, Mma,' said Mma Ramotswe.

Mma Makutsi leaned back in her chair. She was smiling. 'I wondered when you were going to notice, Mma. Do you like them? They're new.'

Mma Ramotswe knew from long experience that Mma Makutsi was sensitive to criticism. The only response one could safely give if asked one's opinion on any aspect of her appearance was to say that it was perfect. Any reservation, even in the form of a momentary hesitation, could give rise to a display of hurt feelings that could quickly become a more than momentary sulk; not prolonged beyond the evening, of course – Mma Ramotswe had never known Mma Makutsi to keep a state of huff going for more than a few hours, but it was best to avoid such occasions altogether, she thought.

'They are very fine glasses,' she said. 'They are clearly very fashionable.'

It was just the right thing to say. Mma Makutsi touched the spectacles gently, repositioning them slightly on the bridge of her nose. 'I saw them in a magazine, Mma,' she said. 'One of those very famous actresses was wearing them.'

3

'Which famous actress, Mma?'

Mma Makutsi shrugged. 'Oh, I don't remember the names of any of those people. But they are very famous, Mma. They go to parties and there are many photographers at those parties. Snap, snap, snap – so that we can all see what was happening at the party even if we never get an invitation.'

'So, this lady – whoever she was – was wearing your spectacles, Mma?'

'The exact same,' said Mma Makutsi. 'And there was a list at the bottom of the page of what she was wearing, and how much it cost. They gave the name of the shop where you could order spectacles like that. It's down in Cape Town; they do not sell these glasses in Botswana. You have to write off for them. These are Cape Town glasses – everyone is wearing them down there, they say.'

Mma Ramotswe wondered whether it was really a model who had been wearing them. 'I think that lady might have been paid to wear them, Mma. I think that is possible, because otherwise they would not have published the details of where you could buy them.'

'It does not matter,' said Mma Makutsi. 'She might have been a model – who knows?'

Mma Ramotswe thought about this. 'If she was a model, Mma, do you think she was really short-sighted, or would she have been wearing them just for the photograph?'

Mma Makutsi hesitated. 'It is possible, Mma, that she was short-sighted. I could not tell from the photograph.'

'You're right, though, Mma,' said Mma Ramotswe. 'It doesn't matter whether or not she needed them. The point is: they look very good on you, Mma.'

'You're not just saying that, Mma?'

Mma Ramotswe shook her head. 'I am not just saying it, Mma Makutsi. I am sitting here thinking it as well. I am sitting here thinking: those spectacles look very good on Mma Makutsi. They are a big improvement.'

As soon as she said this, Mma Ramotswe realised that she had said the wrong thing. She was about to rephrase her words, but it was too late.

'What was wrong with my old glasses, Mma? Why did they need improvement?'

'There was nothing wrong with them,' said Mma Ramotswe hurriedly. 'They were very fine glasses. It's just that these new ones are even finer.' She repeated, even more emphatically, 'Even finer, Mma.'

Mma Makutsi seemed appeased. She looked at her watch, and Mma Ramotswe noticed that she was peering at it more closely than usual. Perhaps it was the light, as the sun had just gone behind a cloud and it was darker in the office than it had been a few minutes earlier.

'I think it is time for tea, Mma,' she said. 'I shall make it.'

She got up from her desk and crossed over to where the kettle was perched on top of the filing cabinet. As she pressed the switch, she said to Mma Ramotswe, 'Have your new neighbours moved in now, Mma?'

Mma Ramotswe nodded. 'They have, Mma. I watched their furniture arrive this morning. It was very interesting, Mma.'

And it had been, because there are few things more interesting in neighbourhood life than to witness the unpacking and the installation of one's neighbours' effects. People can say all sorts of things about themselves, can portray themselves in all sorts of false lights should they choose to do so, but their furniture is incapable of lying. Your furniture always tells the truth about you, and if the furniture is unvarnished, then so too is that truth.

The furniture van, a lumbering pantechnicon, had pulled up outside the neighbour's house at seven in the morning, at a time when Mma Ramotswe had just served breakfast to Motholeli and Puso. Mr J. L. B. Matekoni always breakfasted early, and he had already driven off in his truck to Tlokweng Road Speedy Motors. An early departure meant that he would beat the morning traffic, which, as was happening everywhere else, was getting worse and worse. Gaborone had grown, and its traffic problem had grown with it, although it was by nowhere near as bad as it was in many other cities. They had discussed that over morning tea in the office a few days earlier, a discussion that had led to a spirited exchange between Charlie, the junior assistant detective and part-time mechanic, and Mma Makutsi. Mma Makutsi had introduced the topic by mentioning the traffic jams that could now be encountered in Nairobi.

'I've heard that there are people who live in their cars these days,' she said. 'It takes so long to drive into work that they don't bother to drive back. They just pull in to the side of the road, change into their pyjamas, and sleep in the car. Then they reverse back to the office the next morning.'

Charlie had laughed. 'You cannot live in a car,' he said. 'Where would you cook your meals? Where would you go to the bathroom? Those are very important questions, Mma Makutsi.'

Mma Makutsi had dismissed these objections. 'I'm not saying that I have seen people doing these things, Charlie. I'm simply telling you what I have read in the newspaper – or it might have been a magazine. Somewhere I read it. They called them the "car people". That is what they said. They said they take their food with them. They did not say anything about the bathroom.'

Mma Ramotswe had expressed the view that it would help if the government spent more on public transport. 'We need more buses,' she said. 'We need more of these big buses that take a whole lot of people. One hundred people, sometimes, all in one bus.'

'The government says it has no money,' said Mma Makutsi. 'They say it is not their job to buy these buses.' She paused. 'Anyway, even if we had more buses, there are still too many cars. Too many people are buying cars and then driving them round. What can you expect but traffic jams if people have too many cars?'

Charlie frowned. 'So what do we do?'

Mma Makutsi had the answer. 'We take cars away from people. The government should say: there are too many cars, and so you cannot have a car any longer. They would give them compensation, of course, but they would take their cars away.'

'Whose cars?' challenged Charlie.

'People's,' said Mma Makutsi.

'Including yours?' Charlie asked Mma Makutsi. 'And Mma Ramotswe's white van? What about that? Should the government take Mma Ramotswe's van away from her?'

Mma Makutsi made a dismissive gesture. 'Of course not, Charlie. I'm not suggesting that anybody should take Mma Ramotswe's van from her. She needs it to get into work.'

'Ha!' crowed Charlie. 'And your car, Mma Makutsi? You have that red car of yours with its big exhaust pipe. Think of all the smoke you make, Mma Makutsi, racing round in that red car. Think of that. And Phuti Radiphuti, too. He has a car with a big engine – I've serviced that engine and so I should know. It is a very thirsty engine, I can tell you. Think of the Limpopo in full flood, and that is how much petrol goes into that engine. Ow!'

Mma Makutsi glared at the young man. 'You're talking nonsense, Charlie. Nobody is going to take my car. I need it to get into work and Phuti uses his car for his furniture business. Our cars would be ... '

'Exempt?' offered Mma Ramotswe.

'Yes,' said Mma Makutsi. 'That's the word: exempt.'

Mma Ramotswe looked down at her desk. Everybody wanted to look after the world, but nobody wanted to give up anything they already had. Mma Makutsi was right when she said there were too many cars, but the business of reducing the number of cars would never be easy. That was particularly so in Africa, where so many people had never had the chance to own a car, and now, just as they were able to afford one, along came people who said they should not have one. And the same thing applied to beef, she thought. Many people had not been able to afford much meat in the past; now, when they could, people who had been eating meat for a long time said it was time for everybody to stop. There was something unfair in that, she thought, and yet we only had one world, and only one Botswana in that world, and we had to look after them both.

But now Mr J. L. B. Matekoni was off to the garage – in his truck, which was not particularly economical to run and not at all green, she suspected – and she had just fed the children, and at that moment the removal van happened to draw up outside the neighbours' house. In such circumstances all that one could do was to tell the children to hurry up and finish their breakfast and get ready for school. Puso, of course, could walk there, as the school was just round the corner, but Motholeli, who was in a wheelchair, could not. On occasion, Puso would push her to school, taking pride in helping his sister, but in this hot weather, with all the dust the heat seemed to bring, Mma Ramotswe preferred to take the chair in her van. She would do that this morning, she thought, and then return to the house so that she could keep an eye on what was going on next door.

She was back at the house after the school run just in time to see the men, who had been perched on the tailgate of the removal van, eating sandwiches, now roll up their sleeves and begin to unload the furniture. This was the interesting part – more interesting, perhaps, than the actual meeting of the new neighbours themselves, whom she had already spotted over the fence when they were viewing their intended purchase. She felt a thrill of excitement, but then, a moment or two later, she felt something quite different. This was doubt. Should she allow herself to take such an interest in the household possessions of her new neighbours, or was this no more than nosiness – the sort of thing that idle village people loved to do because they had nothing better with which to fill their time? The otherwise unoccupied took a great interest in what everybody else had and did. And then they went off and talked about it, sometimes stirring up feelings of jealousy amongst those whose lives were less exciting and less blessed with material goods. Envy was a real problem in villages, where there were plenty of people ready to resent those who had more than they did. It was not an edifying characteristic, and if Botswana had any faults, then this was one of them. It did not help, and people who encouraged it should feel real shame.

She thought about this, and almost persuaded herself that she should turn away and drive off to work, leaving the removal men to do their heaving and carrying unobserved. But then she thought: no harm will be done if I watch, but do not tell anybody about anything I might see. She thought about this for a few moments, closing her eyes, the better to facilitate judgement. Decisions made with closed eyes were, Mma Ramotswe thought, often weightier, more balanced. And now she made up her mind: if she watched, but did not speak about, what was unfolding next door, it would be a perfectly acceptable compromise between natural curiosity and a decent respect for the privacy of others. Her decision made, she settled on her veranda, in a cool spot away from the slowly rising morning sun, with a cup of freshly brewed redbush tea to hand. In that position she watched as the drama of the arrival took place.

Mma Ramotswe watched as the kitchen effects emerged. There was a large fridge, of newish manufacture, which required three men to carry it in, and this was followed by a fancy-looking cooker. This required careful manhandling out of the van and lifting onto a sturdy-looking trolley. On this it was wheeled round to the back of the house from where various shouted instructions emerged as men manoeuvred it into the kitchen. Next came boxes of pots and pans, handles sticking out of splits in the cardboard, and several boxes given over, she thought, to current provisions, judging by the trail of flour that one of them left as it was carried in. Mma Ramotswe smiled at that. It would be a good clue for a detective, she thought, and could imagine what Clovis Andersen, author of *The Principles of Private Detection*, might write about that. *If you find a trail of flour, you can be reasonably sure that somebody has been making their way into or out of a kitchen.* Beyond that conclusion, of course, there would be little one could say.

It took a good hour for the kitchen furniture and equipment to be offloaded and installed. It was now time for Mma Ramotswe to go to work, but she was enjoying herself far too much to do that. There were one or two matters to be dealt with in the office that morning, though none of them was urgent. Mma Makutsi would be there and she could deal with any new business that arose – not that this was likely. For some reason it was a quiet time, and new clients were few and far between. It might be the weather, Mma Ramotswe thought: the heat had been building up steadily, and in hot conditions people tended to behave themselves. Suspected unfaithfulness, the bread and butter of any private detective agency, was seasonal: the hot weather seemed to inhibit it, while the cooler weather brought it on. Clovis Andersen said nothing about this in his book, but then he was used to a climate in which people had the energy to engage in affairs at any time of the year. Here, who could be bothered, in the heat, to flirt with anybody, let alone embark on something more serious?

Of course, temptation could strike at any time, and in any circumstances, and there would always be a trickle of enquiries, no matter what the season was. The previous day they had heard from a prospective client, a woman in Lobatse who had witnessed a small child running up to her husband in a shopping mall. The child had shouted 'Daddy, Daddy' and flung his arms around her husband's legs. 'Silly child,' the husband had said. 'He has mistaken me for his daddy.' But he had been flustered – far more than one might expect an innocent person to be in such circumstances. The child had been retrieved by a young girl who was clearly a nanny, and had been dragged away protesting and still shouting, 'Daddy!' Could the No. 1 Ladies' Detective Agency look into this matter? Of course they could, and Mma Makutsi had agreed to drive down to Lobatse the following week and interview the client about her concerns. 'My husband is a good man,' the woman had said, 'but you know what men are like, Mma. They are not good all the time.'

'The only men who are good all the time,' Mma Makutsi had said, 'are the saints, and they are all dead now, Mma.'

Charlie, who had overheard this conversation in the office, had scowled. 'You have no right to talk about men like that,' he protested. 'There are many men who are good all the time. Many, Mma.'

'Name one,' said Mma Makutsi, adding, 'Apart from Mr J. L. B. Matekoni, of course. He is a very good man on a permanent basis.'

Charlie tried a different tack. 'And women? Are women always good, Mma?'

Mma Makutsi did not reply immediately. Mma Ramotswe, who was amused by this exchange, decided to keep out of it.

At last Mma Makutsi said, 'Women are human, Charlie. That is well known.' She glanced at Mma Ramotswe as she said this. 'That is well known' was Mma Ramotswe's phrase – the clincher of any argument, the settler of any point of dispute. But there were occasions when Mma Makutsi employed it, although she always glanced at Mma Ramotswe as she did so, as if to confirm she had the licence to use it.

'So,' said Charlie, 'if they are human, then they will be just as bad as men. All humans are equal, I think. Isn't that what the Constitution of Botswana says?'

'This has nothing to do with the Constitution of Botswana, Charlie,' snapped Mma Makutsi. 'This is psychology, and there has never been any doubt that women have better psychology than men when it comes to ...' She waved a hand in the air. '... when it comes to these things.'

'What things, Mma?'

'To behaviour,' said Mma Makutsi. 'Women are always thinking of what is best for children, for instance. They think: what is going to make children strong and happy? What is going to make sure that there is food on the table? What is best for everybody? Those are the questions that women are always asking.'

'And men?' Charlie demanded. 'Do men not think about those things too?'

Mma Makutsi replied that men sometimes thought about those things, but they often acted impulsively because they were impatient. Or they acted without thinking because ... well, they didn't think in the same way as women. They thought that something needed to be done, and they did it. They did not think about the consequences.

And that was where the discussion had ended, as the office telephone had rung with another call, and human psychology was left for another day. Now, on her veranda, watching the removal men, Mma Ramotswe thought about the exchange between Mma Makutsi and Charlie, and reflected on the fact that there could be discussions between two people where both were wrong. You might even embody that in one of Clovis Andersen's rules, she thought: *Do not think that in any case where there are two competing arguments one of them has to be right: both can be wrong.*

Her thoughts were disturbed by a shout from one of the removal men, who had stumbled while carrying a small table. The table had landed on his foot and he had shouted out in pain. One of the other men had laughed, calling out some comment about carelessness. Mma Ramotswe was concerned; the man was crouched down now, rubbing his foot, clearly in considerable pain. Instinctively she rose from her seat and made her way to her gate.

'Are you all right, Rra?' she asked.

He looked up. He was a man of about forty, with the lightish brown skin that suggested a touch of San blood somewhere in his ancestry. His shirt was soaked in sweat, under the armpits, along the chest, around the collar.

'I have hurt my foot a bit,' he said. 'But I think it will be all right, Mma.'

He stood up now, wincing slightly as he tested his weight on his foot.

'I have some of that stuff you can rub on your foot,' Mma Ramotswe said. 'You know that green ointment? Zam-Buk? The one that is very good for bruises?'

He shook his head. 'That is kind of you, Mma, but we must

finish this load.' He looked inside the van, and Mma Ramotswe followed his gaze. There were still a few items remaining – bedroom furniture, she noted. She saw a wardrobe, still tied to the side of the van's interior to prevent its toppling over; two chests of drawers; a standing mirror. And then there were the beds. She counted them. One, two, three, four.

The man was looking up at the sky. 'When is it going to rain, Mma?'

Mma Ramotswe sighed. 'I ask myself that every morning, Rra. I go out into my garden and I look at my beans and I think, when is it going to rain? And the beans are thinking that too, I believe.'

The man laughed. 'And the grass. And the cattle. And the snakes down in their holes. They are coughing, I think, because of all the dust – the snakes are coughing.'

Mma Ramotswe smiled. 'That is a very odd thought, Rra. I can imagine a snake would have a long cough – a very long cough.'

She looked into the van again. One of the other men was untying the beds, making them ready for removal. Four beds. Four single beds.

On impulse she asked, 'Are there only four beds, Rra?'

He glanced into the van. 'Yes, there are four. We loaded four, and we shall be unloading four. That is how it works, Mma.'

She thought, *single* beds. She looked at the man. 'No double bed,' she muttered.

The comment had not been addressed to him, but he answered. 'We do not ask about these things, Mma. We are removal men. You give us the furniture; we put it in the van; we drive wherever: one hundred kilometres, two hundred, one thousand if you want to go and live up in Zambia. We will take your things anywhere.'

He looked at her, and then said, 'We do not think about these things, Mma – not in our job.'

She lowered her eyes, chastened. She felt that she wanted to tell him that she was not a gossip, that she was not one of those people who pried into the affairs of others. She wanted to explain to him that she was a detective and that it had become second nature to her to look at the world and then wonder what lay behind the things one saw. But she did not say any of this, because she felt ashamed, and he had his work to do, and she should leave them to it now.

He thanked her for the offer of the ointment and returned to his work. She went back to her veranda, where she finished her cup of redbush tea, and prepared to drive into the office. No double bed, she thought. And this was followed by the thought: this is not my business. It was important to think that particular thought, she reminded herself as she drove off towards the Tlokweng Road and the premises of the No. 1 Ladies' Detective Agency. There are things in this world that are one's business, and things that are not. It was sometimes a challenge to find exactly where the boundary between these two lay, and to act accordingly. That was the challenge. Yet here it was obvious: whether or not one's new neighbours slept in a double bed was no business of anybody but themselves. Others should not even think about it. So she told herself not to think about it, which of course is the surest way of guaranteeing that you will think about exactly the thing you do not wish to think about.

Chapter Two

Late People Talk to Us

Mma Makutsi had not been idle. 'Since you are so late this morning, Mma Ramotswe,' she said, 'I have used the time to go through old files. I have taken out ones that we can get rid of now, I think.'

Mma Ramotswe crossed the office and deposited on her shelf her bag and the keys to her van on her desk. Glancing at Mma Makutsi's desk she saw a pile of brown manila files, papers protruding here and there from between the covers. The sight made her think of the hours of work that each of these represented, and also of what lay behind each and every folder: the human emotions, the plans, the disappointments – and, in some cases at least, the triumphs. One or two of them, she noticed, had a familiar large red sticker on the outside denoting *Payment of Final Bill Pending*. That was a forlorn hope, now, she thought. And then there were the green stickers – not many – that signified *More Developments Possible*. Again, that was unlikely, Mma Ramotswe told herself. She tried to think of recent developments in any of these old cases, and could think of none. Perhaps a rewording of the sticker might be called for: *More Developments Possible, but Unlikely* would be more realistic, she felt.

'You have been very busy, Mma,' she said.

Mma Makutsi studied her fingernails in a vaguely prim manner. 'Well, I thought that it would be a good idea to tackle something that we've been talking about for some time now.' She paused, looking up from her fingernails. 'Talking about, yes, but not getting done.'

Mma Ramotswe was not sure whether there was a note of reproach in Mma Makutsi's voice. It was true that they had been planning to go through the filing cabinet in order to weed out dormant files, and on one or two occasions had almost embarked upon the task, only to be interrupted by the arrival of a client or the ringing of the telephone. There were other routine administrative tasks that needed to be tackled but that had been put off for one reason or another; this one, though, was more pressing than the others as the filing cabinet was now almost full and more recent files had been stacked, in no particular order, on a shelf next to the well-thumbed copy of Clovis Andersen's *The Principles of Private Detection*.

Mma Makutsi picked up one of the files. 'This one, for example, Mma. Remember that man who ran the store and said his wife was having an affair? And then his wife came into the office and said the same thing about him? And we had to sit there with a straight face?'

Mma Ramotswe did remember, and she laughed at the recollection. 'And then they both decided that it was a mistake and got back together.'

There was more. Mma Makutsi lifted up the file and held it over the wastepaper bin. 'And then they argued about who should pay the bill, and neither of them paid.'

'I think we can throw that one away, Mma,' said Mma Ramotswe. 'Case closed.'

The file fell into the bin. It was almost like an act of forgiveness, although there were no witnesses, save the two of them. Mma Ramotswe found herself raising her eyes briefly, almost guiltily, to the ceiling. At school in Mochudi, all those years ago – in that small school perched on top of the hill, with the village beneath it and the sound of cattle bells drifting up on the breeze; there, standing before the class, her teacher, the infinitely patient Mma Kenosi, had told them about the Recording Angel who noted down everything – 'And I mean *everything*, boys and girls, that you do. So even if you do a good deed and nobody is there to witness it, that will be written down.' And at that, she would raise her eyes heavenwards, and thirty-five pairs of eyes watching her would be raised in unison, as if in an orchestrated display. The habits of childhood, instilled by the Mma Kenosis of this life, may be overwritten by the demands of the years, but some vestiges remained – thoughts, ways of doing things, odd beliefs, superstitions ... these things had a power over you that ensured their survival, even if it was in weakened form. And so it was that Mma Ramotswe thought briefly of the Recording Angel as Mma Makutsi tipped the defunct file into the bin. She had long since abandoned belief in such a person, because a moment's thought was enough to explode the notion: how could anybody keep an eye on the millions – no, billions – of good, and bad, deeds that people did every day? Such a task was clearly impossible, even if you believed in angels, which she did not. Well, not *completely*: there were times when you *wanted* to believe in angels, and when you might just allow yourself a few moments of such a belief. When you were in danger, perhaps, you might secretly wish for angelic assistance, and might be forgiven for believing in something that you didn't believe in. Or when you wanted something so badly – that a grievously ill friend might be relieved of her suffering, one way or another, for example; then you might clutch at such a belief. And when your silent prayer was answered, was it not tempting to think that an angel had brought about that which you wanted? Was this not just an ordinary human way of thinking – or hoping, perhaps?

As she thought of this, she remembered the loss of her old friend, Charity, who had been a friend, too, of Mma Potokwani. Together, she and the matron of the Orphan Farm had spent the last two days of Charity's life nursing her through the cruel blows that her illness brought; the struggles for breath, the relentless coughing that racked her frail system. They had watched as their friend became thinner and thinner until there seemed so little of her, far too little to survive another night. But she had, and then, in the morning, as the sun rose over the acacia trees, she had suddenly become still and Mma Potokwani had turned to her and said, 'That is the angel that has come for her, Mma.' And Mma Ramotswe, through her tears, had simply nodded, and kissed her late friend's brow. Then she had gone outside, because Mma Potokwani, who had been a nurse before she became a matron, knew what was required as a last service to those who have become late, and would do what was needed in private. The husband was there in the garden, watering the melons, and she saw from his eyes that he knew the news that she was bringing him from the sick room. And she said to him the first thing that came to her mind, which was, 'An angel has visited this house, Rra.' And that somehow made it easier for both of them; and so she had decided that even if there were no angels, we might still wish to believe in them because that made our life more bearable, and she was not ashamed to think like that.

Mma Makutsi brought her back to the present. 'I saw them, by the way,' she said, gesturing towards the freshly abandoned file. 'They came into Phuti's store. They were looking for a new table. They seemed very happy. They were both laughing.'

'I'm glad it all ended well for them,' said Mma Ramotswe. And she was: she believed there came a time when debts had to be forgiven – and that applied to countries as well as people, she felt. There were some countries in Africa that were still paying for the spending sprees of their early post-independence rulers. It was not the fault of today's children, but then the world was a hard place and there always seemed to come a time when the wells of generosity ran dry.

Mma Makutsi grinned. 'They saw me, you know. They saw me in the furniture shop. I was standing there with Phuti, and they saw me.'

Mma Ramotswe raised an eyebrow. 'And what happened, Mma?'

'They ran,' Mma Makutsi replied. 'He ran first, and then she ran after him. Phuti was very surprised. He asked me what was going on and I told him. He shook his head. He has problems with bad debts too.'

'It is sometimes not easy to forgive,' observed Mma Ramotswe.

'It's like stealing,' said Mma Makutsi. 'If you don't pay what you owe, it's like stealing. I am not so quick to forgive as you are, Mma Ramotswe.' She leaned over to retrieve the file. 'In fact, I am going to write to these people again and tell them I have not forgotten the bill.'

Mma Ramotswe sighed. 'You could try, Mma. But what about asking for half?'

'Ninety-seven per cent,' said Mma Makutsi firmly. 'I will ask them for ninety-seven per cent of what they owe. That will give them a three per cent discount.'

They spent the next half-hour looking at some of the other files. It was slow work. With the day's quota of generosity expended, the remaining unpaid bill files were retained by Mma Makutsi for what she described as 'one last push', while others, cases in which they had either solved the client's problem or been unable to help, were one by one disposed of and dropped into the wastepaper bin and an overflow cardboard box retrieved by Mma Makutsi from the small storeroom at the back of the garage.

Now it was time for mid-morning tea. 'One last word on these unpaid bills,' Mma Makutsi said. 'When I lived up in Bobonong, there was a man who had a little business selling stock food. You know those cattle licks, Mma – the ones with salt and this and that? You know those ones?'

Mma Ramotswe did know them. She was, after all, the daughter of the late Obed Ramotswe, fine judge of cattle, whose large herd had, after his death, provided her with the means to buy her house and start her business. She had absorbed a great deal of knowledge about cattle from her father, and knew what it was that cattle needed. He had said to her, 'Cattle, Precious, will eat anything if they don't get the salt they need. You don't want your cattle to eat sticks and stones, do you? Or dirt? That is why they must have their licks.' And then he had talked about potassium and zinc and vitamin D, and she had remembered some of these, but not all. She had remembered about magnesium, though, and the way he had spoken about the risk of the disease he called staggers if the cattle did not get the magnesium they needed.

She heard his voice again, as she heard it in her head now and then, at unexpected moments. Late people talk to us, she thought; they talk to us, but most of the time we are not listening because we are so busy with what we are doing here and now and there are so many problems to be dealt with. But then, when we stop for a moment and catch our breath, we might just hear the voices of the late people who love us, and they are whispering to us, quietly, like the wind that moves across the dry grass; and we know that it is them, although we also know that it cannot be them, for they are late. And so we try hard to hear, just to be sure, and their voices fade away and there is nothing once again.

Now it was Mma Makutsi talking, and she was telling her about the man in Bobonong who sold salt licks for people's cattle. 'He let people buy them on account,' she said. 'If people did not have the money to pay, he would never send them away. Because that would mean their cattle would not get the salt they needed and you would never want to be responsible for another person's cattle dying. So he let them buy on credit and pay later. But ...'

'Not everybody paid?' suggested Mma Ramotswe.

'That's right. Not everybody paid. But this man – the salt-lick trader – he had a very good way of getting them to pay, Mma. It always worked. One hundred per cent of the time – it worked.'

Mma Ramotswe waited for the secret to be revealed. Was Mma Makutsi going to use a special Bobonong way of getting the agency's debtors to pay up?

'He used witchcraft,' said Mma Makutsi. 'He found this old witch doctor – you know, a *sangoma* – and he paid him a few pula to put a curse on the people who didn't pay their bills. Then he told them, and they all paid up very smartly – the next day, in fact. It was very effective.'

Mma Ramotswe shot a disapproving look across the room. 'But you're not going to do that, are you, Mma Makutsi?'

There was a note of disappointment in Mma Makutsi's answer. 'No, Mma, I shall not do that.'

Mma Makutsi got up to start making the tea. She had just switched on the kettle when the door opened and Mr J. L. B.

Matekoni, who had been inspecting a car in the garage workshop, came into the office, wiping the grease off his hands with a piece of the blue paper he kept for this purpose.

'There is a woman,' he said to Mma Ramotswe. 'There's a woman outside to see you, Mma.'

Mma Ramotswe glanced at her diary. 'We don't have anybody booked in, do we Mma?'

Mma Makutsi shook her head. 'There is nobody.'

'I'm not sure if she's a client,' said Mr J. L. B. Matekoni. 'She said it's personal. I told her to come and knock on the door. I told her that the garage was a separate business, but she seemed very shy. She wanted me to speak to you first – to find out whether you would see her.'

'Show her in, Rra,' said Mma Makutsi. 'I will make an extra cup of tea for this timid lady.'

Mr J. L. B. Matekoni finished wiping his hands. 'She said she is a cousin.'

Mma Makutsi spun round. 'Of mine, Rra?'

'No.' He looked across the room towards his wife. 'Of Mma Ramotswe's.'

Mma Ramotswe frowned. 'Did you recognise her, Rra?'

Mr J. L. B. Matekoni was uncertain. 'No, not really. Well, maybe slightly. She looked a little bit familiar, but not really.'

'Well, that's clear enough,' said Mma Makutsi.

Mma Ramotswe looked disapprovingly at Mma Makutsi. Then, turning to Mr J. L. B. Matekoni, she said, 'I think you should bring her in, Rra.'

Blessing Mompati sat in the client's chair directly opposite Mma Ramotswe, holding a mug of tea across which she blew a cooling breath.

'This tea is very hot,' she said. 'I am not complaining, Mma – it is very welcome, but it is hot.'

'It will cool, Mma,' said Mma Ramotswe. 'And we are in no hurry. There is plenty of time to drink tea.'

Blessing put the tea down on Mma Ramotswe's desk. 'I have been trying to cut down on sugar.' She had asked for three spoons. 'But it is not easy, Mma.'

From behind her, Mma Makutsi said, 'It is a question of will-power, Mma.'

Blessing half turned to answer Mma Makutsi. 'I do not have much of that, Mma. Maybe that is my problem.'

'I'm sure you do,' said Mma Ramotswe.

Blessing shook her head. 'I do not think so, Mma. It is the same thing with fat cakes. I know we shouldn't eat too many, but when I see a plate piled high with fat cakes, well—'

'Willpower again,' interjected Mma Makutsi. 'Sugar, fat cakes, cigarettes – it is all the same thing. Willpower.'

Blessing spoke over her shoulder. 'You must be very strong, Mma. Not all of us are strong.'

Mma Ramotswe took control. 'When you came in, Mma, it was a moment or two before I remembered who you are. I'm sorry if I looked blank. You should not look blank when a cousin comes to see you – even a distant cousin.'

Blessing assured her that no offence had been taken. 'We have not seen one another since we were girls, Mma. That is a long time ago.'

'Many, many years,' said Mma Ramotswe.

'I think we came to see you in Mochudi on our way down from Francistown. I remember your father.'

'He is late now.'

'I knew that. I'm very sorry. All the best people are late, Mma – or that's sometimes how it seems.'

24

Mma Ramotswe took a sip of her tea. 'The tea is cooler now, I think, Mma.'

Blessing tested it, and agreed. 'It is good to see you with your own business now, Mma,' she said. 'That man out there – the mechanic – is he the man you married?'

Mma Ramotswe nodded. 'That's Mr J. L. B. Matekoni. He's my husband.'

'I've heard that he is a very kind man,' said Blessing. 'That's what they say, anyway.'

'He is. He's a good man. I am very happy with him.'

A wistful look passed over Blessing's face. 'I was not so lucky. I was with a man who drank. He was always drinking – all the time.'

'There is no cure for that,' said Mma Makutsi. 'If men are drinkers, then that is what they are.'

'Oh, I don't know,' Mma Ramotswe said. 'They can join these groups they have. There is one in that church near the stadium. They sing hymns. If you are tempted to have a drink, you can call them and they will send two or three people round to sing hymns with you until the need to drink passes. They say that it works.'

'It is too late for him,' said Blessing. 'He fell into a ditch. You know, Mma, that is what they say about these people. They say that it is only when they end up down in the dirt that they will do anything about their problem.'

'And did he?' asked Mma Makutsi. 'Did he go to these people near the stadium?'

Blessing shook her head. 'It was the rainy season, Mma. The ditch was full of water.'

They fell silent. Mma Ramotswe caught Blessing's eye and then looked away. 'I am very sorry, Mma.'

'He is late, Mma?' Mma Makutsi asked – a little insensitively, thought Mma Ramotswe.

'He is late,' said Blessing. 'He fell into the ditch at night-time. He walked into it. The police said they thought it was about midnight. Somebody found him on the way to work the next morning. The water had drained out of the ditch, and so they wondered how you could drown in a ditch with no water. The police doctor said he had definitely drowned.'

'I am very sorry to hear all this, Mma,' said Mma Ramotswe.

'Thank you, Mma. It is some years ago, now. I am over it, I think.'

'And you didn't meet anybody else?' asked Mma Ramotswe.

Blessing shook her head. 'It is not easy, Mma. There are not many men these days. I don't know what has happened to the men.'

This brought a reaction from Mma Makutsi, who snorted. 'Men? Where are all the men? Good question, Mma – very good question.'

Blessing turned round to face Mma Makutsi. 'Well, Mma. Do you know the answer to that?'

'I do not,' said Mma Makutsi. 'But I have some ideas. I think that women have let men get away. They have let them run off. In the old days, women made men marry them because if they did not marry them, then they would not let the men kiss and cuddle them – if you know what I mean, Mma. They said: no kisses, no cuddles until you have bought the ring, spoken to the father and the uncles, and paid the lobola. Then there can be that sort of thing. But now? Kisses and cuddles straight away and then the men say, "Thank you very much, Mma, but I am going away because there are all sorts of things that I would like to do – and getting married and settling down is not one of them."' She paused. 'That is what has happened, Mma.'

'Possibly,' said Mma Ramotswe. 'Possibly, Mma.'

'No, Mma Ramotswe,' said Mma Makutsi. 'Not possibly – definitely. And then there are men who say that they do not like women. They say, "I do not like ladies and so you can cross me off your list." I am not making this up, Mma – that is what they say. And so they go off and that's the last any of us girls see of them, Mma, I can tell you.'

Mma Ramotswe shifted in her seat. This was a difficult topic in Botswana society and people did not like to talk about it openly. Perhaps that was the trouble: if they talked about it, it would be different.

'I think the important thing is that people should be happy,' she said. 'There are some people who like one thing and others who like another. That is not something we should worry about too much. Why make people unhappy by saying they cannot be with the people they want to be with? Why, Mma?'

Mma Makutsi was tight-lipped. 'I do not want anybody to be unhappy, Mma. I did not say that. I just said that some men have decided they do not like ladies, and so there are fewer men for the ladies who like men. That is all.'

Mma Ramotswe decided to bring the conversation back from these major issues of demography and marriage. Discussions of those subjects tended to get you nowhere, she felt, interesting though they might be. If you thought there were too many people – or too few – then talking about it did not change the number of people there were.

'I am very pleased to see you, Mma,' she said to Blessing. 'But I was wondering whether there was anything that I could do for you. You aren't in need of a private detective, are you?'

Blessing smiled. 'I am not, Mma. No, I came to see you because there is something I need to talk to you about – and you are my cousin.'

'I am happy to talk to you, Mma,' said Mma Ramotswe. 'I am listening right now. What do you need?'

'Money,' said Blessing.

Chapter Three

Rule No. 1

That evening, Mma Ramotswe did not tell Mr J. L. B. Matekoni about Blessing's request. She had intended to do so over dinner, having made him his favourite stew of Botswana beef, and having served it with his favourite vegetable, pumpkin – moistened, of course, with a large pat of butter and covered in a rich gravy from the roasting tin in which the beef had been prepared. After that, all that was required was salt and pepper sprinkled on the top, and there was a meal that would keep anybody happy, from the President down to the humblest of men in his remote cattle post. Not that such distinctions were encouraged in Botswana, where everybody was equal, in theory at least: in practice, it was not hard to pick out those who had more beef and pumpkin than others, and were, perhaps, not quite as ready to share their beef and pumpkin as they might be. But although that was a troubling issue, and one that certainly worried Mma Ramotswe, she was not thinking of that as she and Mr J. L. B. Matekoni sat down to their meal and he, sniffing at the steamy aromas rising from his plate, asked, 'Is there a luckier man in all Botswana, my Precious, than the one you see seated at this table? Is there?' And she had smiled, because she loved receiving compliments of that nature – and who does not? – before replying, 'But is there a luckier woman in all Botswana – or maybe even in all Africa – than this woman *you* see seated at this table?'

That would have been a good time to broach the subject of Blessing's visit to the agency, but somehow she missed the moment, and the conversation veered off in another direction. Then, at the end of the meal, Mr J. L. B. Matekoni had yawned and announced that he was too tired to talk any longer because of the long day in the garage and the difficulties with a gearbox that had proved to be resistant to all reason. So it was not until the next morning, when she brought him a cup of tea in bed, that she felt able to raise the delicate issue of Blessing.

It was delicate because Mma Ramotswe knew that Mr J. L. B. Matekoni had his views on people who relied on distant family connections to get some sort of favour from others. In his view it was this idea of obligation that led to corruption, the canker that had held Africa back from achieving its full potential. Corruption was the devil, he said, that led countries rich in resources to the begging bowl. It had happened so many times in so many different places, but never in Botswana. 'And why?' he asked. 'Because Seretse Khama would not tolerate corruption – that is why.' And he, the first President, that good man who spoke with all the authority that came from his origins in the first family of the Bamangwato people, had said that there should be no corruption in Botswana and that those who had power should wield it for the good of all rather than for the lining of their own pockets. And that had worked, when all about them, in Angola, and South Africa, and Zimbabwe, officials and politicians had taken their cut and slowly drained the blood from their economies. Some had become immensely rich, funded by stolen diamonds or the bribes paid for large construction contracts – there were hundreds of ways of taking money that should not belong to you – and honest men and women had suffered as a result.

'And how does this happen?' Mr J. L. B. Matekoni asked. 'It happens because of that thing you boast about, Mma Ramotswe. It happens because one person can go to another and say: you are my cousin, or my cousin's cousin, or even my cousin's cousin's cousin, and this means that you must give me the job or the contract. And so this thing grows, and puts down deep roots, just like the mopipi tree, deep roots that go right down into the heart of a country. Deep, deep. And soon nobody can do anything about it, because everyone is doing it, and there are no honest people left, and that is what corruption is, Mma.'

Yes, thought Mma Ramotswe, yes, but ... And the but was a big one. She thought he was right about how some people took advantage of family connections to get the things they wanted; he might be right about that, but at the same time she would not want to see that tradition abandoned, because that would make Botswana just like anywhere else where people did not think they had to help others. You had to look after other people because if you did not, then the world was a cold and lonely place, a place where, if you stumbled, there would be no hand to pull you to your feet. So even if Mr J. L. B. Matekoni was right about how people had abused this idea of mutual reliance, she could not bring herself to reject it.

Now, as she sat on the edge of their bed, while he sipped the tea she had made him, she said, 'That woman who came to see me yesterday, Rra. You remember her?'

He nodded. 'What did she want, Mma?'

'She wasn't a client, you know.'

He took a further sip of his tea. 'I know. She said something about being a cousin. I meant to ask you about her, but that gearbox I was busy with ...' He shook his head. Gearboxes were the cross he bore in life. He did not mind shock absorbers or fuel pumps, or brake drums, but gearboxes were another matter altogether.

'Her name is Blessing. She is a very distant cousin – you know how it is: daughter of a cousin who married a cousin – that sort of thing.'

Mr J. L. B. Matekoni smiled. 'That makes all of us cousins,' he said. 'You, me, Mma Makutsi – even Charlie, I suppose. We're all related.'

'Yes, we are,' said Mma Ramotswe. 'And if you trace it far back enough, we all come from the same place – way, way back. East Africa. Even people up in Iceland – they come from East Africa originally. So everyone is a cousin.'

'That is this DNA they talk about,' said Mr J. L. B. Matekoni, adding, with mock seriousness, 'I should like to see some of this stuff one day. I wonder if it looks like motor oil. High-grade motor oil, naturally.'

She laughed. 'We are not motor cars, Mr J. L. B. Matekoni. Well, I'm certainly not ...'

He drank the last of his tea and put the empty cup down on his bedside table. Putting his hands behind his head to act as an extra pillow, he prepared to enjoy the last few moments in bed before getting up. He closed his eyes.

'You aren't going back to sleep, are you?' asked Mma Ramotswe. 'It's a working day, remember.'

His voice was drowsy. 'I'm not going back to sleep. I'm just thinking.'

'About?'

'About those early people back then – you know, the ones in East Africa – the ones whose skulls they dug up. I was thinking about them having a sort of *kgotla* meeting and saying, "It's about time we got moving."' He opened his eyes and smiled. 'And then one of them says, "How about going off to Europe or India? There will be big opportunities there."'

'This Blessing,' Mma Ramotswe persisted. 'She came to tell me about one of our relatives. She says that he is not well.'

Mr J. L. B. Matekoni sighed. 'People are always falling ill, Mma. That is the way we are.' He paused. 'I'm sorry, of course, it is not very pleasant being unwell, but it is always happening, I'm afraid.'

'And—'

He interrupted her. 'And they need money? Right?'

Mma Ramotswe lowered her eyes. He knew how these things worked, just as she did. She gave a wordless reply, nodding to confirm what he had said.

Mr J. L. B. Matekoni sat up and began to get out of bed. 'It's always the same, Mma. This one, that one – everyone needs money. There's never enough, no matter how careful you are, no matter how hard you work. There is always a need for more money.'

'It is a man called Tefo Kgomo. He worked in the mines up at Selebi-Phikwe and is now living down here – just outside town. You get to his place from the Lobatse Road. Down that way.'

Mr J. L. B. Matekoni donned a clean shirt. He gave another sigh. 'And what is wrong with him, Mma?'

'His hips,' she said. 'He has arthritis in both his hips. It is very difficult for him to walk now. It is always very painful.'

'Can't they do something? I thought that these days they have an operation.'

'Yes,' said Mma Ramotswe. 'They do have an operation. They can put in new joints.'

'It's amazing,' said Mr J. L. B. Matekoni. 'Just like cars, Mma, don't you think? A new set of engine valves. A new suspension system. Just like cars.'

'You're right, Rra. It is amazing. But Tefo cannot get these things, she said.'

Mr J. L. B. Matekoni paused in his dressing. 'But there's that big hospital down in Lobatse. That's close to where he lives, surely. They have plenty of doctors there. My friend, Thomas, who has his garage down that way says that he looks after the cars of at least seven doctors at that hospital. They come from all over the place – there are some very well-trained doctors, Thomas says. Big experts in blood and hearts and so on. There will be a bone doctor there – definitely.'

'I'm sure there is,' said Mma Ramotswe. 'But there's a problem. Tefo cannot get treatment in the government hospital. Not this special treatment, anyway.'

He was puzzled. 'But I've heard of people who've had that operation here in Gaborone. In the government hospital. There hasn't been a problem.'

'Citizens, Rra.'

He frowned. 'Citizens?'

'Those people will be citizens. This man, this Tefo, is South African. He's a Motswana, yes, but from over the border. He has worked in this country for many years, but he isn't a citizen.'

Mr J. L. B. Matekoni asked why not. There were procedures for obtaining citizenship and if you were in the country long enough and qualified, then it might be granted.

'That's true,' Mma Ramotswe said. 'It's ten years. You have to be in the country for ten years if you want to be naturalised.'

'But you said that he had worked here for many years . . . '

She looked down at her hands. Mr J. L. B. Matekoni was a kind man – there was none kinder in Botswana, she had always thought, but he was slow to get involved in the affairs of others. And now she had to reveal the most uncomfortable aspect of the whole story.

'He has worked for a long time, Rra, but . . . but there is something that means he will not get citizenship.'

Mr J. L. B. Matekoni waited.

'He has a conviction.'

Mr J. L. B. Matekoni shook his head ruefully. 'I thought that, Mma. The moment you said "but". I thought: this man has been convicted of something.' He paused. 'What is it?'

'Stock theft.'

It was the worst answer she could have given, short of saying that Tefo had been convicted of murder. The ownership of cattle lay at the heart of Botswana's culture, and stock theft was widely and roundly condemned.

Mr J. L. B. Matekoni shrugged. 'That's it, then. If that's on his record, Mma, then I'm surprised they didn't send him back over the border.'

'He has two children,' said Mma Ramotswe. 'They are still young – or they were young when he was convicted. He was supporting them and since their mother is a Motswana they would not deport them. So they let him stay under a residence permit.'

'Did he go to jail, Mma?'

Mma Ramotswe relayed what Blessing had told her. It had not been a serious case of stock theft – he was accused of taking a heifer belonging to a neighbour and putting his own brand over the original owner's. Since it was only one animal, the magistrate had been lenient and not sent him to prison. But it was a conviction, nonetheless, and that remained on his record.

'Blessing said that she was convinced he was innocent and that the neighbour had done the rebranding himself. He had hoped that Tefo would be sent to jail.'

'Why?' asked Mr J. L. B. Matekoni. 'What had Tefo done to him?'

Mma Ramotswe shrugged. Rural feuds were complicated, and as often as not went back a very long time. Sometimes they were handed down from parent to child, with the result that they could simmer away when everybody had forgotten the original cause of hostilities.

'There must be few things worse than being wrongly accused of a crime,' Mma Ramotswe said. 'You know you are innocent, but you also know that most people will not believe you – even your friends.'

'It must be very bad,' agreed Mr J. L. B. Matekoni. But what, he wondered, could one do about it? The world was like that. There were things that were wrong about it that were very difficult to change, and no matter how careful the police and the courts were, they would sometimes get the wrong person.

'I want to help her,' said Mma Ramotswe.

He was pulling on his socks. He stopped. 'You want to help with the operation?'

She nodded. 'I can't give a great deal,' she said. 'Just a small amount.'

Mr J. L. B. Matekoni stared at his feet. This was what he had feared. 'But, Mma,' he said. 'If we give money to every distant relative who needs it, we will have none left for ourselves. Word gets out – you know that as well as I do. People will say, "Oh, that Mma Ramotswe will always help you," and then, before you know it, there's a line of people halfway to Lobatse, all wanting a bit of financial help, and every one of them – every single one of them – a distant cousin.'

She did not say anything. She knew that what he said was right.

'And do you know how much those operations cost?' he continued. 'Tens of thousands of pula, Mma. If you can't get the government to pay, then you have to pay a very big bill. As much as a car costs, Mma. Did you know that? Easily as much as a car costs.'

'I was only going to give a little,' she said.

He shook his head. 'You can't, Mma. Look at what you pay Charlie – hardly anything. If you want to be charitable, then I think you should start at home – right under your nose – and give Charlie more money, rather than help this distant cousin – so distant that we'd need binoculars to see him, Mma.'

Mma Ramotswe did not argue. Before she and Mr J. L. B. Matekoni married they had not discussed their financial situation in any detail. Both had assumed that they would pool resources, and that each would decide which part of their joint patrimony he or she wished to manage. Without there ever having been any real debate about it, Mma Ramotswe found herself looking after the bills, drawing upon the common account into which they paid their separate regular incomes – hers from the profits of the No. 1 Ladies' Detective Agency, his from the takings at Tlokweng Road Speedy Motors. In addition to those sources, they each had a small amount of money from the occasional sale of cattle. In that respect, Mma Ramotswe was considerably better off than Mr J. L. B. Matekoni, as Obed Ramotswe had left her a good-sized herd and there were still many head of these out at her cattle post. Some people were loath to sell cattle, treating them almost as family members, but Mma Ramotswe had never been sentimental about this. She loved her cattle, yes, but she understood that there was a time for selling just as there was a time for cherishing.

Mr J. L. B. Matekoni's cattle had been taken into the herd of an elderly uncle of his, a man who, like Obed Ramotswe, knew almost everything there was to know about cattle husbandry. Mr J. L. B. Matekoni liked this uncle, who had in his time been a railway mechanic, and he admired his judgement – when it came to cattle and to the care and maintenance of railway engines. But what he found trying was the uncle's inability to talk about anything other than cattle. There had been a time when he had been prepared to converse about trains *and* cattle, but lately the trains seemed to have been forgotten about and the conversation focused entirely on cattle. But whatever his shortcomings as a conversationalist were, he took good care of his nephew's cattle, even though he never had more than ten head at any one time. This was very little when compared with Mma Ramotswe's one hundred and fifteen.

Mma Ramotswe could not recall ever having a single argument about money with Mr J. L. B. Matekoni. Now, as he told her about charity and its demands in her back yard, she realised that this was a disagreement. She could have argued with him, but she felt reluctant to do that. In her mind, consensus and the doing of things together was the key to a good marriage. Once you began to argue about little things, the stage would be set for much bigger disagreements, and she did not want that. So all she said was, 'It's all right, Rra – I won't give them any money.'

He looked abashed. 'I didn't say you *couldn't*, Mma. I didn't say that. I would never tell you what you should do with our money.'

She looked away. He had. He had said 'you can't'. She was sure of that.

'All I said,' Mr J. L. B. Matekoni went on, 'or all that I *meant* to say is that there are too many people looking for money. If you decide that one of them actually deserves it, then there is no reason why you shouldn't help them. But you have to be careful, Mma – that's all.'

'I don't think we should argue about this, Rra,' she said. 'I know that you are careful when it comes to money, and that is a good thing. Money should be looked after by the head, rather than by the heart. I will find out a bit more about this man. But I won't do anything foolish.'

'You'd never do anything foolish, Mma,' said Mr J. L. B. Matekoni, relieved that a potentially difficult issue had been satis-factorily resolved – at least for the moment.

They spent the next few moments in silence. And then, just as Mma Ramotswe was about to rise to her feet and take Mr J. L. B. Matekoni's teacup back to the kitchen, they heard the sound of voices outside.

'Is there somebody in the garden?' asked Mr J. L. B. Matekoni. He crossed to the window and peered out. 'No, there's nobody there.'

The voices returned. A woman's voice was raised, and it was followed by a lower voice in answer. Then the woman spoke again, shouting this time.

'It's coming from next door,' said Mr J. L. B. Matekoni. 'Our new neighbours.'

Mma Ramotswe joined him at the window. The voices were clearer now, the volume of the exchange having been turned up. It was possible to pick out some of the words, although no full sentences could be heard.

Mma Ramotswe looked at Mr J. L. B. Matekoni. 'They're arguing, Rra.'

Mr J. L. B. Matekoni winced. 'Did you hear what she just said, Mma?'

She shook her head.

'Just as well, Mma,' he said. 'She is being very rude to him.'

The woman's voice rose to become even more shrill.

'That was not a nice thing to say,' said Mr J. L. B. Matekoni. 'She called him an anteater.'

Mma Ramotswe smiled. 'That is a rather rare insult, Rra. I have not heard that used very much. And what is wrong with anteaters, I wonder?'

'They are very greedy,' said Mr J. L. B. Matekoni. He was not sure about that, but he thought it might be true, as they seemed to gorge themselves once they found a colony of ants. 'And they have these very long tongues, Mma. Perhaps he has a very long tongue, this new neighbour of ours.'

'Or a long nose,' suggested Mma Ramotswe. 'They have a long nose that they put down ant-holes. If his nose is long, then that might be why she is calling him that.'

'If she didn't like his nose,' said Mr J. L. B. Matekoni, 'then why did she marry him, Mma? Before you marry somebody, surely you should make certain that you don't have a problem with his nose? Would you not agree, Mma Ramotswe?'

Mma Ramotswe hesitated. In general, she took the view that a person's physical appearance was neither here nor there, and that when it came to choosing your life partner, how the other person looked had little or no bearing on how successful the marriage would be. She was aware of many cases where a woman had been very happy, for many years, with a husband who was unprepossessing in the extreme. Phuti Radiphuti was a case in point: he was not the most good-looking of men, and yet he had been a wonderful husband for Mma Makutsi. And then there was that man who worked in the supermarket – his ears were so large that they made him look like a jackal, and yet Mma Potokwani, who knew his family, had told her that his wife said that the day she met him was the luckiest day of her life. And, speaking of noses, that senior civil servant who brought his car to be serviced at Tlokweng Road Speedy Motors had one of the largest noses in the country – so large and dominating that it was almost impossible to see his eyes or mouth – and yet his wife seemed to love him and had borne him seven children, which was always a good sign in a marriage.

'I think it is more important, Rra,' she replied, 'to make sure that you and your future spouse have the same interests. That's more important than things like noses.'

Mr J. L. B. Matekoni waited for her to explain.

'You see,' she continued, 'if one person in the marriage is interested only in cattle, or cars, or whatever it is, then it will be very important that the other person is not going to get too bored when they talk to one another. There are some marriages where the wife goes to sleep the moment the husband opens his mouth – I have seen that happen, Rra.'

'And the other way round, of course,' said Mr J. L. B. Matekoni. Although it was fashionable to run men down, he did not think that this discrimination was fair. Mma Makutsi, he thought, was a little bit too ready to write men off, although Mma Ramotswe never did that herself.

And she was not going to do it now. 'Yes,' she said. 'And the other way round. There are some men who go to sleep when their wives are talking. That happens too, Rra.'

Raised voices were heard once more, briefly, and then they subsided into silence. Mr J. L. B. Matekoni spoke quietly now, although there was no possibility that their conversation would carry over to next door.

'I hope that they are not going to fight every day,' he said.

Mma Ramotswe agreed. 'I fear that things might not be ...'

She searched for the correct expression. '... might not be quite right over the fence.'

Mr J. L. B. Matekoni, having a few minutes previously pulled on his shoes – his old, oil-spattered garage *veldschoen* that he refused to trade in for a newer pair – was now ready for his breakfast. He looked at his watch. Fanwell, his junior mechanic and ex-apprentice, would already be on duty in the garage, ready to deal with any early customers, but he did not like to leave him single-handed for too long. And yet what was Mma Ramotswe hinting at here? Neighbours were important, as troublesome relations with any neighbour could cast a shadow over anybody's life. It was rule no. 1, Mr J. L. B. Matekoni told himself, to remain on good terms with neighbours – even in the face of difficult or even provocative behaviour over the garden fence. Mind you, he admitted, there were other candidates for that rule no. 1 status, including the rule that you should be ready to say sorry when sorry was required. Or the rule that you did not tell a lie to get yourself out of trouble. The wisdom behind that last rule proved itself time and time again: lies created a sticky spider's web that quickly enmeshed those who uttered them. A single lie was rarely enough to conceal the truth, but soon had to be topped up with supplementary lies to confirm the original, until eventually the whole edifice of concealment and distortion toppled over.

He gave Mma Ramotswe a searching look. 'In what way, Mma, are things ... What did you say? "Not quite right"? In what way, Mma?'

Mma Ramotswe did not like to gossip, but the neighbours' behaviour here – the shouting at such a volume that it was inevitable that others would hear – surely justified her voicing her concerns to Mr J. L. B. Matekoni.

'I think they may not be on normal terms with each other,' she said.

It sounded odd – even to her as she said it – and Mr J. L. B. Matekoni was made no wiser by this remark.

'Normal terms?' he asked. 'What are normal terms, Mma?'

Mma Ramotswe now used a traditional Setswana expression that covered very neatly this sort of situation without spelling things out too explicitly. 'I think they may not be under the same blanket, Mr J. L. B. Matekoni. That is what I think.'

Mr J. L. B. Matekoni shrugged. 'Well, that's not surprising, surely. Would you expect somebody who is calling another an anteater to want to share a blanket? Can you imagine, Mma, what it would be like to share with an anteater?'

'It is not just because of what we have heard,' she said, lowering her voice. 'It's because . . . ' She pointed vaguely towards the fence. 'It's because there is no double bed, Rra. When I watched their things being taken in, I saw that there was no double bed. I noticed that.'

She felt slightly ashamed to be telling him this; ashamed that she had been the sort of person who looked out for such things. And ashamed, too, because she had forgotten her earlier resolve not to talk about what she had seen. Of course, if you talked only to your husband, perhaps that did not count . . .

Mr J. L. B. Matekoni sighed. 'So we have got neighbours who are at war,' he said. 'Not at war with us, but with each other.'

'I'm afraid so,' said Mma Ramotswe.

'I suppose we can live with that,' he said. 'We keep out of it. As long as they shout at each other and not at us.'

'I do not like shouting,' said Mma Ramotswe, a note of sadness in her voice. She liked to think of Zebra Drive as being a haven of peace. The wider world was as the wider world so often was – consumed with all sorts of arguments about all sorts of things – and she wanted Zebra Drive to be an exception to that. So far, it had been, but now that seemed to be imperilled.

She turned away from the window. It was time to make Mr J. L. B. Matekoni's breakfast. There were some husbands who made their own breakfast. Not only that, there were some husbands these days who made their wife's breakfast as well. She had read that this was the case in *progressive* households, where *new men* did their share – and more, sometimes – of the household tasks. Mr J. L. B. Matekoni, though, was not a new man. He was a traditional man who was not much use in the kitchen, and who would probably be unable to make his own breakfast even if he tried. Should she try to make a new man out of him? Should she show him how to make breakfast and then suggest that he might care to put his new-found skill to good use?

She looked at him and smiled. There were some men you could imagine being reformed in this way, but she did not think it likely with Mr J. L. B. Matekoni. And yet that did not matter too much, she told herself. He worked longer hours than she did, in conditions that were far less comfortable than hers. She had her desk and her comfortable office chair. She never had to crouch underneath an inspection platform while oil dripped onto her face. Nor did she have to struggle with bolts that had been stripped so that their nuts would not travel down the wrecked thread. He had to do all that – and more. And for all his old-fashioned approach to life, he was a kind and considerate man who had never said a cross word to her and never would. Nor did he think of himself and his creature comforts, as new men might be tempted to do. He had few possessions – look at his shoes, those awful old boots that no new man would dream of wearing. Look at his shirt, which although washed clean and neatly ironed, told the story of his daily struggles with machinery.

No, Mr J. L. B. Matekoni is perfect as he is, she thought. And then she thought: I shall give him extra bacon this morning – two more rashers than she usually allowed. And an extra egg, too, because eggs were full of iron, she believed, and iron was just the sort of thing that men who were *not* new men might be assumed to enjoy. Men clearly needed iron because ... well, because they just did.

She gave him his breakfast, which he polished off quickly and with evident enjoyment.

'You have been very kind to me, Mma,' he said, as he handed back his empty plate. 'All these years, you have been kind to me.'

She basked in the tenderness of this unexpected tribute, and thought: those poor people over the fence – had they ever tried this? Had they ever said to one another the sort of thing that Mr J. L. B. Matekoni had just said to her, out of the blue? Could one suggest to them that they try it, rather than calling one another anteaters – and worse? She pondered that, and as she did so she suddenly heard, or thought she heard, the voice of her father, Obed Ramotswe, saying to her, 'Precious, remember this: the business of your neighbours is their business.' It was not him, of course, for he was late, and when we hear the voices of late people, we are only hearing an echo. It was true that the world was full of echoes, but those echoes were of our own making, and reminded us, perhaps, of what we should try not to forget.

Chapter Four

A1 Excellent Fine

When he came into the office that morning, Charlie, having greeted Mma Makutsi perfunctorily, said to Mma Ramotswe, 'There is something that I would like to ask you, Mma.'

From behind her desk, Mma Makutsi sniffed loudly. She had several sniffs at her disposal: one, the basic sniff, was purely functional, designed to clear the nose; another was the sniff of doubt, a sniff that carried a message of scepticism as to what had just been said; and then there was the sniff of disapproval, an unmistakably negative sniff, leaving those at whom it was directed in no doubt at all as to Mma Makutsi's feelings.

This was the sniff of disapproval, and prompted a sideways look from Charlie. Mma Makutsi stared pointedly at the papers on her desk in front of her.

'I said good morning,' Charlie muttered. 'You heard me, didn't you, Mma Ramotswe?'

Mma Ramotswe raised an eyebrow. Charlie's greeting of Mma Makutsi had been offhand, but she did not think it had been deliberately rude. Young men often sounded rude even when they were intending to be polite – it was something to do with their difficulties in doing more than one thing at a time: occasionally they were too preoccupied to hear remarks addressed to them. Either that, or they heard what was being said and tried to respond, but did not give sufficient attention to their response. That, she thought, was what had happened here.

'Perhaps you mumbled,' said Mma Ramotswe. It was a gentle reproof, but it was enough to provoke a spirited rebuttal from Charlie.

'I didn't mumble, Mma. I said good morning loud and clear.' He paused. 'There are some people who need to get their ears washed out, I think.'

Mma Makutsi shot him a stern look. 'There is nothing wrong with my ears, Charlie. I can hear perfectly well. When people say good morning in the correct, polite fashion, I can always hear them when they do that. Interesting, isn't it?'

Mma Ramotswe cleared her throat. 'I am sure that we all wish one another a very good day,' she said. 'But tell me, Charlie: what is it you want to ask me?'

Charlie, who had been standing a little way away from Mma Ramotswe's desk, now came closer. Lowering his voice in what could only have been an attempt to prevent Mma Makutsi from overhearing, he said, 'I was hoping to borrow your van this morning, Mma. Just until lunchtime. Then I will bring it back to you.'

Mma Makutsi sniffed. This was a sniff somewhere between the sniff of doubt and the sniff of disapproval. Reacting to this,

Charlie said, 'I shall definitely bring it back by two this afternoon, Mma.'

Mma Ramotswe occasionally lent Charlie the tiny white van. She had done this when he was helping a friend move house, a friend whom Charlie had described in glowing terms. 'He is one of those people who always helps others, Mma,' he said. 'He was a big figure in the boy scout movement too. He was at the scout meetings every week, Mma, every week, doing all sorts of good deeds.'

She had tried not to smile.

'No, Mma,' Charlie insisted, 'I am not making this up. He helped a lady find her false teeth when she dropped them in a ditch. He was the one who found them. It was almost in the papers.'

This had brought a burst of laughter from Mma Makutsi, who had been listening to the conversation. 'How can anybody lose their false teeth in a ditch?' she asked. 'What was this lady doing there? Eating her breakfast? And how can something be "almost in the papers"? Either it is in the papers, or it is not.'

Charlie had put up a spirited defence of his friend. 'You may think I'm lying, Mma Makutsi, but it's true. She might have been going somewhere and maybe she tripped up and lost her teeth. These things can happen, you know.' He paused. 'I am just telling you one of the good things he has done.'

'And he turned water into beer at somebody's wedding?' said Mma Makutsi. 'And walked across the dam – on top of the water? Just a few things like that?'

Mma Ramotswe had ended that contretemps by giving Charlie permission to use the van, and had done so on two occasions since then: on one to take a relative to hospital, and on another to take a supply of animal food out to his uncle's cattle at the height of the last drought. That had been an errand of mercy of which no person in Botswana would disapprove. At a time of drought, the tragedy of starving cattle touched something very deep in the national psyche and it would be unthinkable not to help another to save a herd.

Now she asked, 'What for, Charlie? What do you need the van for?'

Charlie hesitated. From behind him he thought he could hear the faintest of sniffs, but perhaps it was just the breeze against the fly-screen gauze.

'It's to help a friend move something.'

Mma Ramotswe waited, but when no further explanation was forthcoming, she asked, 'What does your friend want to move?'

Charlie said, 'I'll put petrol in, Mma. I'll put ten litres in. That will be more than I'll use, but I don't mind. You can keep the extra, Mma.'

'That's not what I asked you, Charlie. I asked you what your friend wants to move.'

Charlie shrugged. 'Just something, Mma. He hasn't told me exactly what it is.'

This was too much for Mma Makutsi. 'He hasn't told you? Oh, Charlie, you're being very naïve. Do you know what that word means? It means you are being very stupid.'

He glared at her. 'I am not being nave,' he retorted.

'Naïve,' said Mma Makutsi. 'It's *naïve*. And that is what you're being.' She shook her head. 'You're exactly the sort of person they're talking about at airports, Charlie. At airports they say, "Do not carry anything for people you don't know." That's what they say. And you know what they're talking about? I'll tell you: bombs, Charlie.'

Charlie laughed. 'Bombs, Mma? I can tell you – I am not going to be moving bombs in Mma Ramotswe's van. Ha!'

'I didn't say you were going to put a bomb in the van,' snapped Mma Makutsi. 'I said that was what foolish people do. They agree to carry something for somebody they meet at an airport and then they find they've been carrying a bomb. And they are very sorry, I can tell you.'

Charlie laughed again. 'You say they're very sorry, Mma Makutsi. But how can you be sorry if you're blown up? You won't be around to feel sorry about anything. You'll be blown up.' He paused. 'I'm surprised you didn't know that, you being a detective.'

'Do you think I don't know what happens when you're blown up, Charlie? What I meant – and I'm sorry you're finding it a bit hard to grasp – is that those people are very sorry when they are caught carrying these bombs. That is before the bombs have exploded, you see. They are caught and then they say, "Oh, I'm very sorry – I didn't know that the parcel had a bomb in it." That's when they are sorry.'

Mma Ramotswe felt it was time to bring the discussion to an end. Mma Makutsi and Charlie could argue for hours once they got going, and she did not want that. So she said, 'You can borrow the van, Charlie, but be careful with it, please.'

He thanked her effusively. 'You're very kind, Mma Ramotswe. You're kinder than ...' He glanced at Mma Makutsi and then quickly looked away. 'You're kinder than some other people.'

A final shot came from Mma Makutsi. 'Make sure they don't hand you a bomb, Charlie. That's all I'd say to you. Look at the thing your friend asks you to carry before you carry it – not after.'

Mma Ramotswe reached for the van's keys from her drawer and handed them to Charlie. He put them in his pocket and, with a polite nod to both of them, left the office.

'What's he up to, Mma?' asked Mma Makutsi.

Mma Ramotswe shrugged. 'Helping a friend out, I think. Perhaps taking somebody somewhere. These young people move about a lot – they're always getting a new room in somebody's house. And then they have to take all their things – their sound systems and . . . and . . . ' She struggled to remember the sorts of things that people of Charlie's age possessed.

'Clothes,' said Mma Makutsi. 'They have lots of clothes these days. Even young men. Lots of clothes. Trainers and so on.'

Mma Ramotswe smiled. 'Would you like to be that age again, Mma Makutsi?'

Mma Makutsi shook her head. 'I would not, Mma. I would hate to have to worry about what other people thought of me. You know, they all worry about that – all the time. I heard a programme on the radio about it. They were talking about anxiety in young people. They said that it's a big problem these days. They're all anxious.'

'But we—'

Mma Makutsi was confident. 'We have stopped being anxious, Mma. Now we say to ourselves, "What is going to happen is going to happen." And once you say that to yourself, you stop being anxious.'

'I hope so,' said Mma Ramotswe. 'Though, now you come to mention it, I worry about Charlie. I worry that things will go wrong for him because he is a young man and he doesn't always think things through as carefully as he should.'

'Do you think he's going to do something foolish with your van, Mma? Such as carrying stolen goods in it?'

'I hope not.'

'Because if he did that,' Mma Makutsi continued, 'you could be in serious trouble, Mma. You could go to prison.'

Mma Ramotswe said that she thought that unlikely. But even as she downplayed Mma Makutsi's suggestion, she remembered that innocent people *did* go to jail. It did not happen very often, especially in Botswana, with its careful judiciary and its largely honest police force, but there were always exceptions and she knew of several law-abiding men who had ended up being wrongfully convicted of an offence. Honest men ... she did not know of any honest women who had been convicted of things they had not done, but there was always a first time. And for a few moments she imagined herself in an ill-fitting prison outfit, cutting grass along the side of a road in a working party, perhaps, while along the road drove the righteous and the respectable. And she imagined one car in particular driving past and slowing down so that the driver could get a good look at the convicts, and she would look up from her scythe and see none other than Violet Sephotho at the wheel, staring at her with an expression that would be a mixture of pity and intense satisfaction. That would be hard to bear – far harder than any shame at the fall from respectability, or any anger at the wrongfulness of conviction. It would be unbearable, she decided, and she felt a rush of relief as she reminded herself that this was fantasy, that it had not happened, and that it was highly unlikely ever to occur, even if Charlie really was planning to do something illegal with the van. No, surely he would not do that – not Charlie, whom she had known for years now, and who was maturing at long last. Not him. And yet, and yet ... how many victims of the bad behaviour of others ever imagined that the person they trusted would behave badly towards them, would let them down? None of them, she suspected, and that conclusion made her ask herself whether she should have insisted that Charlie give a fuller explanation of why he wanted the van.

She arose from her chair and made her way to the window, through which she could look out over the small stretch of cleared bush at the back of the garage; it was here that she parked the van under the shelter of an acacia tree. Now, the van was just moving away and it was too late to run after Charlie, demanding further details.

'Too late?' asked Mma Makutsi.

Mma Ramotswe nodded. 'He'll be all right. I trust Charlie.' She did – to an extent. In the essentials, Charlie was a good young man. His fecklessness – and fecklessness is never the fault of a young man, in the same way as a tendency to bite or chew things is never the fault of a puppy – was improving, and anyway did not detract from the goodness of his soul. That, Mma Ramotswe thought, was what counted: the goodness of the soul. She knew that people sneered at that idea – especially now, when it was unfashionable to talk about such things, but she still believed that we all had a soul. And how could one not believe in such a thing, given that it was so obvious when we looked into the eyes of others and we were able to understand what they were feeling, without a single word being uttered? Or when we were walking in the bush and heard the sound of cattle bells, and looked up and saw the sky over Botswana, and felt the wind against our cheek? Of course there was a soul; of course there was.

Mma Makutsi sniffed – the doubtful sniff this time. 'You believe him, Mma? I don't,' she said.

Mma Ramotswe and Mma Makutsi were busy for the rest of the morning and neither noticed the passage of time. Mma Makutsi went off to collect the mail – in her own car – and when she returned, shortly after twelve, she reported to Mma Ramotswe that she was sure she had seen Charlie in the white van. 'He was driving somewhere,' she said, adding, 'very fast.' She paused, and gave Mma Ramotswe a meaningful look. If you lent your van to somebody like Charlie, then could you expect anything but that he push the engine to the maximum?

'I didn't have the time to look closely,' she continued. 'Whoosh! He was gone. Just like that, Mma. Whoosh!'

Mma Ramotswe smiled. She suspected that there was a considerable amount of exaggeration in the report of this sighting. She felt tempted to quote Clovis Andersen, who said – if she recalled correctly – *never overstate what you see. Just report – don't embellish. If you see a husband you are observing holding the hand of a young woman, do not say that you saw him kissing her. It never helps a case to try to make it stronger with hyperbole.*

Hyperbole ... Mma Ramotswe had been delighted to make acquaintance with that word, which she had never encountered before. She had a good vocabulary in English – as well, of course, as her natural command of her mother tongue, Setswana – and she had a small and shaky understanding of Zulu, acquired from a friend in her schooldays. But even with her excellent English, there were occasional words that sent her to the dictionary, and hyperbole had been one of them. She liked the sound of the word, with its sharply rising consonant at the beginning and its round vowels at the end. This was a word that could be shouted out at the top of one's lungs, if one wished. It would also be a good name for a favourite cow, she thought, or even for a child – a girl, she thought, as it would hardly suit a boy.

And she had been able to use it on occasion, too, which was an additional bonus when it came to newly discovered words. She had tried it on Mma Potokwani, casually suggesting that reports of a large snake that had frightened residents of Tlokweng village involved hyperbole. 'People are always making small snakes into large snakes,' she said. 'And innocent grass snakes all become black mambas, too, Mma. People are given to hyperbole in these matters, Mma Potokwani.'

But Mma Potokwani had taken it in her stride. 'There is no

hyperbole, Mma Ramotswe,' she retorted. 'I saw the snake myself, and I am not one to exaggerate. It was two metres long, at the very least. And it was a mamba. I know those snakes. It was a mamba – not a hyperbole.'

'I would not like to be bitten by a hyperbole,' muttered Mma Ramotswe. She could not stop herself; she had to say this, although more or less immediately she regretted it.

'They are very dangerous, Mma,' said Mma Potokwani.

Now, on hearing Mma Makutsi's report, she said, 'That's a bit of hyperbole, Mma. My van cannot go *whoosh*. It is a very slow van.'

Mma Makutsi stared at her through her new glasses, adjusting their position on her nose as she did so. 'I am not a hyperbole, Mma. He *was* driving fast. You know how Charlie is.' She paused. 'And where is he, Mma? He has been away for hours now. He said he would not be long – but where is he? I am just asking, Mma – that is all I'm doing. I am not criticising you in any way – I'm just asking where Charlie is and wondering when he will come back.'

Charlie eventually returned shortly after two. It was Mma Makutsi who heard the van approaching and rose from her desk to look through the window.

'He's parking now, Mma,' she reported. 'Now he's getting out and he's looking at the van. I wonder why he's doing that, Mma? Surveying the damage, perhaps?'

Mma Ramotswe joined her at the window. She saw that Charlie had moved to the other side of the van and was bending down to examine something, possibly the near-side front wheel. Then he straightened up, walked to the back of the van, and examined something there.

'He might have scraped it,' said Mma Makutsi. 'You remember how he scraped Mr J. L. B. Matekoni's truck once? You remember that? And he said that the scrape had been caused by lightning, but it hadn't of course. You remember?'

'It's very easy to scrape against something,' said Mma Ramotswe. 'Let those who have never scraped a car throw the first stone, Mma.'

'I am not throwing any stones,' retorted Mma Makutsi. 'I am just saying that if it were my van, Mma, then I would be out there, checking the van for scrapes and bangs and such like.'

'Do you think so, Mma?'

Mma Makutsi nodded. 'I will come with you, Mma. Just to check up.'

They went outside and made their way over to the acacia tree and the van. Charlie saw them coming, and waited for them nonchalantly, his hands in his pockets. 'I am back now,' he called as they approached him.

'Is everything all right, Charlie?' asked Mme Ramotswe. She did not want to be seen examining the van too obviously, but she did shoot a glance in the vehicle's direction. Mma Makutsi was less reticent; she moved over to stand beside the van and peered down at the open loading area at the back.

Charlie watched Mma Makutsi nervously. 'Everything is A1 excellent fine,' he said.

Mma Makutsi looked up. 'A1 excellent fine, Charlie? That sounds very good. No lightning strikes this time?'

Charlie ignored this. 'My friend was very grateful to you, Mma,' he said to Mma Ramotswe. 'He said you are very kind and will certainly go to heaven when you die – which he hopes is not for a long time yet, of course.'

'What did you transport?' asked Mma Makutsi, peering again at the loading area. 'It must have been something rather heavy.'

Charlie frowned. 'Personal effects, Mma Makutsi. And they were just average heavy.'

Mma Makutsi reached out to rub the metal surface of the tailgate. 'This bit,' she said, 'I don't know what you call it – this bit here.'

'Tailgate,' said Charlie, glancing at Mma Ramotswe.

'Yes,' continued Mma Makutsi. 'This tailgate is a bit bent, Charlie. Or am I imagining something? Can you see it, Mma Ramotswe? If you come over here and take a look, you'll see that the whole tailgate seems to be a bit bent.' She paused. 'Not that I'm accusing anybody of anything – least of all you, Charlie.'

Mma Ramotswe joined Mma Makutsi at the rear of the van. She could see what the other woman meant – the tailgate appeared to have buckled slightly. She turned to Charlie. 'Did something happen, Charlie? I think that Mma Makutsi may be right. This bit is bent, see? Look, see the way it goes down there and then comes up again.'

Charlie struggled to look unconcerned. 'An old van always has irregularities, Mma. Even a new one sometimes is not quite straight.'

Mma Ramotswe shrugged. 'I don't think it matters,' she said. 'It still works, does it?'

Charlie stepped forward, brushing Mma Makutsi aside as he closed the tailgate. 'It still works,' he said. 'Look.'

Mma Ramotswe hesitated. It was clear to her what had happened: Charlie and his friend had overloaded the van with whatever they were transporting – perhaps a heavy sofa. They had rested the sofa on the tailgate while they decided how to manoeuvre it into the van, and the weight had caused the buckling. It was entirely excusable damage – the sort of thing that could happen to anybody who underestimated the strain that an object could place on a surface. Who had not done that sort of thing at some point in their lives? And yet one part of her thought that Charlie should not get away with it. If he had confessed to what had happened, nobody – not even Mma Makutsi – would have been able to make much of it. But he had not confessed, and in one view he should be confronted with the damage and told to apologise. But now, she thought, was not the time. Mma Makutsi would make a big thing of it, and there was no call, she felt, to do that.

'That's fine,' she said. 'Let's not worry. It's too hot to be standing out here.'

Charlie breathed out in relief. 'I have bought you a box of chocolates,' he said to Mma Ramotswe. 'They are to thank you for lending me the van.' He reached inside the van for a small box of chocolates and handed it to Mma Ramotswe.

'You don't need to do this, Charlie,' she said. 'But these are very nice. I like these chocolates.'

Mma Makutsi peered at the box. 'You need to be careful of those, Mma Ramotswe,' she said. 'They are very full of calories, those chocolates. I have read about them in a health magazine. They said, "These chocolates are very full of calories – thousands and thousands of calories – and are best avoided by healthy people." I am just telling you what the magazine said, Mma. I am not saying that I think you shouldn't eat them. I'm not saying that.'

Mma Ramotswe opened the box. 'Would you like one yourself, Mma?'

Mma Makutsi hesitated, and Mma Ramotswe saw at once that she was torn.

'One won't do you any harm, Mma. Two might – but not one.'

Mma Makutsi reached for a chocolate. 'You're quite right, Mma Ramotswe. One chocolate is always going to be all right.'

They went inside. Charlie had agreed to work in the garage that afternoon, so they did not see him in the office. And he was still working there when Mma Ramotswe left the office shortly before five. As she drove home, she sniffed the air. There was a strange smell, and it seemed to be inside her van. She opened a window, and the smell largely disappeared. But not altogether, and when she pulled up outside her house on Zebra Drive, she got out and peered into the back of the van. There was definitely a smell, but there was no sign of where it was coming from. What was it? A musty smell – an unfamiliar smell. The smell of an old sofa, perhaps – one that had had numerous cups of tea and beer spilled on it in the course of its career. Perhaps, she thought; but then she thought, perhaps not.

Chapter Five

All Needs Foodstuffs and Household Good

M ma Makutsi accompanied Mma Ramotswe on her visit to Blessing Mompati the following morning. They had closed the office, leaving a note on the door saying 'Back after Lunch, God Willing'. That qualification was Mma Makutsi's idea. 'It doesn't matter if you believe in God or not,' she said. 'Saying "God Willing" is a good idea anyway – it shows that you're not taking anything for granted.'

'I never do,' Mma Ramotswe assured her. 'I never take anything for granted.'

'Just as well,' said Mma Makutsi. 'Anything can happen, Mma Ramotswe. You could have a heart attack, for instance. Just like that. We could be driving off to these people we're going to see and halfway there, maybe even as we approach their house, you might have a heart attack.'

'Oh, I hope not,' began Mma Ramotswe. 'I don't—'

Mma Makutsi did not let her finish. 'I'm not saying this *will* happen, Mma – God forbid! It's just that it sometimes *does* happen. People are driving along and suddenly they feel a pain in their arm. You know that the pain is often in the arm first, Mma Ramotswe? People think it will be in the middle of their chest, where the heart is, but no, it can be in the arm. A very strong pain.'

'I've heard that,' said Mma Ramotswe. 'People say—'

Again, she was cut short. 'I've said to Phuti Radiphuti that if he ever gets a pain in his arm, he must tell me immediately. I said, "Don't assume it's a pulled muscle. Let the doctor decide that."'

'Very wise, Mma.'

'There are many heart attacks,' Mma Makutsi continued. 'It is a very common thing these days, when people are eating the wrong sort of food and putting on too much weight.'

She paused. This conversation had started as they placed the notice on the door of the agency and they were now making their way to the white van in its parking place. She glanced at Mma Ramotswe, as if to calculate whether she had put on any recent weight.

'Traditionally built people need to be aware,' she said. 'Not you, of course, Mma. You are very healthy. But in general, traditionally built people must be more aware of the risks.'

'I think many of them are,' said Mma Ramotswe. 'There are many people, Mma, who are very careful about what they eat and yet they become traditionally built as the years go by. I would not criticise such people, Mma.'

'Of course not, Mma,' protested Mma Makutsi, a picture of

injured innocence. 'I wouldn't criticise them – all I would do is say, "Be careful." That is all.'

'Anyway,' said Mma Ramotswe briskly. 'We have written "God Willing", and let's hope that we are back safely, and in good time.'

'Quite right,' agreed Mma Makutsi. 'Although, even if you don't have a heart attack, Mma, you have to think of the roads. Look at how bad they are these days, with all these drivers rushing around, breaking the speed limit all the time, Mma. All the time. No wonder there are all those accidents. We're going on the Lobatse Road, right? That's a bad place for accidents. People overtake because they're in a hurry to get down to Lobatse and then there's an accident.'

'We shall drive very slowly,' Mma Ramotswe said. 'My van does not overtake easily. In fact, Mma, it does not overtake at all.' She smiled. 'It was even passed by a donkey cart once. And several bicycles.'

That was an exaggeration – indeed a hyperbole. But Mma Makutsi had more to say, and now she sounded a serious note. 'That makes it more dangerous. If you don't have power, then you can't get out of trouble. That's what Phuti always says. He likes to have a car that can go faster than other cars on the road for that very reason, Mma.'

'We shall be all right, Mma Makutsi. If a dangerous situation arises, I shall just drive off the road and into the bush. That is the best thing to do. Just leave the road altogether.'

In spite of these dire misgivings, Mma Makutsi was pleased to be accompanying Mma Ramotswe on her mission that morning. Unlike Mr J. L. B. Matekoni, who had voiced his doubts about Blessing, Mma Makutsi had not voiced any opposition to Mma Ramotswe's proposal to respond to the appeal for help. 'I am not altogether sure about this, Mma,' she said, 'but I can see why you might want to help. I know what it's like to have no money.'

She did not say this reproachfully, or with any bitterness – it was simply the way things had been. She had come from a poor family in Bobonong – not as poor as some, but hard up by any standards. They had sold livestock to finance her journey to Gaborone and her enrolment in the Botswana Secretarial College, and at the end of every month, when they sent money down to her in Gaborone, she knew that every pula she received had involved a sacrifice by someone up in Bobonong. And not just a sacrifice by her immediate family, but one that was made by more remote relatives – uncles, aunts and cousins. She was never to forget how the system of wider family responsibility had enabled her to get that ninety-seven per cent and then launch herself upon her career. Not that her troubles had been over that quickly – even after she'd talked herself into the agency, it had been a struggle for Mma Ramotswe to pay her a decent salary out of the agency's initially tiny takings. Her impecuniosity had persisted until she had been able to earn a bit more from the part-time typing school she set up for men, and then, at last, quite unexpectedly, she had met Phuti Radiphuti at a dance class and all her scrimping and saving had been conclusively and gloriously brought to an end. Phuti was a wealthy man, with his Double Comfort Furniture Store and his large herds of cattle, and their engagement marked the end of penury for Mma Makutsi. Not that she contrived any of that: she and Phuti loved one another, and the match was made without regard to material considerations. When she first got to know him, she was unaware that he was well off and had, in fact, been surprised when she learned the truth. And she had handled the change in her circumstances with tact and consideration. It would have been easy to stop work, but she declined to do that; it would have been tempting for her to over-indulge herself, but again she was careful – even if she had acquired a considerable number of pairs of new shoes and dresses, too. Observing this,

Mma Potokwani, whose relationship with Mma Makutsi had not always been easy, paid handsome tribute. 'She has not allowed all this to go to her head,' the matron pronounced, adding, 'Except now and then – but we're all human, aren't we, and who amongst us would not occasionally splash out on some frippery if we had the money to do so?'

The traffic was light, as the morning rush that saw people streaming into Gaborone for the day's work was over by the time they pulled away from the outskirts of the town, the small office blocks and other commercial buildings that gradually spread out into the surrounding bush. They left the dam behind them and the riverbed that had been dry for long, parched months; they drove past the turn-off to Mokolodi Reserve and the first of the farm roads that joined the main highway at irregular intervals. On a rutted track running alongside the tarred road, they saw a cart laden high with firewood, pulled by a rickety donkey. An elderly man, his hat battered to the point of being barely recognisable for what it was, raised his whip in greeting. Mma Ramotswe sounded the van's horn in response, and Mma Makutsi waved from her wound-down window. 'The old ways,' said Mma Makutsi. 'There are still some people who believe in the old ways. Nobody waves to one another any longer, Mma.'

Mma Ramotswe agreed, in spite of her optimistic conviction that things were never as bad as they seemed. The old ways had been superseded in so many places by an indifference to others; how else might one explain the failure of people to notice one another, let alone to utter the greetings that strangers in Botswana had always exchanged.

It took them half an hour to reach the turn-off to the village mentioned by Blessing when she'd come to see Mma Ramotswe. She lived there, she said, with her mother and an unmarried sister, who was away at present; Tefo lived next door in a house she said he had built himself a few years earlier. 'Unofficially,' she explained. 'It is an unofficial house, Mma, because the headman would not give him permission to build a proper one.'

The road to the village was untarred, and although in the dry season the baked earth surface was easily passable, Mma Ramotswe imagined that in the rainy season it would quickly become impassable. Here and there, where erosion had been particularly bad, the surface of the road degenerated into long cracks, like small fault lines, that had to be avoided by steering onto meandering deviations made by previous traffic. Stunted acacia lined the road, along with thorn bushes and the occasional tree, and these were covered with a fine red dust from the surface of the road.

'This is not a good place,' said Mma Makutsi, gazing about her. 'It is hot down here, and there is very little grazing for cattle.'

'We are seeing it at a bad time,' said Mma Ramotswe. 'When the rains come, this will be different.'

'When the rains come,' said Mma Makutsi, longingly. 'But will they ever come, Mma? Each year they seem to be later and later, and when they do break, they are sometimes no more than a wind with a few drops of water in its eyes.'

Mma Ramotswe did not respond. She had been busy guiding the van round the obstructions that impeded their journey at every turn, and now, at last, the village came into sight. At first it was just the occasional roof, popping out above a canopy of thorn trees, but then there was a shop, with a brightly painted blue sign above its door: All Needs Foodstuffs and Household Good. Mma Makutsi surveyed it critically. '"Goods", I think, Mma. They have lost an "s". Household Goods. Plural.'

'These stores have everything,' said Mma Ramotswe. 'And you need these places if you live out here.'

There was a school, a low-level building painted yellowish-cream, in front of which a sign proclaimed: Tshekedi Khama Junior School. This was no more than a couple of small, square buildings, each endowed with a veranda, and surrounded by a dusty playground dominated by two large oil drums painted in the national colours. There was a minuscule clinic, marked by a red cross on its front wall. Underneath the cross was a painting in naïf style of a nurse holding a thermometer and, in a dialogue bubble above her head, saying, 'Don't ignore the signs!'

'Of what?' asked Mma Makutsi, pointing to the mural. 'Signs of what, Mma?'

Mma Ramotswe was not sure, but ventured that the message was perhaps that a high temperature should be taken seriously. 'A high temperature is a bad sign,' she said. 'That is well known, Mma.'

'Yes,' said Mma Makutsi. 'You cannot ignore a high temperature.'

The village was somnolent, with few signs of activity other than that which surrounded a small roadside stall where a woman was selling maize cobs. Several women were standing beside her – customers, thought Mma Ramotswe – and they all paused their conversation to stare at the visitors in the van.

Mma Ramotswe drew up to the stall and addressed the women through the car window. Greetings were exchanged before she asked if they could direct her to Blessing Mompati's house. It was a short distance down the road, the stallholder replied, and then added, 'Why do you want to see her, Mma?'

Mma Ramotswe smiled. 'I am a cousin.'

'And I am this lady's colleague,' chipped in Mma Makutsi.

It was an unwise addition, thought Mma Ramotswe as she gave Mma Makutsi a quick, discouraging glance.

The woman nodded. Then another asked, 'Colleague in what, Mma? In an office?'

Mma Ramotswe replied quickly. 'Yes, in an office.'

She had given her answer in the tone of one who would not welcome further questioning, but this was the countryside, where everybody felt entitled to know everybody else's business.

'What sort of business is that, Mma?'

The question hung unanswered in the air as cicadas, somewhere in the dryness, kept up their incessant shriek. It was Mma Makutsi who eventually replied, 'We are enquiry agents, Mma. We make enquiries – general enquiries.'

Mma Ramotswe could not help but smile at the admirably vague answer, and, what was more, it was true. There were times, she thought, when Mma Makutsi showed complete brilliance. No wonder she had got ninety-seven per cent ...

The women at the stall looked at one another. None wanted to be shown to be ignorant of what an enquiry agent did, and so there were nods of understanding. They repeated their directions.

'You will find her in, Mma,' said one. 'I saw her go into the house a few minutes ago.'

As Mma Ramotswe parked a short distance down the road, she complimented Mma Makutsi on her handling of the question. 'If we had said we were detectives, it would have been all round the village. There would be rumours that Blessing was in trouble with the police. People would have said all sorts of things.'

'These village people can be big gossips,' said Mma Makutsi. 'The biggest gossips are found in the places where the least is happening, you know. Go to a place where nothing has ever happened, and you will hear a lot of gossip – that's for sure.'

They approached the house pointed out by the women. It stood just off the road, and next to it, across a straggling single-strand fence, was a house that was half-shack, more of an outhouse or garage than anything else, with a decrepit motorbike parked outside it. A few discouraged-looking paw-paw trees clustered about the back of this house; otherwise, the yard was bare.

They walked up a narrow path that led to Blessing's home. All along the edge of this path, empty bottles, upended, had been half sunk in the ground to provide an ornamental border. The bottles, mostly green, were coated with dried mud and dust, lending them a forlorn appearance; an attempt at beautification that seemed only to make more pronounced the slight air of desolation that hung over the village. This was not a prosperous place; this had none of the bustle of Mochudi, where Mma Ramotswe had been born and brought up. If the inhabitants of this village nursed any hope, Mma Ramotswe imagined, it was a hope of getting away rather than of making anything of local life.

She glanced at Mma Makutsi, who she imagined was thinking much the same thing.

'I haven't seen a village stand-pipe,' muttered Mma Makutsi. 'I wonder if these people have water. A well, maybe.'

'It is hard for them,' said Mma Ramotswe. 'Everywhere in Botswana is getting better, but there are some places ... ' She sighed. The benefits of progress had been unevenly spread. There was affluence in the big towns, but this did not always trickle down as the politicians said it would.

They approached the *lelapa*, the yard around which a knee-height wall described the curtilage of the home. From the gateway, Mma Ramotswe called out, "*Ko ko,*" the greeting for an invitation to enter. Blessing had seen them from a window, and the front door was quickly opened, from which she called out her own greeting. She was evidently pleased to see them, and enquired solicitously, and at some length, about their journey from Gaborone. Had there been much traffic on the road? Had there been many bad drivers?

'Yes,' said Mma Makutsi, 'almost all of them are bad these days.' Had they found the turn-off without difficulty?

The house was a small one – four rooms – the first of which served as kitchen and sitting room. There was a table, four hard-backed chairs, and an ancient couch covered over with a bright blanket which served as a throw. The shelf above the couch was lined with provisions – the familiar foodstuffs of the simple kitchen: a packet of sugar, a couple of tins of corned beef, a small bag of dried beans, sweetened condensed milk.

Because the room was gloomy, even in the noon light, Mma Ramotswe had not noticed the door at the back, which was slightly ajar. Now it opened, and an elderly woman entered, a shawl wrapped round her shoulders.

'This is my mother,' said Blessing.

Mma Ramotswe and Mma Makutsi issued the traditional greetings, referring to her politely as Mma Blessing – mother of Blessing.

'So you are Precious Ramotswe,' said Mma Blessing to Mma Makutsi.

Mma Makutsi put her right. 'No, Mma. This lady here is Mma Ramotswe. I am Mma Makutsi. She works with me.'

Mma Ramotswe noticed that. Mma Makutsi worked with *her*, but this was not the time nor the place.

Mma Blessing nodded as she absorbed this information. 'So you are the lady,' she said to Mma Ramotswe. 'You are the daughter of Obed?'

It had been years since her father had died – her daddy, as she still called him, but even now, after all that time, it made her catch her breath to hear his name on another's lips. He came to her mind every day – every single day – but it was different when his name was brought up by somebody else. That made her feel all the more that he was still there somewhere, in that Botswana that had existed, but had faded, and that he had not yet been forgotten. The past was a vast congregation of people, countless, crowded; a Botswana that was slipping away now, as must inevitably happen, but that still harboured those whom we might recognise, who were special to us, and whose name, even if uttered by chance, triggered memories of warmth and love.

'I am his daughter, Mma,' she replied.

Mma Blessing moved towards her to place a hand upon her right forearm. There was surprising strength in the grasp, as often is the case with the grip of the elderly – who might hold on to others as if clutching at a world they knew they must lose. Mma Ramotswe put her own left hand over Mma Blessing's extended fingers: the skin was dry, not really flesh but just a cover for the bone beneath.

'Obed and I were children together,' the old woman said. 'Our grandfathers were cousins, you see, and that made us cousins too, although far-away cousins, of course. But that makes no difference, does it? It is the same blood, isn't it?'

Mma Ramotswe nodded. She looked into Mma Blessing's eyes, and saw that they were white with cataracts. 'It is the same blood,' she said.

'And that never changes, does it?'

Mma Ramotswe inclined her head in agreement. She wondered what Mma Blessing could see through the tiny white discs that were in the pupils of her eyes. They said that it made the light fade, as if the world was seen through a milky screen, though seen less and less as the condition progressed. But surely she could have them removed, because Mma Ramtoswe had been told that it was a very simple procedure now, not nearly as complex, or expensive, as the replacement of a hip.

Mma Blessing relaxed her grip, and, feeling for the back of one of the hard-backed chairs, she sat down. 'The last time I saw you,

Mma, you were a little girl. It was not long after your mother became late, and you were being looked after by your aunts, or it might have been a cousin. I do not remember all that well now, although I remember you. I remember seeing you and you were wearing a red dress and you were laughing.'

Wearing a red dress and laughing . . .That was a memory anybody might herself wish to have of her childhood. Yes, she had been fortunate, because there had been so much laughter in her childhood. Some people remembered only tears and anxiety, and even fear; she remembered laughter.

'And now,' continued Mma Blessing, 'now you are this lady living in Gaborone, and you have a husband and a business and everything. And they have even had your photograph in the paper, I'm told.'

'Only once,' said Mma Ramotswe. 'And there were other people in the photograph with me.'

'That is still very important, Mma. Back in my day, nobody put photographs of women in the papers. Or if we were in photographs, they did not put our names. They put the names of the men under the photograph, but not the names of the women.'

Mma Makutsi had been silent, but now she spoke. 'That has all changed, Mma Blessing. Now the women are deciding who should be in the photographs. There are ladies working on the newspapers and they put photographs of ladies on the front page, and there are men in the background.'

Mma Ramotswe laughed. 'Sometimes, Mma. Sometimes.'

'Soon men will be in the back seat,' Mma Makutsi continued. 'And we will be the ones who are driving the car.'

Mma Blessing drew in her breath. 'That will be a big day, Mma. I shall be late by then, I think, but it will be a big day for Africa.'

'You must have tea,' interjected Blessing. 'And I shall call Tefo.

He will come over from his place.' She waved a hand in the air, in the direction of the shack they had seen next door.

There was no electricity in the house, and the tea had been brewing on a fire at the back. Mma Ramotswe had detected this, as there was a smell of woodsmoke in the air. Sometimes people would use a small paraffin stove; sometimes they would rely on the embers kept warm in a stone hearth. She suspected that Mma Blessing would be the one in this household to prefer a real fire.

As Blessing went out to make the tea, her mother continued the conversation. 'It's good of you to come and see Tefo,' she said. 'He is your cousin too, you see. His grandfather was a cousin of the second wife of my uncle. The first wife went away. She was not much good, Mma. She went away.'

'It is sometimes best if people who are not much good go away,' said Mma Makutsi. 'That is what I think, at least.'

There was the sound of a throat being cleared, just inside a dim back room, and then a man appeared in the doorway. This was Tefo, a tall man neatly dressed in khaki trousers and shirt. He had a walking stick, and was leaning heavily on it, taking the weight off his left leg.

They greeted one another.

'I have heard all about you,' said Mma Ramotswe. 'And now we are meeting.'

'I have heard all about you, too, Mma,' he said. 'I have heard that you are a famous detective up in Gaborone.'

Mma Ramotswe laughed. 'I am not famous, Rra. It is just a little business.'

'Two people,' said Mma Makutsi. 'Two directors, and one boy.'

'I'm sure you do very important work,' said Tefo.

He made his way towards the chair next to Mma Blessing. He walked with a pronounced limp.

'I'm sorry to hear about your hip,' said Mma Ramotswe. 'These things are very painful.'

'Yes, very painful,' said Tefo.

'And I'm sorry to hear that you cannot get the operation at the government hospital.'

Tefo sighed. 'There is a problem for me. I am not a citizen, you see. I was born over on that side – in South Africa – and so they say, "Go over there and get it done in one of their hospitals." But if I go over there, they say to me, "You are not a citizen because you have lived for a long time in Botswana. You are their problem – not ours."'

'That is what bureaucracy is like,' said Mma Makutsi. 'They make up rules so that they can say that it is nothing to do with them. They are very clever, these people.'

Mma Blessing shook her head. 'There are many people who are not wanted. In the old days, everybody was wanted by somebody, Mma Ramotswe. Now it is different. Nobody wants other people.'

This remark was followed by silence. Then Mma Makutsi said, 'Your place is next door, Rra?'

Tefo nodded. 'That is my place. I built it myself.' There was a note of pride in his voice.

'You're very lucky to be able to build a house,' said Mma Makutsi. 'If I tried to build a house, I'm sure it would fall down.'

Tefo laughed. 'I don't think so, Mma. I'm sure that you would be very good at building houses.'

'I don't think so,' Mma Makutsi retorted. 'Not me.'

Mma Ramotswe glanced at Mma Makutsi. The exchange between her and Tefo was badinage, but it had a slightly flirtatious air to it.

Suddenly Mma Makutsi said, 'Would you show it to me, Rra? Could I see this place you've built?'

Tefo hesitated. He looked briefly at Blessing and then at her mother. 'Now, Mma?' he said to Mma Makutsi.

'Why not?'

He rose to his feet. As he did so, his stick fell to the floor. As he started to bend down to retrieve it, Mma Makutsi stepped forward. 'You must let me pick that up, Rra,' she said. 'Your hip ...'

He shook his head. 'I am all right. Or mostly all right. I can do these small things.'

'It must be very painful,' said Mma Makutsi.

Tefo patted his leg. 'If I do not ask it to do too much for me, it is all right,' he said.

Mma Makutsi looked at Mma Ramotswe. There was a message in the look, but Mma Ramotswe was unsure what it was. So she said, 'May I come and see your place too, Rra?'

Tefo said that he was happy to show anybody his house. 'I used breeze blocks for the foundations,' he said. 'There are very good foundations in my house. And the lower parts of the walls are made of those blocks too. Termites cannot eat concrete, you see. Or only those termites who have metal teeth ...'

Mma Makutsi laughed. 'I wouldn't like to be bitten by one of those,' she said.

'It depends where you get bitten,' said Tefo. 'I should not like to sit on a termite like that.'

To Mma Ramotswe's surprise, Mma Makutsi giggled girlishly. 'No, that would not be good. Definitely not.'

'The tea will be ready when you get back,' said Mma Blessing. 'You can drink it after you have seen the house.'

They went outside. 'You have a very nice view from this place,' said Mma Makutsi. 'The hills over there. The trees ...'

Tefo seemed pleased. 'It is a good place to be, Mma. People who live in big towns don't know what they're missing.'

'They don't miss everything,' muttered Mma Makutsi.

Mma Ramotswe looked at her quizzically. Mma Makutsi, meeting her look, gave a small signal with her hand. Mma Ramotswe shook her head, as discreetly as she could.

They stepped over the wire fence, held down for them by Tefo. 'I am very pleased with these trees,' he said, pointing to the paw-paws. 'I get fruit from them. I shall plant some more one day, I think.'

'Paw-paw is very good for you,' said Mma Makutsi. 'Now, Rra, show us this place of yours. You must be very proud of having built it all yourself. Look at it, Rra! Very good.'

At the end of their visit, after the drinking of the tea and the making of farewells, they walked the short distance to the parked van in silence. It was not until they were back on the main road that the conversation began, as Mma Ramotswe had been busy negotiating the obstacles on the badly maintained track from the village. 'Don't talk to me just yet,' she said to Mma Makutsi. 'I do not want to end up in a ditch.'

'There is much that I want so say.'

'Me too,' said Mma Ramotswe, swinging the steering wheel to avoid a place where the track had collapsed into a ditch.

On the main road, a tarred surface once again beneath their wheels, Mma Makutsi began. 'Did you see it, Mma? Did you see it?'

Mma Ramotswe sighed. 'I am very disappointed. I must say that.'

'Disappointed?' exclaimed Mma Makutsi. 'Maybe we should be disappointed that acting standards have fallen so low. Maybe we should be discussing how sad it is that nobody in this country could ever get a job in the films. Maybe we should say that there's a big need for a drama college in these parts. Maybe we should be saying all that, Mma.'

She was right, thought Mma Ramotswe. 'You put it very well, Mma.'

Mma Makutsi snorted. 'Did you see how many times he changed legs, Mma? First, he said it was his left hip. Then he said something about his right leg, I seem to recall. Then, when we went over to his house, he had his stick in his right hand, having held it in his left hand just a few moments before.'

'I saw that,' Mma Ramotswe replied. 'It was a good idea of yours to get him to show us his house.'

'Oh, I knew immediately, Mma Ramotswe. I knew the moment he came into the room. I knew.'

'But how, Mma?'

Mma Makutsi hesitated. 'There's something I call the *guilty look*, Mma. You can't mistake it. You take one look at somebody and you know straight away.'

Mma Ramotswe was intrigued. 'But can you be sure, Mma?' There was nothing about that in Clovis Andersen's book – nothing remotely like that. *The Principles of Private Detection* was all about observation and conclusions based on the evidence of one's eyes. It was not about unfounded suspicion. And yet, thought Mma Ramotswe, and yet ... She had never been deaf to her feelings and the instincts that occasionally moved her to conclude one way or the other, but she was not convinced that you would ever know *straight away* ...

'I am sure.'

There was another reason for immediate distrust of Tefo, but Mma Makutsi did not mention it to Mma Ramotswe. Her shoes had said something. That tiny voice that apparently only she could hear had whispered to her as he came into the room. *Don't trust these people, boss.* That was what they had said. She was sure of it, although she knew, of course, that shoes could not talk. And yet hers seemed to do just that. Unless the voice came from within, she told herself. If it did, then there was a rational explanation for the phenomenon. And yet she was sure she had heard them. The voice had come from down below, not from up in the head. And it had spoken with that small, nasal voice that shoes have. It was all very puzzling, but the message, at least, was clear. *Don't trust these people, boss.* What could be less ambiguous than that?

Chapter Six

Vehicles Have a Smell

It was quite by chance that Mr J. L. B. Matekoni should have decided that afternoon to change the oil in Mma Ramotswe's tiny white van. At the last minute an important client had cancelled an appointment for the routine service of his two Mercedes-Benz delivery vans and this meant both Mr J. L. B. Matekoni and his junior mechanic, Fanwell, found themselves with time on their hands. It was the sort of cancellation that would normally be extremely irritating, but, in this case at least, Tlokweng Road Speedy Motors was prepared to forgive more or less anything. This client, who ran a business providing sound equipment for weddings and other special occasions, had made a point of bringing his expensive vans to Mr J. L. B. Matekoni when many in his position would have taken them to one of the large garages on the other side of town. 'I do not like those big places,' he announced. 'They charge you hundreds of pula just to drive over their threshold. They say, "How are you, Rra?" And then the next thing they say is, "That will be three hundred pula." And then they ask, "When do you think the rains will arrive?" That's two hundred and fifty pula. "Now then, what is the trouble with your vehicle?" Five hundred pula please. And so on.'

These ruminations, already producing a grin of pleasure on Mr J. L. B. Matekoni's face, became even better. 'And then their mechanics, Rra,' the client continued, 'oh, my goodness. Are those people trained to take an engine to pieces and then put it back again? They are not. They are computer operators, that's what they are. They call themselves mechanics, but I may as well call myself a brain surgeon – which I am not, by the way. They plug your car into their computer – "One thousand pula, please, payable now" – and the computer says there is big rubbish going on somewhere, and it tells them where it is. But do you think they know how to fix that rubbish? They do not, Mr J. L. B. Matekoni. What the computer says is, "You must take out that part and replace it with a new part, number 678a/b (three thousand pula). Then everything will be all right again and we shall all be happy." That is what the computer says.'

'Ha!' exclaimed Mr J. L. B. Matekoni. 'You have diagnosed what is wrong with those places, Rra. You are one hundred per cent right about all that. I do not have a computer, of course.'

'No, you do not have a computer, Rra, because you are a proper *mechanic*, rather than an IT person. You have *tools*. You have oil cans. You have your instruments, just like a surgeon has his scalpel. That is the difference, you see. And you know how an engine works. Those fellows in those places know how a cash register works. Oh yes, they are very good at that, I can tell you!

'So,' the client went on, 'I am very happy to be bringing my vans to you, Rra, because I know that I will not have to take out a bank loan to pay your bill. I also know that you will try to fix anything that needs to be fixed rather than just giving up and throwing some part away. That is the difference.'

'Thank you, Rra. It is good to hear that you approve of what we do at Tlokweng Road Speedy Motors.'

Any relationship based on such sentiments can survive the occasional cancellation at short notice. In addition, Mr J. L. B. Matekoni knew that the calling-off of the service was for a very good reason: the client was required to provide sound amplification for a major funeral taking place out of town. This was for a well-respected retired politician who, as a young man, had served under Seretse Khama himself and who, full of years, had died out at his cattle post, on the land that he loved, amidst the cattle that he cherished. There would be large crowds at the ceremony in his village, and the speeches would be long. There was nothing worse than listening to a speech you could not hear, and the family was keen to have good loudspeaker arrangements to ensure that everybody could pick up every word of what was said.

The cancellation, justified though it was, left the garage idle. For this reason, when his eye fell on Mma Ramotswe and Mma Makutsi returning from their visit to Blessing, it occurred to Mr J. L. B. Matekoni to service the van and perhaps attend to the suspension. Suspension was the van's main weak point – amongst rather a lot of weak points, if the truth be told – this being particularly so on Mma Ramotswe's side of the vehicle. 'Your van sags a bit,' he had said to her, 'because the weight is mostly on one side, Mma ...' And he had added quickly, 'That is quite normal, of course. It is nothing to do with—'

'Being traditionally built?'

'No, it is nothing to do with that, Mma. It is a distribution issue. That is all.'

Now he turned to Fanwell and suggested that he get the key from Mma Ramotswe and move her van onto the inspection ramp. 'We can spend a bit of time on that front suspension,' he said. 'And the oil will need changing. Give an old engine clean oil and she'll thank you.'

'Who'll thank you, Rra? Mma Ramotswe or the engine?'

Mr J. L. B. Matekoni smiled. 'I meant the engine,' he replied. 'But Mma Ramotswe will thank you too.'

Fanwell drove the van over and positioned it on the pneumatic ramp. As he got out of the cab, he remarked to Mr J. L. B. Matekoni, 'Funny smell, Rra.'

Mr J. L. B. Matekoni frowned. You had to watch the electrics on an old vehicle, as cables had a habit of burning out when their plastic sleeves rotted. 'Something burning, do you think?'

Fanwell shook his head. 'You stick your nose in there, boss. It's not that sort of smell. That plastic burning smell is different. I always recognise that. No, this is ... Well, it's a sort of ... sort of cattle smell.' He frowned; something was puzzling him. 'But not quite.'

Mr J. L. B. Matekoni opened the driver's door and sniffed at the air inside. He looked puzzled as he walked round to the back of the van and lowered the tailgate. He sniffed inside the back of the van.

'It's coming from in there,' he said. 'And yet, it's empty. There's nothing in the van.'

Fanwell scratched his head. 'But you must admit that there has been *something*, boss. It's not there now, but there was something there earlier on. Has Mma Ramotswe been carting cattle dung around? Maybe for use in somebody's fire, do you think? Or for making one of those traditional floors?'

Mr J. L. B. Matekoni was at a loss. 'Vehicles have a smell,' he said to Fanwell. 'We all know that. But this . . . I have never smelled a van that has *this* particular smell.' He paused. 'Perhaps I should ask Mma Ramotswe what she's been carrying in here. Sometimes she goes to that garden centre, to Sanitas, and gets those unusual fertilisers for her beans. Some of them smell a bit strange, if you ask me. But this smell . . . ' He shook his head. 'This is what I would call a mysterious smell, Fanwell.'

Fanwell shrugged. 'Or Charlie might know?'

'Why Charlie?' asked Mr J. L. B. Matekoni.

'Because he's been driving the van. Mma Ramotswe lent it to him. Did she not tell you?'

Mr J. L. B. Matekoni did not answer, but turned on his heel and made his way into the office to have a word with Mma Ramotswe. She was busy talking on the telephone, but signalled to Mr J. L. B. Matekoni to sit down in the client chair while she finished the call. Mma Makutsi was filing – an activity that always engaged her attention completely, and so she just nodded curtly and continued with her task.

'Well, Rra,' said Mma Ramotswe as she put down the receiver. 'Are you ready for a cup of tea?'

Mr J. L. B. Matekoni shook his head. 'I'm about to change the engine oil in your van,' he said. 'And give it the once-over too.'

She thanked him. She remembered what he had told her about the importance of regular oil changes in an old vehicle.

'But there is one thing,' Mr J. L. B. Matekoni said. 'One thing is puzzling me, Mma. And it's puzzling Fanwell too. There is a smell, you see. I was wondering what you had been carrying in the van.'

For a few moments, Mma Ramotswe did not answer. But then she remembered; yes, there had been a smell, and she had noticed it the previous day, when she had been driving home. She had opened the window to try to get rid of it, but it had lingered. She had made a mental note to ask Mr J. L. B. Matekoni about it, but it had slipped her mind. Now she said, 'Yes, Rra. You are absolutely right. There *is* a smell. I smelled it yesterday.'

'And did you have anything in the van that might have caused it?'

She shook her head. There was always a reason for a smell. She did not think that Clovis Andersen had said anything about smells in *The Principles of Private Detection*, but had he addressed the subject he would undoubtedly have said something like, *There is no smell without a reason for a smell. That is basic. Rotten smell, rotten situation* ... Perhaps she could write that in the margin in the chapter on 'Drawing conclusions from the evidence of your senses' – a very important chapter that she and Mma Makutsi had often discussed.

Mr J. L. B. Matekoni raised the question of Charlie's use of the van. 'What did Charlie do with your van? Fanwell said that you lent it to him yesterday.'

'He needed it to help a friend with something.'

'With *something*?'

Mma Ramotswe shrugged. 'Yes, Mr J. L. B. Matekoni. He did not tell me what it was. He was helping a friend to transport something.'

Mma Makutsi now detached herself from her filing. She had warned Mma Ramotswe that Charlie might be up to something, and here was the fallout she had worried about. She fixed Mr J. L. B. Matekoni with a quizzical stare. 'Has he done something to the van, Rra? This morning I thought there was something wrong with it.' She threw a glance at Precious. 'I said that, didn't I, Mma Ramotswe?'

'The van is all right,' said Mr J. L. B. Matekoni. 'It's just that there's a smell.'

Mma Makutsi's eyes narrowed. 'A smell, Rra? An illegal smell? Do you think it's an illegal smell?'

'I wouldn't say that,' replied Mr J. L. B. Matekoni. 'It's certainly not *dagga*. You can always tell if somebody's been smoking *dagga*. No, it's not that.'

'But still illegal, do you think?' pressed Mma Makutsi.

She wanted him to say yes, it was, but he did not. And perhaps I should not be surprised, she thought; she would be hard pressed to think of any other illegal smells, although undoubtedly there were some. The smell of money being laundered, for example – that might be a memorable smell, if one were ever to encounter it, although of course nobody ever actually put dirty money in the wash …

'I'm not saying anything about illegality,' said Mr J. L. B. Matekoni. 'All I'm saying is that Charlie must have been carrying something unusual yesterday. Now there is a smell. And there is also a bit of buckling on the tailgate.' He paused. 'Where is Charlie, by the way?'

'It is his day off,' said Mma Ramotswe.

'I'd like to have a word with him,' said Mr J. L. B. Matekoni. 'I'd like to ask him to explain himself. If you borrow somebody's vehicle, you don't abuse it.'

He said that with conviction. But it was not only his deep-seated respect for vehicles that had been offended here; there was the additional issue of truth-telling. Mr J. L. B. Matekoni felt strongly about the truth – as did Mma Ramotswe – and the idea that somebody should fail to mention damage done to a borrowed item was anathema to him.

'He'll be at his uncle's place, where he used to stay,' said Mma Makutsi. 'He hangs about there on his day off. That new wife of his … Queenie-Queenie … She works, and so he can't see her until after five.'

Charlie had recently married, and was living in a rented flat near the village, courtesy of his new father-in-law.

Mr J. L. B. Matekoni looked at Fanwell. 'I think I'm going to go and have a word with him. You come too, Fanwell.'

Fanwell looked uncomfortable. If Charlie was going to be berated – which looked likely – he was not sure that he wanted to be party to that. Charlie asked for this sort of thing to happen, but he and Fanwell had been through a lot together over the years, and there was an old bond between them.

'But there are things to do here,' he began. And then, rather lamely, 'Work and . . . ' He trailed off.

Mr J. L. B. Matekoni's expression suggested the subject was closed: Fanwell would be accompanying him. He was a mild man, not given to strong views or displays of anger, but the young mechanic could tell that his boss was rattled.

'I'll come, boss,' Fanwell said quickly, wiping his hands on a twist of the blue absorbent paper dispensed from a large roll on the wall. He looked down at the ground: he had warned Charlie that he would take matters too far one day – he had told him. Whatever could have possessed him to think that he could damage Mma Ramotswe's van, fail to mention what had happened, and then get away with it? As a very young man – an eighteen-year-old – Charlie had been able to get away with virtually anything through sheer charm. People forgave him because of his jaunty good looks and his winning smile. Those seemed to work with everybody – they were particularly effective with women; but men, too, seemed susceptible to them. It was a different effect with them, thought Fanwell: men saw in Charlie the boy they once were – or would have liked to be. Older women saw him as a wayward son – they wanted to mother him – while to young women he was seditiously attractive: a bad boy who wasn't quite as bad as all that, who would calm down once a wedding ring was placed on his finger and he was staked off as occupied territory.

Fanwell was not a risk-taker. When attending to car engines he tested nuts before he attempted to take them off the bolt; Charlie would use brute force, not caring about stripping the thread. When connecting a wire to a terminal, Fanwell would use a carefully positioned drop of solder, just to be sure, whereas Charlie would simply make a loop with the end of the wire and wind it round the screw. The difference was stability and permanence; Charlie's mechanical interventions might fix a problem, but they would do that only for a short while. Sooner or later the patch would be shaken off by the vibrations that pass through any car in motion, and the problem for which help had been sought would recur. 'People don't like bringing their cars back to the garage,' Mr J. L. B. Matekoni explained. 'Mechanics are like dentists: people don't want to see them too often.'

Charlie had raised a finger to make a point. 'Me,' he said, 'I've never been to the dentist. Not once. Ever.'

Mr J. L. B. Matekoni had ignored this, but Fanwell had expressed surprise. 'Never? Never ever, Charlie? You mean you've never gone, even if he didn't do anything to your teeth?'

Charlie had struck a nonchalant pose. 'Never. That's what I said. Why go to the dentist unless your teeth are sore. Mine aren't.' He opened his mouth and tapped his front teeth. 'These teeth – see them – they're never sore. Never. And all the teeth behind them are in first-class condition A1. I don't need a dentist to tell me that.'

Fanwell shook his head. 'Everyone needs to go to the dentist, Charlie. They told us that at school. Remember that science teacher who gave lessons on personal hygiene? Remember him? What did he say, Charlie? What did he say?'

Charlie shrugged. 'He was always saying things. That's the

trouble with teachers – they spend a lot of their time saying things. If they said fewer things – hardly anything – then people would listen to them. But they don't.'

Fanwell looked to Mr J. L. B. Matekoni for support, which was forthcoming. 'Fanwell is right. Things can be going on inside your teeth, Charlie. Outside, they can look fine, but once you get inside they can be full of rot.' Mr J. L. B. Matekoni paused. 'You should see a dentist, Charlie. I will pay for you to have a check-up.'

Charlie was unconvinced. 'That's good of you, boss. But I don't want to waste your money. If I went to a dentist he'd take one look and then say, "First-class teeth – nothing needed there." But we'd still have to pay, you see, and I don't want to waste your money, boss.'

'But it's not just about teeth,' Fanwell persisted. 'There's something called gum disease, Charlie. If your guns get sick, then your teeth drop out. You wake up one morning and you have no teeth. That has happened many times. And if you had no teeth, what would the girls say?'

'They'd say, "No thanks,"' offered Mr J. L. B. Matekoni. 'Girls like a man to have teeth.'

Charlie laughed. 'How do you know that, boss? I don't want to be rude, but how do you know what girls want?'

Mr J. L. B. Matekoni took the question in a good-natured way. 'I might surprise you, Charlie,' he said. 'You may not know that I was a big man with the women back in the old days. Oh yes, you can smile at that, but I was. There were always women watching me, waiting for their chance.'

Even Fanwell was surprised. 'You must have been very popular, Rra. What happened?'

Mr J. L. B. Matekoni looked hurt. 'What happened? Are you saying that . . . ' He made a helpless gesture.

Fanwell quickly apologised. 'I did not mean that, Rra. I did not mean to say that you are not popular still. I think you are. Women are still watching you, Rra. I have seen it.'

Mr J. L. B. Matekoni was suddenly interested. 'Oh, really, Fanwell? Where are these women? I have not seen them, I'm afraid. I'm prepared to accept they are there, but I have not seen them myself.'

Charlie caught Fanwell's eye. 'You shouldn't be winding the boss up,' he said. 'There are no women, Rra. Or not that we have seen.'

'There could be,' said Fanwell. 'You know what women are like, Charlie. They are always on the lookout for a better man. They look at the man they already have and think: there must be better men than this one. That's what I believe they think.' He lowered his voice. 'I have heard women say that – using those exact words. It is very shocking.' He paused. 'Even that Queenie-Queenie of yours. I don't want to make you feel insecure, Charlie, but how do you know what goes on in her head? How do you know that she isn't thinking: there must be men who are a bit better than Charlie? That's what I would be thinking if I were going out with you. That's what I'd be saying to myself.'

They drove in Mr J. L. B. Matekoni's truck to the street in the heart of Old Naledi where Charlie's uncle's house occupied a corner lot. It was a shabby part of town, one of the cheapest suburbs, ignored by the wave of prosperity that had moved across so many other parts of Gaborone. Many of the houses here were not much more than shacks, even if there were none of the tarpaulin and tin shelters of the real shanty town. Such places had not come into existence in Botswana because the poverty that produced them had been kept at bay, but even so, there were still families who lived in cement-block houses of one room and a make-do kitchen, where people washed in small tin tubs, and where the characteristic odour of penury, that smell of cheap soap and rancid frying oil, of rubbed-in dirt, was never far away. This was nothing like that; indeed, Charlie's uncle's house was well appointed by comparison, had a sound roof of red-painted tin, and, being at the end of a street, enjoyed a large plot of scrub land on which structures of any sort were yet to be built. This land boasted a thicket of trees and an unruly hedge of rubber plant with its friable branches and its viscous white sap.

Mr J. L. B. Matekoni parked the truck at the gate and gestured for Fanwell to follow him up the short path that led to the house. Fanwell dragged his feet; he was not relishing this encounter with his friend.

'Don't be too hard on him, boss,' he said as they closed the gate behind them.

Mr J. L. B. Matekoni sighed. 'I am not like that, Fanwell. I haven't come to punish him. I've come to ask for an explanation.'

Fanwell nodded. He understood.

'And if nobody asked Charlie to explain himself,' Mr J. L. B. Matekoni continued, 'if nobody tackled him about a thing like this, then it would be doing him no favours. He has to learn that he can't do this sort of thing and get away with it.'

Fanwell nodded again. 'I know that, Rra. I know that.'

They approached the house. The front door, a rickety-looking construction painted green and with a gauze fly-screen across its top half, was held open by a propped-up stick. Inside the house, the legs of a table could be made out, and a burning light bulb. Mr J. L. B. Matekoni called out, and then moved to knock on the door.

A boy of about ten appeared. His torso was bare, his only garment being a pair of skimpy khaki shorts. He raised his eyes to the visitors, and then lowered them again. A child did not stare at older people; most children had that instilled in them at an early age.

Mr J. L. B. Matekoni greeted the child politely. 'We have come to speak to Charlie.'

The child said nothing, his gaze still fixed on the floor at his feet.

'You're Charlie's cousin, aren't you?' said Fanwell. 'I've met you, I think. Have I met you?'

The boy nodded. 'You are my cousin's friend, Rra. I know you.'

'So where is Charlie?' asked Fanwell, and added, 'We haven't come to give him trouble, you know. That is not why we are here.'

The child seemed relieved by the assurance. 'He is not in the house. He is outside.'

Fanwell frowned. 'We did not see him. We came in that way.' He gestured behind them.

'He is not that side,' said the child. 'He is over there – behind the house. But he will not want to see you, I think. I think he will want you to go away.'

Mr J. L. B. Matekoni smiled. 'How do you know that, young fellow? How do you know he will not want to see us? I'm his boss at the garage. Did you know that?'

The boy cast his eyes down once again. 'He told me to tell anybody to go away.'

Fanwell shook a finger at the boy. 'We are not anybody. I am Charlie's friend from a long way back. Back, back. And this is his boss. We are not just anybody.'

The boy pointed again. 'I can take you. He is just back there.' He paused. 'But he told me that nobody was to see what he has there. He told me that, and I am scared because he will be very angry and will hit me.'

Fanwell tried to reassure the boy. 'You can stay here. The boss and I will go and find him. He will not blame you.'

The boy looked miserable. 'He will say I told you about the elephant.'

This brought sudden silence as Fanwell and Mr J. L. B. Matekoni exchanged glances.

'An elephant?' asked Mr J. L. B. Matekoni. 'What is this elephant?'

The boy pursed his lips.

'You must tell us,' said Fanwell. 'You cannot say "elephant" and leave it at that. What elephant are you talking about?'

The boy looked up. 'He has an elephant now. Charlie has an elephant.'

Fanwell laughed. 'Charlie has an elephant! Yes, and I have a giraffe. Or maybe a lion. Yes, I have a lion.'

The boy shook his head vigorously. 'No, Rra, I am not talking about any of those animals. I am talking about the elephant that Charlie has out at the back there. Behind the hedge. There is a very small elephant. Very small.'

Fanwell looked to Mr J. L. B. Matekoni for guidance. 'What do we do, boss?'

'We go and take a look,' said Mr J. L. B. Matekoni.

Fanwell followed him out of the house and along a path that led to the hedge and the cluster of trees on the wasteland. 'There can't be an elephant,' he said. 'That boy is imagining it.'

'We'll see,' said Mr J. L. B. Matekoni. 'I can't imagine there's an—'

He stopped. Through the body of the hedge they could make out the figure of Charlie, bending over a small, humped shape. And then the shape moved, and its ears and its trunk could be made out. There was a baby elephant; it could be nothing else.

'Charlie!' called out Mr J. L. B. Matekoni.

Charlie straightened up. He opened his mouth to say something, but then closed it again. The elephant raised its minute trunk and ran it across Charlie's forearm gently, tentatively.

'See,' said Charlie. 'See. He thinks I'm his mother.'

Mr J. L. B. Matekoni and Fanwell said nothing.

'You see?' Charlie repeated.

Fanwell shook his head. 'You've really done it now, Charlie.'

If Charlie noticed the reproach, he did not show it. He smiled. Addressing Mr J. L. B. Matekoni with a note of triumph, he said, 'You see, boss? You see how this little elephant likes me?'

Mr J. L. B. Matekoni shook his head. He turned to Fanwell. 'Did you know about this?' he asked. 'Did you know that Charlie had an elephant?'

Fanwell was indignant. 'Of course I didn't, boss. Charlie has never done anything like this before.' He paused. 'So that was the smell in the van, Rra. That was the reason for the dent in the tailgate.'

Mr J. L. B. Matekoni sighed. 'Did you transport an elephant in Mma Ramotswe's van, Charlie?'

Charlie stroked the tiny elephant behind its ears. 'Maybe, boss. Maybe.'

The elephant turned to face Mr J. L. B. Matekoni and took a few steps towards him. Mr J. L. B. Matekoni stood stock still.

'There,' said Charlie. 'He likes you too, boss. Maybe he thinks you're his father.' He laughed, and patted the calf on its head. 'Me, I'm the mother, and you're the father, Rra. And this little one . . .' He gave another pat on the head. 'And this little one is our child.'

Mr J. L. B. Matekoni was silent as the tiny elephant's trunk explored his shoes and ankles. He turned to Charlie. 'What are you going to do with this poor little creature, Charlie?'

Charlie shrugged. 'I don't know, boss. But that's not really my problem. My friend says he's working something out.'

'And what will that be?' pressed Mr J. L. B. Matekoni.

'Don't ask me, boss. I'm just looking after him for a few days.'

They stayed a few minutes longer, and then, leaving Charlie with the elephant, they made their way back to the front of the house. The young cousin came out to meet them.

Mr J. L. B. Matekoni looked at the boy, who was frowning, as if worried about something. 'Are you all right?' he asked.

The boy stopped in his tracks, staring at the ground. Then he raised his eyes to meet Mr J. L. B. Matekoni's gaze.

'They're going to eat that elephant,' he said.

Nobody moved. At last Fanwell broke the silence. 'Who's going to eat him?'

The boy's voice was no more than a whisper. 'Not Charlie. It is not Charlie.'

'Who then?' asked Mr J. L. B. Matekoni, bending down so that he was looking the youngster in the face.

The boy closed his eyes. 'I heard Charlie's friend talking to his brother on his phone. Charlie was not here. The friend's brother is a butcher, Rra. He said that he would take the elephant. I heard him talking about money.'

'And you're sure Charlie doesn't know?'

'He does not know, Rra.'

Fanwell frowned. 'But why have you not warned Charlie?'

The boy shifted his weight from foot to foot. 'Charlie always does what that friend tells him to do. He is a bit scared of him, I think, Rra.' He paused. 'And I do not think he would believe me. That friend of his is a liar, and he would say that he was not going to do this thing he was threatening to do, and Charlie would believe him.'

Mr J. L. B. Matekoni laid a hand on the boy's shoulder. 'Listen, young man, he said. 'Don't talk to anybody about this. Do you understand?'

The boy nodded miserably. 'It is a very friendly little elephant,' he said.

'Yes,' said Fanwell. 'It is.'

Chapter Seven

Morning Boyfriend, Evening Boyfriend

History records only a handful of occasions on which Mma Makutsi rose from her desk to her feet in astonishment, exaltation, or outrage. One was when Mma Ramotswe had announced that for the first month in its history the No. 1 Ladies' Detective Agency had made a profit (astonishment); the occasion when news had come through of the defeat of Violet Sephotho in one of her many machinations (exaltation); and that when apprentices had used her teapot for the temporary storage of diesel oil (outrage). And now there was just such a moment, as Mr J. L. B. Matekoni, accompanied by Fanwell, came into the office and cleared his throat in the way in which he always did when about to say something portentous.

'We have just seen something very ...' He struggled to find the right word. At his side, Fanwell ventured, 'Very unbelievable.'

Mr J. L. B. Matekoni nodded. 'Yes, indeed. Very unbelievable – so unbelievable as to be ...' Once more he floundered.

'So unbelievable that we cannot believe it,' suggested Fanwell.

Mma Makutsi looked up from the letter she was reading. It had come from a woman in Francistown who suspected that her husband was having an affair – a letter of a type that the agency received several times a week from all corners of the country. 'There are far too many affairs going on in Botswana,' Mma Ramotswe once said. 'You'd think that was number four in the list of national activities: diamond mining, wildlife tourism, cattle ... and then, affairs.' Mma Makutsi had smiled, but had doubted whether Botswana was any different from anywhere else. 'Those things are happening everywhere, Mma,' she said. 'Wherever there are men, then you will find that there are affairs going on.'

'But there are men everywhere, Mma. There is no country where there are no men.'

'That is true,' said Mma Makutsi. 'But what I said is also still generally true. Men are great ones for having affairs.'

Mma Ramotswe thought about this. She was all for the rights of women, and she was not one to tolerate men who tried to put women down, but at the same time her sense of fairness was bone-deep, and she did not approve of running down men simply because they were men. Mma Makutsi sometimes generalised on these things, she thought, and was inclined to dismiss men rather too readily. Now Mma Ramotswe pointed out that if so many men were, in fact, having affairs, then there must be an equal – or roughly equal – number of women who were doing the same thing themselves. If that were not the case, she pointed out, then who would those men be having affairs with? 'Unless,' she continued, 'there are some women who were having affairs with more than one man at a time. If that is happening, Mma Makutsi, then it is possible that there would be more men having affairs than there were women up to the same thing – if you see what I mean.'

'Oh, I see what you mean, Mma,' said Mma Makutsi. 'And that is probably true, you know. Look at Violet Sephotho.' She drew a deep breath for the *con brio* performance. 'She is one woman who contributes greatly to that particular statistic, Mma. When we were at the Botswana Secretarial College together she was notorious, Mma – *notorious* – for having more than one boyfriend at a time. She had a morning boyfriend, and then she had an afternoon boyfriend. And people said that there was an evening boyfriend too, although I was never able to confirm that. I could well believe it, though. You didn't have to be Clovis Andersen to work out what was going on.'

Mma Ramotswe shook her head. 'That is too many boyfriends, Mma.'

'Too many boyfriends? You're absolutely right, Mma Ramotswe. But too many for Violet Sephotho? I think not, Mma. I think not.' She lowered her voice. There were some things – indecent things – that should not be spoken about in a normal voice, but should be uttered only in a muted register. 'I can tell you, Mma, that there was one time she was driven to the college in the morning – early, early in the morning, Mma – by a man. He was one of those men who think they are just the thing, Mma – you know the type: sunglasses, even when the sun is only just coming up over the horizon. Gold watch – big gold watch – and gold chain round the neck. That sort of man, Mma. Why does a man need to wear a gold chain round his neck? Those chains are not made for men – they are made for ladies – and yet a certain sort of man comes along and says, "That is a very good chain for me." Anyway, there was this man and he drove up to the college – right up to the front door, Mma, and parked *right next to the Principal's car*. Can you believe that, Mma? An *unauthorised* car parking next to the Principal's car – in the very spot, in fact, in which the Professor of Accountancy would park his car . . . '

Mma Ramotswe listened intently. Mma Makutsi told a good story, with strong emphasis, even if some of what she said had to be taken with a pinch of salt. Mma Ramotswe might have pointed out that none of the staff at the Botswana Secretarial College were proper professors, and that it was wrong to give them a title reserved for the real professors at the University of Botswana, but she did not think that this was the time for that objection.

'This man parked in the Professor of Accountancy's place without the slightest hesitation. It is one thing to sneak into a reserved parking place for a minute or two and then sneak out again – who hasn't done that sort of thing, Mma? – but it's quite another thing, I think, to go and park in the Professor of Accountancy's place and then get out of the car, bold as brass, and stretch your legs, and kiss your girlfriend – *kiss her*, Mma – in full view of anybody coming up the drive of the Botswana Secretarial College.

'But that's exactly what Mr Gold Chain did, Mma Ramotswe. He put his arms round Violet Sephotho – right round her, Mma – and then he put his big film-star lips on her stupid over-painted mouth and kissed her. *Smack*, Mma. Just like that. *Slurp*. You can just imagine the germs that were flowing between them, Mma. A Limpopo River of germs. And then he pulled away – *slurp* – and she started to pat his face, Mma, like this – pat, pat – and she started to laugh, and he laughed too. But I was not laughing, Mma. I was walking up the drive as this thing happened, and I was too shocked to do anything but struggle for breath. Honestly, Mma, if I had fainted there and then and they had found me lying flat out on the ground, I would not have been in the least bit surprised.

'But then, Mma, I took a deep breath and tried to forget what I had just seen. We were told by a reverend up in Bobonong that if you saw something like that happening and you were truly shocked, then you should just sing a hymn under your breath. Not too loudly – you don't have to let everybody in the vicinity know that you are singing a hymn, but you sing it very quietly. The reverend said that this was the way to protect yourself against such things. So I sang a hymn under my breath, Mma. I sang "Shall we gather at the river". Do you know that one, Mma? It is a very good hymn, and I can recommend it for situations when you are very shocked by what you have just seen. The words are inspirational, Mma. They are very good words to remember. *Shall we gather at the river / Where bright angel feet have trod* ... And then the next verse goes, *Yes, we'll gather at the river / The beautiful, the beautiful river / Gather with the Saints at the river* ... Oh, it is a very good hymn, Mma Ramotswe.

'As I walked past, Violet looked at me and nudged her boy-friend – or Morning Boyfriend, as I should perhaps call him. And she said to me, "So what are you singing, Grace Makutsi?" That is what she said, Mma. And you know what I said to her? I said, "Mind your own business, Violet. It is none of your business what I am singing."'

'That would have shown her,' said Mma Ramotswe.

'It did. But then, Mma, I saw that there was lipstick all over his collar and the front of his shirt. She had been kissing him *all over the place*, Mma.'

This brought silence, which lasted until Mma Makutsi continued, 'And then, Mma, later that day – at eleven o'clock, when we ended the morning session early because it was a Wednesday, which was our half-day – at eleven, Mma, another car was at the end of the drive, and this was driven by another, different man, Mma. This was the real, official Morning Boyfriend, which meant that the boyfriend we'd seen in the early morning was not the Morning Boyfriend after all, but was the *Evening Boyfriend*, Mma . . . ' Mma Makutsi lowered her voice even further. 'Coming off shift, Mma. Coming off shift.'

Mma Ramotswe waited a few moments in case there was more, but there was not. So she said, 'That is a very interesting story, Mma Makutsi. Violet Sephotho is clearly a lady who has too many boyfriends, I would say.'

'You can say that again,' retorted Mma Makutsi. 'And then you can say it again – twice over.'

But now, as Mr J. L. B. Matekoni and Fanwell came into the office and announced that they had seen something unbelievable, Mma Makutsi looked up in anticipation. She prided herself on the fact that in her role as a private detective she had seen just about everything there was to be seen – or almost – and, frankly, nothing would be truly unbelievable to one of her experience. So she smiled in a rather condescending way at all this talk of unbelievability and waited for the details.

And what Fanwell said was sufficient to bring her to her feet. She had not been prepared for this.

'Charlie has got hold of an elephant,' Fanwell said. He broke the news in a breathless manner, as if he were a runner who had jogged through the bush with this bombshell.

Mma Makutsi rose to her feet. She looked at Fanwell first, then at Mr J. L. B. Matekoni, and finally, as if she were expecting a refutation of the news, at Mma Ramotswe across the room.

'I'm not making this up,' Fanwell continued.

Mr J. L. B. Matekoni nodded his confirmation. 'No, Fanwell is not making this up. Charlie has an elephant – a very small elephant, but an elephant nonetheless.'

'He's keeping it at the back of his uncle's place,' Fanwell continued. 'There's that wasteland – you know the place with the trees and the rubber hedge. The elephant is in there.'

Mma Ramotswe said nothing at this disclosure, but Mma Makutsi said in astonishment, 'Why has Charlie got an elephant?'

Fanwell had been wearing his hat. Now he took it off and folded it into a ball. 'Why has he got an elephant? It is because there was an elephant, you see, and he heard from that friend of his – you've seen the one, he comes around here sometimes . . . he's called, oh, I forget his name—'

'It does not matter what he is called,' interjected Mr J. L. B. Matekoni. 'He's the one who used to drive a bus for that bus company that belongs to the traditionally built woman who used to own three taxis down behind the President Hotel . . .'

'Her,' said Mma Ramotswe. 'That lady used to be very traditionally built – now she is not so much.'

'They used to say that there was enough there for two ladies,' said Mr J. L. B. Matekoni. 'They said you could get two ladies out of her if you wanted to.'

Fanwell brought the conversation back on track. 'That friend of Charlie's – that one – he drove a bus for that fat lady until he hit a mobile telephone tower. Then he went off and drove for somebody who brought haulage down from Maun.'

Mma Ramotswe was keen to get to the nub of the matter. 'What about him?' she asked.

Fanwell continued the tale. 'Well, he comes down from Maun once a week in a truck owned by the man who brings freight down here to Gaborone. Cattle sometimes, lots of cattle, that he takes on to the Botswana Meat Commission in Lobatse. Well, one day he drives into Gaborone with a truckload of cattle for the BMC and, believe it or not, a baby elephant in with the cattle.'

'This elephant is very tiny,' said Mr J. L. B. Matekoni. 'Charlie is not sure how old it is, but he says he thinks it's only a few weeks. When they're that small they're not much bigger than that chair over there. So high.' He held a hand extended below the level of his waist.

'Elephants get much bigger,' said Mma Makutsi. 'An elephant gets very much bigger than that.'

They all turned to look at her.

'I think we know that, Mma,' said Fanwell.

Mma Makutsi looked defiant. 'I know that sounds very obvious,' she said. 'But what I meant is that the elephant may be very small now, but it won't be that small for much longer. And then what is Charlie going to do with it? Ride into the office on his elephant's back like one of those Indian people? Like that? Mr Charlie, Maharajah of Gaborone? Ha!'

Mma Ramotswe wanted to find out why the elephant had ended up with Charlie.

'He told us why,' said Fanwell. 'Will you tell them, boss? Or shall I?'

'I'll tell them,' said Mr J. L. B. Matekoni. 'Apparently this elephant is an orphan. It was with a herd up there, near Chief's Island. There were poachers – after the ivory. And they shot the she-elephant. She had this calf, though – a very young calf. This one that Charlie has. And what happened was that this friend of Charlie's – the one whose name nobody can remember ...'

'Who used to drive the bus for that woman,' explained Fanwell.

'That one. He was driving his truck to take supplies into one of the safari lodges out there – or rather, he was driving back – and he saw this dead mother elephant with her little baby standing right next to her. He had stayed, you see. The poachers had cut the tusks from two elephants they had shot, including the small elephant's mummy. And the small elephant had stayed while this was happening and was now mourning his mother.'

'They do that,' said Fanwell. 'I've heard that elephants mourn. They are very sad when people shoot them.'

'Charlie's friend asked him whether he would look after the elephant,' continued Mr J. L. B. Matekoni. 'He had to drive on to Lobatse, and then down to Mafikeng for something. So Charlie allowed him to drop the elephant off at his uncle's place.'

'How does he keep it from running away?' Mma Makutsi demanded. 'You can't just put an elephant in your garden.'

'No, you can't,' said Fanwell. 'So he has tied the elephant by its leg to a big metal pole in the ground. The elephant can't run away as long as he's tied to the peg.'

Mma Makutsi made a dismissive sound. 'Tied to a peg? That's not going to last very long. What if the rope gets tangled? What then? The elephant isn't going to stand in one place all day, is it? Elephants don't like that sort of thing.'

'There is a boy,' said Fanwell. 'He is Charlie's cousin. He's the one that Charlie used to share a room with. He's the one who is always wetting the bed. Charlie told me.'

'Poor child,' said Mma Ramotswe.

'It's because children drink those sugary drinks before they go to bed,' said Mma Makutsi. 'If you stop them doing that, then you don't have that problem.'

Fanwell shifted his feet in embarrassment. These were not matters that he would choose to discuss in mixed company. 'It's his job to go and check that the elephant isn't getting the rope all twisted round,' he said. 'So, the elephant is all right.'

Mma Makutsi frowned. 'You can't keep an elephant tied up,' she said.

'It's very small,' Fanwell pointed out. 'When they are that small, Mma, they aren't very strong.'

Mma Ramotswe found herself remembering something she had not thought about for years. When she was a girl back in Mochudi there had been a man who lived on the edge of the village, an ill-tempered man of whom she and all her friends were afraid – he was said by one of the older boys to be a cannibal, a canard swallowed implicitly by the younger children – and this man kept a large baboon chained to a wire. Through the final link of this chain ran a wire strung at the height of a few feet between two posts. This enabled the baboon to run backwards and forwards between the two posts, and in small circles at either end. The baboon, like his owner, was ill-disposed towards the world – understandably, in the animal's case – and would snarl and bare his fangs at anybody who ventured near him. The children would creep through the unkempt field adjoining the man's house and watch the baboon from a safe distance. The boys, who were bolder – and crueller – in these matters would throw small stones at the captive animal, eliciting barks of rage from it, and, occasionally, drawing the man out of his house to investigate. Mma Ramotswe remembered this now, and remembered one of the boys warning her, 'That man will eat you, Precious. If you trip and he catches you, then you will definitely be eaten. It will be in all the newspapers. You will be very famous.'

She thought of that now, and imagined a baby elephant in the same inhumane conditions. 'You cannot chain an animal like that,' she said. 'It is very cruel.'

Mma Makutsi agreed. 'Mma Ramotswe is right. Charlie cannot keep an elephant chained up in his back yard.'

'And he shouldn't have used your van,' Mr J. L. B. Matekoni added. 'That is what damaged it, Mma Ramotswe.'

Mma Ramotswe had to smile. 'I would never have guessed,'

she said. 'If you had asked me what is the most likely cause of the damage to my van, I would not have said because it was used to transport a small elephant.'

'Well it was,' said Mr J. L. B. Matekoni. 'And now ... ' He shrugged. He was not sure what to do. Charlie was no longer his apprentice and so he did not feel responsible for him, and yet, at the same time, the young man was an employee of his wife's and still worked one or two days a week in the garage. He shook his head ruefully. These apprentices had been nothing but trouble from the word go; or Charlie had – Fanwell was a different matter, although he, too, had had his moments. 'No, I don't know what to do.'

'We have to speak to him about it,' said Mma Makutsi. 'We have to find out what his plans are for the elephant.' She paused, before continuing, 'It will get bigger and bigger. And then it will be a danger to people.'

Fanwell nodded. 'True,' he said. 'I know somebody who knew somebody who kept a crocodile. When he got it first, it was only so big.' He held his hands apart to indicate a length of a foot or so. 'But then, oh dear, those things get bigger all the time. He kept it in a pond. He put wire round the pond so that it could not get out. It would eat birds that landed too near to the water. It would also go for any foolish chickens who wandered into its enclosure. And then it ate my friend – or tried to. It grabbed him by the foot and started to drag him into the pond. He poked at its eyes with a stick. That is the only way to get a crocodile to let go.'

They turned to look at him. 'You should not keep crocodiles,' said Mma Makutsi. 'Nor snakes. Those people who keep puff adders or mambas are very foolish. The snake is always lying there thinking: when shall I have the chance to bite this person? That is what snakes think – they are always thinking that.'

Fanwell said, 'Snakes do not think, Mma. They have very small heads. There is not enough room for any thoughts in that head.'

'We should not be talking about snakes,' said Mr J. L. B. Matekoni. 'We should be deciding what to do about Charlie and his elephant.'

'I don't see what we can do,' said Fanwell, glancing at Mr J. L. B. Matekoni. Now was the time, he thought, to disclose the unfortunate fate planned for the elephant by Charlie's friend. Mr J. L. B. Matekoni nodded, a signal to let him know he should continue.

'I'm afraid that the elephant is in real danger,' he said. 'Charlie does not know this, but his friend is planning to pass him on to a butcher.'

This led to silence, eventually broken by Mr J. L. B. Matekoni. 'I don't want that to happen,' he said.

'Certainly not,' said Mma Ramotswe.

'We can take the elephant away from him,' suggested Mma Makutsi. 'He is not a fit person to have an elephant.'

Fanwell made a gesture of hopelessness. 'But what would you do, Mma Makutsi? If you take that elephant away from him, what would you do with it? Sell it? You can't sell elephants these days. They are protected. There is a government department somewhere ...'

'The Department of Elephants,' suggested Mma Ramotswe, smiling.

'It will not be called that, Mma,' said Fanwell, missing the irony. 'The Wildlife Department is in charge of all the wild animals – elephants, lions, giraffes. They are all looked after by the Department of Wildlife.'

'We should speak to Charlie,' said Mma Makutsi. 'We should go round there right now and sort this out. It's no good just thinking of it.'

Mma Ramotswe asked how matters had been left with Charlie.

'We heard his story,' said Mr J. L. B. Matekoni, 'but we didn't discuss what could be done about the elephant.'

'We were too shocked,' said Fanwell.

'Too shocked,' echoed Mr J. L. B. Matekoni. 'And we didn't know then what that friend of his was planning to do. I think he's deceiving Charlie.'

Fanwell was uncertain. 'Is it our business?' he asked. 'If Charlie wants to do these things, then—'

He did not finish. Mma Makutsi was adamant that it *was* their business. 'If we don't do something, we'll find that we're the ones left holding the elephant,' she said. 'I know what Charlie is like. He will be thinking: good, an elephant! today, and then tomorrow, if his friend does not turn up for some reason, he will be thinking: how am I going to get rid of this elephant?'

Mma Ramotswe thought that Mma Makutsi was probably right. There had been many occasions in the past when they had been obliged to clear up some mess left by Charlie. They could remain uninvolved if they discovered somebody else was looking after an elephant – such an elephant would be none of their business – but there was a sense in which any elephant in Charlie's keeping was their problem, or would soon become just that. If somebody else was looking after an elephant . . . somebody responsible, somebody experienced, somebody who knew about the needs of orphans, whether human or otherwise . . . Mma Potokwani. Of course. Mma Potokwani, matron of the Orphan Farm (for human orphans, admittedly); pillar of competence and unflappability; concealer of a heart of pure gold . . .

'Mma Potokwani!' Mma Ramotswe blurted out.

Mma Makutsi looked puzzled. 'Mma Potokwani?' she asked. 'An elephant?'

'She is a large lady,' said Fanwell.

Mr J. L. B. Matekoni laughed, only to be silenced by a reproachful stare from both Mma Ramotswe and Mma Makutsi.

'I think I should go and have a word with Mma Potokwani,' said Mma Ramotswe. 'She is the—'

Mma Makutsi tumbled to the plan. 'Of course,' she said. 'She is the one to advise us about orphans. May I come too, Mma?'

'It would be very useful,' said Mma Ramotswe. 'We may have to make plans, and you should be involved in those, Mma.'

Mr J. L. B. Matekoni asked if they should do anything right then.

'Not just yet, Rra,' said Mma Ramotswe. 'The time to act will come, but it is not just yet.'

Chapter Eight

Government Cherries

They drove out in the tiny white van, bumping along the final section of dirt road that led to the gates of the Orphan Farm. Both Mma Ramotswe and Mma Makutsi were in good spirits – high spirits, even – as they considered their mission to Mma Potokwani.

'You know, Mma Makutsi,' Mma Ramotswe said, 'I've asked Mma Potokwani for some very unusual favours in the past.'

'*You've* asked for favours?' exclaimed Mma Makutsi. 'It's the other way round, Mma! *She's* the one who has asked for favours. Big favours. Borrowing your husband for all sorts of reasons. That's a very big favour in my view, Mma Ramotswe. If somebody came along and asked me if they could borrow Phuti, I would give them a very direct response.'

'No? You'd say no, Mma?'

'Of course I would. You cannot lend your husband to the first person who comes along and asks to borrow him. You say to them, "Get your own husband. Find your own man to fix your kitchen sink or whatever. Don't come round to me and try to take my husband." That's what I'd say, Mma. Straight away. I'd say that.'

'But she has always returned him in good time,' Mma Ramotswe pointed out. 'After he has fixed the pump or sorted out whatever needed sorting out, he is always returned to me – like a library book that's been read – just like that.'

Mma Makutsi was not convinced. 'That's all very well, Mma, but I am sure there are many cases where somebody has lent her husband, and then the husband has not returned. Men are like that, Mma. If they find a place where the food is better, or there is more beer, they often stay there. They say to their wife that she does not understand him, and never has, and then they say, "And the food is better here." And so, the man never comes back. There is a big danger of that, Mma Ramotswe. It is a very big danger in this town these days. There are some wicked women about.'

'You're not saying that Mma Potokwani is a wicked woman, are you, Mma?'

'I am certainly not saying that, Mma. I would never accuse Mma Potokwani of stealing husbands, or even of borrowing them and keeping them too long.'

'No, Mma, I see.'

'No, all I'm saying is that if we're counting the favours, then you are very much in credit, Mma. It is you who have done the favours for Mma Potokwani and the Orphan Farm. It's you who fixed their pump – through your husband, of course. It's you who fixed that minibus she uses to take the children about the place – once again, through your husband. So all the favours are stacked up on your side.'

Mma Ramotswe understood what Mma Makutsi meant, but she was still slightly embarrassed to be facing Mma Potokwani with the request she was about to make. Yes, there was an important element of reciprocity in her relationship with Mma Potokwani, but if you set up imaginary scales and put fixing the pump or the minibus on one pan and an elephant on the other, there was no doubt in her mind as to which way the scales would tip.

They parked the van in its usual place, under an acacia tree not far from Mma Potokwani's office. As Mma Ramotswe switched off the engine, she heard a voice call out from a stand of fruit trees a short distance away.

'I am over here, Mma. I'm picking guavas.'

They made their way to where Mma Potokwani, her skirts tucked into a pair of large green bloomers, had climbed into a guava tree to harvest the fruit.

'You must be very careful up there,' called out Mma Ramotswe. 'You must be careful not to fall.'

Mma Potokwani reached for a guava and tossed it down into a small tarpaulin spread out on the ground below.

'I shall come down now,' she said. 'I have picked almost all the fruit on this tree.'

Her descent was an elegant one for somebody so large as Mma Potokwani. And within not much more than a few moments, she was standing before them, extracting her skirt from its temporary constraints, and smiling broadly at her visitors.

'You wouldn't have expected to see me in a tree, would you?' she asked.

'No, I did not expect that,' said Mma Ramotswe. 'But there is no reason why you shouldn't climb a tree, Mma.' She thought, though, that there were very good reasons why people like Mma Potokwani – and like herself, for that matter – should not climb

110

trees. Traditionally built people were not designed for tree-climbing, unless, of course, the tree was particularly strong, with boughs in a position to support their weight. A baobab tree was perhaps the best tree for a traditionally built person to climb, as these trees, with their immense girth, could support the weight of an elephant. Their branches, though, were high up off the ground and there would be the small matter of scaling the great trunk – an impossible task, she thought. For a moment she pictured Mma Potokwani high up in the branches of a baobab tree, her skirts tucked in, waving to those below. She heard her calling, 'Mma Ramotswe! Mma Ramotswe! Come up and join me . . . '

Mma Potokwani's voice brought her back to reality. 'Except that it's a very stupid thing for a person like me to do,' the matron said. 'If you are traditionally built like me – like us, Mma – then if you fall out of a tree it is a big fall. You hit the ground with considerable force.'

'You try to avoid falling out of the tree, then, Mma,' said Mma Makutsi.

'Indeed you do, Mma Makutsi. Falling out of a tree is one of those things in life that you should certainly try to avoid.' She chuckled. 'You cannot go through life wrapped up in cotton wool, but you can avoid taking unnecessary risks. Play it safe – that's what I say, Mma Makutsi. Play it safe.'

Mma Makutsi nodded her agreement. 'I am always playing it safe, Mma Potokwani. I am very reluctant to take any risks – and Phuti is the same. He is Mr Softly-Softly most of the time.' She thought of risks she had taken recently, and found it difficult to call any to mind. Of course, she had an advantage over most people in that regard – she had shoes that would warn her of any untoward danger. She knew that this sounded absurd – possibly even deluded – and yet she had heard them as clearly as if somebody had been right there with her, whispering advice. And there had been more than one occasion when an intervention by her shoes had averted unpleasantness or even physical danger – as when they had seen a cobra on her bedroom floor and had warned her of the lurking peril.

Snakes in the wrong place, of course, could be a nightmare. In the hot weather, when the sun beat down on the land like a hammer, even snakes, cold-blooded sun-worshippers though they were, could find the heat outside too much and would slither into the house for the cool of the cement floor. They liked bathrooms, which were often the coolest rooms in a house, and they liked to lie under the bath itself or around the base of a laundry basket, or, as had occurred in the house of one of Mma Makutsi's friends, in the bowl of the toilet itself, half submerged in the water. That was a situation too terrible to contemplate, although her friend had lived to tell the tale. She herself had not been bitten, but an aunt of hers had, a lady of generous proportions who had not even noticed at first and had only realised that something was wrong when she stood up and discovered the snake still attached to her, its fangs stuck in her flesh. Fortunately, it had not been a poisonous snake, and there had been no ill effects, at least of a physical nature. The psychological consequences of such an episode, though, could be profound. And then, of course, there was that man down in Lobatse whose bed had been invaded by a python and who had, in his half-awake state, imagined that what was wrapped around his right leg was his wife's leg rather than the coils of a large constrictor. He, too, had survived unscathed – on a physical level.

Mma Potokwani, having now invited them into her office, led them along the rough path that ended up at her veranda. 'I have just baked a fruit cake, as it happens,' she said. 'I imagine that you ladies will have a slice.'

'We have been looking forward to that, Mma,' said Mma Ramotswe, adding, 'That is not why I come to see you, Mma Potokwani. I know that there is often a slice of your delicious cake awaiting me, but even if there were not, I would still come to see you.'

'Although perhaps not quite so often,' quipped Mma Makutsi.

Mma Potokwani laughed. 'I know, Mma Ramotswe.' She paused. 'Although we often have a favour to ask of our friends when we go to see them. That is only human. If I come to see Mr J. L. B. Matekoni it is not always just for the pleasure of his company – much as we all enjoy that, of course – but it is also to ask him to do something.'

'That is what men are for, Mma,' said Mma Makutsi. 'If they weren't good at fixing things, I'm not sure we would really need them.'

This brought a swift rebuttal from Mma Ramotswe. 'No, Mma,' she said, 'you cannot say that. Men are not as bad as some women say they are. They are different – yes – they do not see things in the right way sometimes, but they are still nice to be around.' She paused for a moment. Mma Ramotswe was charitable, but even so, there were one or two men she considered to be beyond the pale. These were men whom one would avoid, if at all possible, rather than seek to confront. So she qualified her remark with, 'I mean *most* men are nice to be around, even if there are one or two who . . .'

She saw that Mma Makutsi was watching her, and she knew Mma Makutsi was only too aware of whom she was thinking – Note Mokoti, the man she had once been married to. Mma Ramotswe had been much younger then, and the things we do in youth should not be laid too readily at our door, but even so she had reproached herself one hundred times for allowing her head to be turned by that trumpet-playing wastrel; that selfish, preening charmer; that silver-tongued abuser … She stopped herself. She had forgiven him; she had made that supreme, conscious effort to forgive the man who had fractured her young heart and who had almost broken her spirit, too, and it was wrong for her now to think about him in these terms. Hate was a welcoming host and would always encourage you to join its parties. So whenever she thought about Note, rather than dwell on the painful memories around him, she would deliberately think of something else. And what better to think of, when one is trying not to think of one man, than another man? If the man you were trying not to think about was a bad man – as Note unquestionably was – then the antidote was to think about a good man – and there were plenty of men lining up to be thought about. Her father, for example, the late Obed Ramotswe; that kind, good man who stood for everything that Botswana stood for – decency and honesty being the main values that underpinned the country. Yes, and why not? It was fashionable to pour scorn on patriotism; she had heard people do that – and even go so far as to laugh at the Botswana flag – but she would never, never do that. Those values – the values her daddy had taught her – were still there and she would never be ashamed to talk about them.

So, her father was one man she could think about when wanting to cancel memories of Note. And then there was Mr J. L. B. Matekoni, the man she had married after she had finally got rid of Note. Mr J. L. B. Matekoni was the best of men, as everybody who had any dealings with him quickly discovered. And her old friend, Bishop Mwamba, was a good man, and Seretse Khama, of course, and Professor Tlou, who had written that history of Botswana and who had been so wise, and Dr Moffat, who had run the hospital at Mochudi and had looked after and comforted so many, and Mma Makutsi's husband, Phuti Radiphuti, who was so protective of the interests and welfare of his staff at the Double Comfort Furniture Store. And Mma Potokwani's husband, too – not that they saw much of him, as he was very much what Mma Potokwani herself described as a 'background husband'. And Fanwell, now that she came to think of it – he was a nice young man, and if he had been a bit feckless in the past, then that was almost certainly because of Charlie's influence. Even Charlie himself, although he still had a lot to learn; his heart was in the right place, she was sure of it, as was apparent from this business he had got himself into with the orphan elephant. Charlie would not have thought it through before acting, but the impulse to help had been there, and he deserved full credit for that.

Mma Ramotswe's thoughts were interrupted by Mma Potokwani, who remarked as they entered her office, 'Oh, there are plenty of no-good men. I have been thinking of keeping a list of the no-good men of Botswana and publishing it, price eighty pula, and worth every thebe. This would be a list of all the scoundrels – all the drinkers and boasters and idle men. It would have a picture of each of these men, perhaps, and a few lines about their typical habitat . . .'

'Like one of those bird books,' exclaimed Mma Makutsi. 'Or those wildlife guides that tell you where you can find certain animals. Sand veld. Mopani forest. And so on.'

'It would be a very dangerous list,' said Mma Ramotswe. 'Some of the men would surely claim to be on it by mistake.'

'There would be what we call a margin of error,' said Mma Makutsi. 'At the Botswana Secretarial College . . .'

Oh no, thought Mma Ramotswe. The Botswana Secretarial College again . . .

'At the Botswana Secretarial College,' Mma Makutsi continued, 'one of the professors . . .'

Not professors, thought Mma Ramotswe.

'One of the professors was a big expert on the margin of error. He used to tell us, always allow for a margin of error. If you allow for a margin of error, then you will never find yourself wishing, Oh, if only I had allowed for a margin of error. So, allow for it.'

Mma Potokwani invited them to sit down while she switched on the kettle and took the cake tin off a shelf.

'As I told you,' she said, 'I have been busy baking. I made four cakes yesterday: one for myself – and you, of course – and then three for the housemothers. We have three birthdays this week, one after the other, three of the housemothers, and so I have to make a cake for each of them. It is a tradition we have here at the Orphan Farm.'

'Perhaps you should be like the Queen over in England,' said Mma Makutsi. 'I was reading in a magazine that she has two birthdays – her real birthday, and then an official birthday that comes at a more convenient time. The housemothers' official birthdays could be staggered that way.'

Mme Ramotswe nodded. She was an admirer of the Queen, who she thought was just like Mma Potokwani – one of those people who were single-minded in the performance of their duties. Such people just went on and on doing what was expected of them. The Queen went round opening things and shaking hands with people; Mma Potokwani spent her days chasing people up to support the orphans, to donate surplus food, to pass on children's clothes and trainers, to find jobs for the children once they were grown up and ready to leave school. She never took no for an answer; she never gave up.

And there was Prince Charles, who she knew loved Botswana. When he came again to visit the country, she would try to invite him for tea. He would be too busy to come, of course, and there were people around him who would fend off invitations, but she knew they would have a great deal to talk about: about the rains and the crops; about looking after the world; about remembering that when all was said and done we lived on the land and had to give the land the love that it needed if it was to continue to provide for us.

'It would be good to have two birthdays,' said Mma Potokwani. 'But I think we have to be content with one.'

The kettle having boiled, she made the tea. Then, once that had been poured, a jug of milk was passed around. Mma Makutsi took no more than a dash of milk in hers, while Mma Ramotswe, who liked her tea milky – even when she was drinking her favourite redbush tea – poured a generous volume of milk into her cup.

And then there was sugar. Mma Makutsi hesitated, as if conscious of an invisible censor – her shoes, perhaps, who had once ticked her off for eating three fat cakes in a row – but then helped herself to a half-spoon, passing the sugar bowl on to Mma Ramotswe. She did not hold back from helping herself to one and a half spoons – but filled so generously as to be the equivalent of three more modest spoonfuls. Then the bowl was passed to Mma Potokwani, who took three and a half.

The cake was served by Mma Potokwani, who told her guests that there were more cherries than usual in the mixture. Cherries had been on promotion at the supermarket, she explained, and she had stocked up. 'Children like cherries, you see, and I give them as a reward if a child does something especially good.'

Mma Ramotswe smiled as she imagined a well-behaved child having a sticky and glistening cherry popped into its mouth by Mma Potokwani. 'Perhaps the government could do that too,' she mused. 'Not for children, but for adults. There could be special ceremonies at which people who have done good things would line up to get a cherry from one of the government ministers.'

Mma Makutsi chuckled. 'That's a very good idea, Mma. That nurse – Sister Banjule – you remember her? She would be at the top of the list.'

Mma Ramotswe nodded. Sister Banjule, who ran the Anglican Hospice, would be a very good candidate for this reward. She had looked after so many people at the end of their days, and done so with kindness – the greatest compliment anybody could pay a nurse or a doctor. Kindness. It was not a complicated thing, kindness – we all knew how to be kind, and we all recognised it when we came across it. Sister Banjule had looked after Mma Makutsi's late brother, Richard, when he had died. His life had not been of much importance or significance to others – he was a very ordinary man, who had not really done very much – but she had made him feel cherished in those final few days, and Mma Makutsi had never forgotten that.

'Yes,' said Mma Ramotswe. 'She would be at the top of the list – right up at the top of the list, Mma Makutsi.' She looked at Mma Potokwani. She was another person who should be given a cherry by the government, but Mma Ramotswe would not mention that now, as Mma Potokwani was modest and expected no reward.

They bit into their cake. The taste of cherries, liberally sprinkled through the dried fruit that made up much of the cake's bulk, came through strongly. Mma Makutsi closed her eyes in a transport of delight. 'This is very fine cake, Mma,' she said to Mma Potokwani.

'I am in complete agreement with Mma Makutsi,' said Mma Ramotswe.

'I am very happy,' said Mma Potokwani, taking a sip of her tea. 'It would be a different matter if I had guests who did not like cherries.'

The conversation moved on. 'There is something we need to tell you about,' said Mma Ramotswe. 'It is a very strange thing. You will not have heard of something like this, I think.'

Mma Potokwani grinned. 'You cannot shock me, Mma Ramotswe – if that is what you are worried about. Remember I am a matron – with hospital training – and if you are a matron you have usually seen everything.' She paused, to shake her head, as if remembering some of the more shocking things she had seen in her career. 'No, I am never surprised to hear what people get up to – especially men.'

Mma Makutsi agreed with that. 'Especially men,' she said.

'And sometimes ladies, surely,' said Mma Ramotswe. 'We must not be too hard on men.'

'That's true,' said Mma Potokwani. 'Ladies are not always as innocent as they appear. For instance . . . '

She did not need to finish. All three of them were thinking of the same person, and there was no need to spell out the name. Violet Sephotho.

'But let's not worry too much about all that,' said Mma Potokwani eventually. 'You were about to tell me, Mma Ramotswe, of some shocking thing. Well, I am listening now.'

'It has nothing to do with Violet,' Mma Makutsi said. 'I could tell you some shocking things about her, Mma Potokwani, but . . . '

Mma Ramotswe shared her reservation. 'We could do that some other day, perhaps. We would not want to burden Mma Potokwani unduly.'

Mma Potokwani protested that she was perfectly happy to be burdened with disclosures about Violet Sephotho. She was by no means a gossip, but she enjoyed a scandalous story as much as the next person, and when you lived out at Tlokweng you sometimes felt that you were missing out on some of the juicier goings-on in Gaborone itself. Not that Gaborone was a hotbed of such things, but a large town inevitably had a spicier life than a small town, and those who lived in small towns, or in the country, might be forgiven for taking an interest in what their urban cousins were getting up to.

'Well,' said Mma Makutsi, 'as I was telling Mma Ramotswe only recently, when she was at the Botswana Secretarial College – at the same time that I was there, Mma—'

'And where you got ninety-seven per cent, if I'm not mistaken,' interjected Mma Potokwani.

Mma Makutsi inclined her head. 'Yes, that was indeed the case, Mma, but what I was going to mention was the fact that Violet had three—'

Mma Ramotswe interrupted her. 'I really think we should talk about that some other time. I really do.'

'—boyfriends,' Mma Makutsi finished.

'Three boyfriends!' exclaimed Mma Potokwani.

'A morning boyfriend, an—'

Mma Ramotswe cleared her throat. 'The thing that we came to tell you about, Mma Potokwani, concerns Charlie.'

Mma Potokwani seemed disappointed to be leaving the subject of multiple boyfriends, but now gave Mma Ramotswe her full attention. 'Ah, Charlie,' she sighed. 'He is always getting himself into difficulties. So, what's it now, Mma Ramotswe? More girl trouble?'

'He is not having girl trouble at present,' interjected Mma Makutsi. 'That is a thing of the past, now. He went off and got married. He did it very quietly.'

Mma Potokwani approved. 'That will be very good,' she said. 'It is always the best thing for a young man like Charlie. If a young man finds a nice girl, then everything works out well. I have seen that time and time again with the boys here. When they grow up and make their own lives, I watch the ones who had a bad start and who may have been a bit difficult. I watch them, and see what happens. If they come back with a nice girl to introduce to me, then I know straight away that everything will be fine. That will go for Charlie too, I think.'

'I hope so,' said Mma Ramotswe. 'But at the moment there is a more pressing matter. Charlie has been looking after an animal that I'm afraid is going to cause problems for him.'

Mma Potokwani shook her head. 'Don't tell me, Mma Ramotswe. A dog. I've seen young people do that. They get a puppy and they forget that having a puppy is like having a baby. It's almost as much work. And then the puppy gets bigger and bigger and some of them are badly behaved and start biting people, and then there is all sorts of fuss. And the poor dog gets kicked out and ends up wandering around until it's run over or a leopard eats it or something like that.'

'Leopards like to eat dogs,' said Mma Makutsi. 'And so do crocodiles. Phuti knew a man who had a boy hunting dog called Simba. He was a very strong dog, that one, who had jaws like a hyena. Have you seen hyena jaws, Mma Potokwani? They are very big and powerful. You do not want them to bite you if you can avoid it.'

Mma Ramotswe began to steer the conversation back to Charlie, but Mma Makutsi was determined to continue her story. 'This dog,' she went on, 'went with its owner down to the Limpopo one day. He was looking for guinea fowl, I think, because they have them in the bush out there. Anyway, he decided to walk down to the edge of the river to see what was going on down there, and there were some flat rocks that stretched out into the water. There was quite a lot of water, as there had been good rains and the Limpopo was in flood.'

Mma Potokwani winced. 'You have to be careful, you know. That river can be dangerous.'

'Yes,' said Mma Makutsi. 'It can. But this man – this friend of Phuti's – was not careful. He walked out onto those flat rocks and his dog followed him – this horrible big dog called Simba. And since he was thirsty, the dog put his head down to drink some water from the river, and that was when it happened. Right in front of that man, a crocodile suddenly came up out of the water, grabbed the dog by the nose, and pulled him into the river. There was a lot of splashing, and the man threw some rocks into the water where the crocodile had disappeared with the dog, but there's not much you can do, Mma Potokwani, if a crocodile has you by the nose. They do the death roll, you see. Phuti told me about it. The crocodile spins his prey round and round underwater and he drowns him. That is what happens, Mma.'

There was a short silence as they contemplated the fate of the dog. Then Mma Ramotswe said, 'It's not a dog in Charlie's case, Mma Potokwani. It's an elephant. Charlie has got hold of a baby elephant.'

Mma Potokwani's eyes widened, and then she let out a whoop of astonishment. 'An elephant, Mma? A baby elephant? Oh, that is very funny.' Tears of mirth began to show in her eyes; she wiped them away. 'That is the funniest thing I have heard for many years. An elephant!'

Mma Ramotswe was taken aback by her friend's reaction. The fact that Charlie had ended up with an elephant was, in a sense, amusing – but not *that* amusing. She tried, as gently as she could, to impress on Mma Potokwani the gravity of the situation – a difficult task in any circumstances, as Mma Potokwani's nature was one of breezy confidence. 'It's tethered to a post on wasteland behind his uncle's place,' she said. 'He's tied it to a metal post in the ground. That's all. There are no fences, Mma. No stockade.'

Mma Potokwani shook her head in continued disbelief. 'An

elephant. Would you believe it, Mma Ramotswe? Mma Makutsi, would *you* believe it? Had you said, "Charlie has a puppy," I wouldn't have been all that surprised. But an elephant, ladies – an elephant!'

'You can't keep an elephant like that,' Mma Ramotswe continued.

Mma Potokwani laughed again. 'You can't keep an elephant at all,' she said. 'No, an elephant is not a chicken or a duck. It is not a goat.'

Mma Makutsi rolled her eyes. 'It is definitely not, Mma. But I don't think anybody thought it was. Nobody has been saying, "An elephant is just like a goat." Nobody, Mma.'

Mma Potokwani smiled at this contribution, before continuing, 'Oh, Mma Ramotswe, I thought I'd heard everything until I heard this. An elephant!'

'It's dangerous,' said Mma Ramotswe simply. 'Very dangerous.'

'You don't need to tell me that,' agreed Mma Potokwani. 'Did you read in the newspaper about that poor person up north? That late person?'

Mma Ramotswe shook her head. The *Botswana Daily News* was full of unfortunate things that befell people. And these things were inevitable, given the nature of the world and the things that could go wrong. But you couldn't let all that deter you, she thought. You soldiered on; you carried on doing what you thought was the right thing to do; you soldiered on.

'Well,' continued Mma Potokwani, 'there was a report from up your way, Mma Makutsi – not Bobonong itself, but a bit further west, past the Makgadikgadi Pans. Up there in the middle of nowhere.' She paused. A discouraging look from Mma Makutsi warned her that she was on tricky ground. And so she added, quickly, 'I'm not saying that Bobonong is in the middle of nowhere,

Mma Makutsi. I'm not saying that. Bobonong is an important place because ...'

She had gone too far. Had she stopped immediately after admitting the importance of Bobonong, there would have been no difficulty, but she had unwisely started to explain why this should be so, and she realised she had not the slightest idea what happened in Bobonong.

Mma Makutsi smiled. 'You're right, Mma. There is a lot going on in Bobonong. What were you thinking of in particular, Mma?'

'Oh, it's difficult to say,' said Mma Potokwani. 'These places, you know what they're like. There's always something.' She paused. 'But let's not worry about Bobonong. I wanted to tell you about what happened in this other place – the one I was talking about. You see, an elephant walked into a village and knocked down this poor man's hut. He was sheltering inside it because he had heard the elephant, but its walls were made of straw and mud and the elephant just had to lean on them to knock it down. The poor man had no chance.'

'That's very sad, Mma,' said Mma Ramotswe. 'Imagine what it is like to have your house knocked over by an elephant.'

Mma Makutsi had views on that. 'It's because people are building their places on elephants' land,' she said. 'If you leave elephants alone, they'll leave you alone. They have their own places, and all you have to do is keep away from those and you'll be all right.'

'But there isn't enough land,' said Mma Ramotswe. 'That's the problem, isn't it? There are too many people and many of them want to plant crops in places where the elephants live. So the elephants think: these people are on our land, and they rush round and knock things over and frighten everybody because they're so big and so powerful. And then somebody takes a shot at an elephant and all the elephants feel very strongly about that and begin to eat vegetables from people's gardens and frighten everybody. And then you have a big incident.'

Having delivered her views on the subject, Mma Ramotswe sighed. Mma Potokwani, the attentive hostess, interpreted this as a coded request for a further slice of fruit cake. Reaching for the cake tin, she cut a large slice and tipped it onto Mma Ramotswe's plate. Then she did the same for Mma Makutsi.

'Mma Potokwani,' said Mma Ramotswe. 'You will be responsible for my needing a new wardrobe – all my dresses ...'

'That is just shrinkage,' said Mma Potokwani. 'People blame cake for that sort of thing, but they forget that dresses have a natural tendency to shrink with age.'

Mma Makutsi laughed. 'Phuti's trousers have been shrinking for a long time. He is always complaining about that.'

Mma Ramotswe took a bite of her fruit cake and then washed it down with a swig of tea. 'This elephant,' she said, 'this elephant of Charlie's – you know what I am worried about, Mma Potokwani? I am worried about the children.'

Mma Potokwani frowned. 'The children, Mma? What children?'

Mma Ramotswe looked out of the window. It was a cunning tactic, and it was working – just as Clovis Andersen said it would. He said somewhere in *The Principles of Private Detection* that the way to get people to see things from your point of view was to share their anxieties. *Find out what they're worried about*, he wrote, *and then talk about that*. The one thing that could be guaranteed to trigger concern on Mma Potokwani's part was the welfare of children.

'Oh, there are all sorts of children,' said Mma Ramotswe. 'Old Naledi is full of children, and they like to play on that wasteland. When word gets out among the children that there is a baby elephant there, they will be onto it like ... like ...' She struggled to find the right metaphor, and was about to make some reference to bees and honey when Mma Makutsi interjected: 'Like flies on cattle,' she said.

'Yes, like that,' said Mma Ramotswe. 'And what worries me is the thought that these children will be hurt. Even a baby elephant weighs rather a lot, Mma Potokwani. A baby elephant can crush a child very easily – even without meaning to.'

Mma Potokwani's frown deepened. 'That is very worrying, Mma,' she said.

'Yes,' said Mma Ramotswe.

'You need to go to the police,' said Mma Potokwani. 'Or the Wildlife Department.'

Mma Ramotswe shook her head. 'I wish it were that simple, Mma Potokwani. Fanwell suggested that to Charlie. He said, "Why don't you go to the Wildlife Department, Charlie, and get them to take this elephant from you?"'

'And?' asked Mma Potokwani.

'Charlie told Fanwell that his friend was unwilling to do that for some reason. Perhaps he thinks he'll get into trouble for moving an elephant without their permission.'

'And the police?' asked Mma Potokwani.

'Charlie's friend said the police would just dump it somewhere. They are too busy with all the work they have to do. They can't look after elephants.'

Mma Potokwani poured more tea. 'This is not very good,' she said. 'We can't let it hurt the children in Old Naledi.' She paused. 'Is there something else, Mma Makutsi? Is there something you haven't mentioned?'

Mma Makutsi hesitated. 'I think they may be planning to slaughter it and sell the meat. Not Charlie, but his friend. He knows a butcher, apparently.'

Mma Potokwani put down the teapot rapidly. 'That is very bad news indeed, Mma.' She sank her head in her hands. 'We don't want the poor creature to die. All the time these poor elephants have been dying, dying. They are very intelligent beasts, Mma.'

What she said was heartfelt, and it brought about a short silence. Mma Potokwani had spent her life looking after people who could not look after themselves – her orphans – and she had done so with little fuss and certainly with no thought of personal reward. And it was that same sympathy that had sustained her efforts in that direction, that was now aroused for this small elephant. She was practical, of course – she could not have achieved what she had achieved without knowing how the world worked – and she knew that difficult issues arose when elephants came into contact with human society, but that did not stop the prompting of her heart.

'You can see it in their eyes,' said Mma Makutsi. 'You can see that they are thinking about you when they look at you. They are very wise creatures.'

'And they have very good memories,' said Mma Ramotswe. 'They remember all the sad things that have happened to them. That is why an elephant often looks sad.'

'It's a pity there isn't somebody who can help,' said Mma Makutsi.

'I think there is,' said Mma Potokwani. 'I think I know some people.'

Mma Ramotswe looked relieved. 'I thought you might, Mma.'

'But I will have to get in touch with them,' cautioned Mma Potokwani. 'And in the meantime . . .'

'In the meantime,' ventured Mma Ramotswe, 'we need to find some kind person who—'

'Who is used to dealing with orphans,' interjected Mma Makutsi.

'Yes,' said Mma Ramotswe. 'Who is used to dealing with

orphans and who would be able to find a safe place for this elephant until something is arranged. That would not be too long, I think.'

'No more than a few weeks, I imagine,' said Mma Makutsi.

There was silence. From outside, there drifted into Mma Potokwani's office the sound of children chanting a counting rhyme. Mma Ramotswe caught the words, and raised a finger. 'I remember that,' she said. 'I remember that from a long time ago.' It was a sound from the old Botswana – the Botswana of her child-hood, when everything was quieter and more certain; when people had time for one another. It made her sad to think about that – how people had stopped having time for each other. Well, they hadn't altogether, but it did seem that we all had less time for others in our lives. People had more material things than they used to: they had more money; they had cars; they had more food than they could eat; they had fridges purring away in their kitchens, but what had they lost? What silences, rich and peaceful, had been pushed out of the way by humming machinery?

Mma Potokwani was staring at the ceiling. 'It's always possible that we could—' She broke off.

Mma Ramotswe pressed her. 'Could what, Mma?'

'That we could use the old cattle stockade we have. It's down at the other end of the vegetable garden – on the edge of the bush there. It is still strong – they used tree trunks to make it.'

Mma Ramotswe pretended to be surprised. 'I wasn't thinking of you, Mma, but—'

Mma Potokwani cut her short. Her tone was reproving, but, at the same time, fond. 'Yes you were, Mma Ramotswe. And you too, Mma Makutsi. You were both thinking of me, but I don't mind, Bomma, because I would have been disappointed if you did *not* think of me. Because I'm *the* orphan lady, am I not? And if I won't help, then who will?'

Neither of her guests spoke. There was only one answer, of course.

'This will only be temporary,' continued Mma Potokwani. 'I will have to get in touch with my friend to see if she can provide a permanent home. Young people – and young elephants are probably no different – need a proper place. They need somewhere they can stay for a long time.'

'I think you put it very well, Mma,' said Mma Ramotswe. 'You put it perfectly, in fact.'

'Thank you, Mma,' said Mma Potokwani, reaching for the cake tin. 'And since we are all agreed on that, perhaps we should agree on a final slice of cake.'

'There will be no argument about that,' said Mma Ramotswe. And she was about to say 'Even from Mma Makutsi . . .' but did not, of course, because Mma Ramotswe knew when not to say that which she was about to say – a rare gift, not shared by everybody.

The cake was completely finished, only a few crumbs remaining in the bottom of the tin. But that was no surprise because the adage 'You cannot have your cake and eat it' was one of those sayings that was incontestably true, as Mma Ramotswe, and indeed Mma Makutsi, and Mma Potokwani too, had discovered on many an occasion.

Chapter Nine

Mma Ramotswe Has Few Faults

They returned to the office, where Mma Ramotswe called what she termed an 'extraordinary general meeting'. This was a rare occurrence, justified only in the most pressing or extreme circumstances, and involving the attendance of everybody present in the office and the garage. On this occasion, that meant Mma Ramotswe and Mma Makutsi, Fanwell and Mr J. L. B. Matekoni, the last two participants being dragged away somewhat reluctantly from a particularly interesting gearbox issue in an old Ford.

Mr J. L. B. Matekoni was not one to grumble, but he did so now – in his very mild way – pointing out to Mma Ramotswe that you did not normally call a surgeon out from theatre when he was engaged in a delicate surgical procedure. 'It's the same with gearboxes,' he said. 'If you take them to pieces and then walk away you can end up in a terrible mess.'

'The boss is right,' said Fanwell, nodding sagely. 'A terrible mess.'

Mma Ramotswe explained that a co-ordinated plan of action needed to be decided then and there.

'We can't let this matter ride,' she said. 'That young elephant could cause serious harm. Children are likely to find out about his presence, and you know what they are like. Somebody could get hurt.'

They sat in the office while Mma Ramotswe told the two mechanics about their conversation with Mma Potokwani. 'She was very helpful,' she said. 'We did not have to spend a long time persuading her.'

'We did not have to spend any time at all,' said Mma Makutsi. 'She made her offer very quickly.'

'They have an old cattle stockade,' said Mma Ramotswe. 'They haven't used it for years . . . '

Mr J. L. B. Matekoni nodded his head. 'Yes, I know where that is. At the end of the vegetable gardens. They used it in the old days when the orphan farm had a small herd. The children loved having the cattle but they stopped keeping them when one of them was hit by a truck. The children were so upset by this that Mma Potokwani – or her predecessor, perhaps – said that it was better not to have cattle if that sort of thing was going to happen.'

'It's good for children to be brought up with cattle,' said Mma Makutsi. 'Then they understand. Phuti says that he had his first cattle when he was three.'

Mma Ramotswe frowned. 'That's a bit young, surely. You cannot look after cattle when you're that young.'

Mma Makutsi pursed her lips. 'Phuti was very advanced, Mma. He has always been advanced.'

Mma Ramotswe did not argue. Mma Makutsi was fiercely loyal to her husband. 'The point is,' she continued, 'that Mma

Potokwani has offered to take this elephant while arrangements are being made to get it back up north. Apparently, there is a place up there that will look after elephants who have lost their mothers. But it might take a little while to arrange. It will be safe at the Orphan Farm, in that old stockade.'

'Then that is what Charlie must do,' said Mr J. L. B. Matekoni. 'We must tell him.'

Fanwell looked doubtful. 'But Charlie wants to keep it at his uncle's place. He says that it's fine there. He doesn't see a problem.'

'But there *is* a problem,' said Mma Makutsi. 'That elephant is going to hurt somebody. It's all very well for Charlie to say that it's all quite safe, but it isn't really. What happens when Charlie comes to work? He says everything is looked after by that young cousin of his, the one who wets the bed ... '

Fanwell objected. 'But that is not his fault, Mma Makutsi. He can't help wetting the bed – and anyway it's nothing to do with what we're talking about.'

Mma Makutsi was dismissive. 'If a boy wets the bed when he's as old as that boy, then there's an issue, Fanwell. And that issue is what we call psychological. You can't have boys with psychological issues looking after elephants.'

Fanwell looked outraged. He turned to Mr J. L. B. Matekoni. This was typical, he thought, of the general attack on men. That boy might be a bed-wetter but there were plenty of girls who wet the bed – weren't there? – anyway, the point was that the competence of boys in general should not be called into question over such an irrelevant matter. Now he said to Mr J. L. B. Matekoni, 'She can't say that, Rra, can she? She can't say that that boy can't do something like look after an elephant just because he wets the bed?'

Mr J. L. B. Matekoni, who was sitting in the client's chair next to Mma Ramotswe's desk, shifted his feet uncomfortably. 'I don't think a medical problem should affect your ability to do something like look after livestock. No, I don't think that – on balance.'

'Livestock?' said Mma Makutsi, her voice raised. 'Is an elephant *livestock*, Rra? An elephant is a wild creature – it is not livestock. A lion is not livestock. A giraffe is not livestock.'

'What about an ostrich?' Fanwell challenged. 'What about ostriches then? You answer me that, Mma Makutsi. Look at those ostrich farms – they'd say that their ostriches are livestock, I'd say. And yet, what is the difference between an ostrich and a lion?'

Mma Makutsi snorted. 'If you can't tell that, Fanwell, you'd better keep out of the bush. It would be very bad for you if you were walking through the bush one day and you saw a lion and you thought: oh, that lion will just fly away. That would not be very good, I'd say.'

Mr J. L. B. Matekoni intervened. 'Ostriches cannot fly, Mma. They have wings, but you never see them fly. They are too large.'

Mma Makutsi turned to him. 'What are their wings for, then, Rra? You tell me that. If ostriches cannot fly, then why do they have wings?'

Mma Ramotswe sighed. This was an extraordinary general meeting, and here they were immersed in a pointless argument about the capabilities of ostriches. Of course ostriches could not fly – you saw them running through the bush on those long legs of theirs, but you never saw them fly. But the question as to why ostriches had wings was an interesting one, she reflected, even if it was not one that they should be considering at that particular time.

'Not everything in nature has a purpose,' said Fanwell.

'Fanwell,' said Mma Ramotswe, 'we do not need to talk about that.'

Fanwell looked indignant. 'I didn't start it, Mma. It was Mma

Makutsi who started talking about ostriches and lions and so on. All I'm saying is that there are things that have happened because of evolution.' He cast a glance in Mma Makutsi's direction. 'That is very important, you see – evolution.' He paused. 'Have you heard of that, Mma Makutsi? Have you heard of Einstein and his theory of evolution.'

'Don't think I don't know about evolution,' said Mma Makutsi. 'And, anyway, it wasn't Einstein. He was the person who . . .' She hesitated, but only briefly, not wanting to confuse Einstein with Clovis Andersen. 'He was the person was said *E equals mc squared*.'

Fanwell stared at her defiantly. 'So? So, what does that mean, Mma. It's all very well to say that sort of thing, Mma, but what does it mean?'

Mma Makutsi waved a hand in the air. 'There isn't time to go into that right now, Fanwell. Some other time, I think.'

Mr J. L. B. Matekoni thought of something. 'I read somewhere that we came from fish. Have you heard that, Mma Ramotswe? Have you heard that we were all fish once?'

Fanwell shook his head in disbelief. 'I cannot believe that, Rra. If we were all fish, then how did we get out of the water? How would we have been able to breathe?'

'Perhaps we took a deep breath underwater first,' said Mr J. L. B. Matekoni. 'Then we got out of the water for a bit, holding our breath for as long as we could. Then we went back into the water again. Gradually we would have spent more time out than in, and that is when we would have started to evolve into monkeys.'

Mma Ramotswe had had enough. Clapping her hands, she announced that the topic of evolution, along with the topic of ostriches and lions, was now closed and they should return to the issue of elephants.

'Are you saying,' she asked Fanwell, 'that Charlie will not want to have the elephant moved to Mma Potokwani's place? Is that what you're saying?'

Fanwell said that he feared that was the case. 'You know how Charlie can be, Mma. He is a very stubborn person.'

Mma Ramotswe said that she was very sorry to hear that. 'I know what you mean, though. There have been occasions in the past when Charlie has dug his heels in and has refused to be moved. When he's doing that, you just can't get him to change his views. He is like a Kgale Hill – a great big rock that's going nowhere. There's no shifting him.'

'Do you think he likes having the elephant there?' asked Mma Makutsi. 'Is that the problem?'

Fanwell said that he thought it was. 'I think the idea of having an elephant appeals to Charlie. After all, how many people have elephants? Hardly any.'

Mma Makutsi said she thought Charlie might feel that having an elephant gave him status. 'He's always been very sensitive about status,' she said, adding, 'Largely because he has none, I think.'

Mma Ramotswe was not going to let that pass. 'That's unkind, Mma. Charlie is an employee of the No. 1 Ladies' Detective Agency. He has the status that goes with that.' She paused. Sometimes Mma Makutsi had to be reminded of the country's ideals; not every day, but sometimes. 'And the status of being a citizen of this country. That is a status. And being a person – that is a status too, in the eyes of God. God likes all of us – even Charlie.'

Mma Makutsi looked chastened. 'I didn't say that God didn't like Charlie, Mma. I never said that. He probably likes him a bit – who knows? But I can't imagine that God would want to spend too much time with him. A bit, maybe, but not much.'

Fanwell chose to issue a warning. 'You'd better be careful, Mma Makutsi. If God heard you talking about Charlie like that, he'd be furious. You'd better be careful – unless you've got a very good lightning conductor.'

'Come now, everybody,' said Mma Ramotswe. 'Let us not get bogged down in these things.' First it had been ostriches and lions and evolution, and now it was theology. She would have to steer the discussion back to where it should be.

'If Charlie won't agree to move the elephant,' she said, 'then he could find himself in big trouble. If a child were to be knocked over – crushed, even – then Charlie would almost certainly be arrested. If a life were lost, then it could even be manslaughter, which is a very serious offence in the Botswana Penal Code. It is there, you know, manslaughter, for just this sort of situation.'

'And that can mean years in prison,' said Mma Makutsi. 'We would not want that, would we?'

'I would not want anybody to go to prison,' said Mr J. L. B. Matekoni.

'Except those people who deserve it,' said Mma Makutsi quickly. 'There are some people who should definitely be in prison.'

Mma Ramotswe made another effort to focus the discussion. 'Charlie is the problem here,' she said. 'You know what Clovis Andersen says . . .'

Mma Makutsi looked up. Mma Ramotswe had few faults, she thought, but if there was one respect in which she might perhaps be criticised, it was in her tendency to attribute quotes to people who almost certainly never said anything of the sort. She did that a great deal with Sereste Khama, who, if Mma Ramotswe were to be believed, gave wise rulings on almost every conceivable subject. Some of these were undoubtedly true – Seretse Khama had been a very wise man indeed – but others, Mma Makutsi suspected, were Mma Ramotswe's own opinions falsely, even if quite innocently, attributed to the great man. So, she thought, it was highly unlikely that Seretse Khama had ever said anything about the benefits of redbush tea, even if Mma Ramotswe had on more than one occasion said that Seretse Khama was one of the first public advocates of redbush tea and that he endorsed the view that it was good for the digestion. Similarly, she very much doubted whether Seretse Khama had ever had cause to remark on the need to soak dried beans overnight before cooking them. He *may* have known about that – although it was not the sort of thing that anybody would expect a man to know – but would he have thought it right for him to speak in his role as Paramount Chief of the Bamangwato people and then as President of Botswana, on such a subject? She thought not, and so she maintained a certain scepticism when Mma Ramotswe spoke of these matters. Mma Makutsi did not fully appreciate, of course, that even if Mma Ramotswe was not absolutely certain that Seretse Khama had pronounced on a matter, she restricted herself to attributing a claim to that effect to those instances where she felt that he would almost certainly have expressed such a view had he turned his mind to the matter. That was quite different from making something up – a distinction that Mma Makutsi, for all *her* many merits, was unlikely to appreciate, given her own tendency to see the world in absolute terms. Not that Mma Ramotswe would ever overtly take her to task for that – in a world in which there were far too many people prepared to tolerate the sort of moral ambiguity or obfuscation that was at odds with the old Botswana sense of what was right or wrong – in such a world it was refreshing to come across somebody like Mma Makutsi, who had no difficulty at all in drawing a clear and robust line between right and wrong. And it was quite proper, too, that such standards should be defended by the No. 1 Ladies' Detective Agency, because if you could not trust a detective agency to be on the right side, then what hope was there for anything? If there was any institution in which people might expect to find a firm expression of rectitude, then surely it was a detective agency whose mission statement was to get to the bottom of things in the pursuit of justice and the truth – or something to that effect, the precise wording having been lost when Mma Makutsi inadvertently threw out the file in which she had lodged the relevant piece of paper recording the statement.

But now Mma Makutsi was waiting for Mma Ramotswe to reveal what it was that Clovis Andersen had said that was relevant here. It came after a short delay: 'You know what Clovis Andersen says – he says find the person who has the solution and then you will find the solution.'

Mma Makutsi looked at Mma Ramotswe. 'Did he say that, Mma? Are you sure?'

Any further discussion of the source of this proposition was cut short by Mr J. L. B. Matekoni's intervention. 'That is very true, Mma,' he said. 'And in this case, it means that there is only one way of preventing a disaster – and that is to take Charlie out of the picture.'

This remark brought a gasp of astonishment from Fanwell. 'Take Charlie out?' he stuttered. 'Do you mean *kill him*, boss?'

Mr J. L. B. Matekoni rolled his eyes. 'Kill Charlie? Don't be ridiculous, Fanwell. You mustn't talk like that.'

'But I wasn't talking like that,' protested Fanwell. 'You were, boss. You said—'

Mma Ramotswe raised a hand to silence the debate. 'I think there's a misunderstanding here. I think that what Mr J. L. B. Matekoni meant was that Charlie's views have to be overridden. That is definitely not the same thing as killing him.' She looked nervously at Mr J. L. B. Matekoni. 'I am right, aren't I, Rra . . . I hope.'

Mr J. L. B. Matekoni nodded. 'Of course you are, Mma. I'm a mechanic, not a gangster.'

Mma Makutsi laughed. 'That is very funny,' she said. 'Fanwell has obviously been watching too many films about gangsters and so on. Those people talk about *taking people out* . . . '

'Rubbing them out,' said Fanwell. 'That also happens a lot. People rub other people out.'

Mma Ramotswe shook her head. 'I do not like language like that. We do not speak like that in this country. There can be no rubbing out here.'

'No,' said Mr J. L. B. Matekoni. 'You are right, Mma.'

'So, what *do* we do?' asked Fanwell.

Mma Ramotswe looked thoughtful. 'I think we have no alternative but to get the elephant away from that place . . . '

Mma Makutsi took over. 'And take it to another place – to Mma Potokwani's, in fact. And that means, I think, that we shall have to do it at night.' She smiled. 'I can just see Charlie's face when he wakes up and finds there is no elephant any longer.'

'It would be for the best, I suppose,' said Mma Ramotswe. She felt uneasy, and it showed in her expression.

'I don't think we should do it at night,' said Fanwell. 'The police often patrol Old Naledi at night. You see them driving about in their cars. That is because it's a good place for criminals to walk around at night. They like walking around that place.'

Mr J. L. B. Matekoni looked doubtful. 'But can we drive through the streets of Gaborone with an elephant in the back of the van? I don't think so. In fact, I don't think we should go behind Charlie's back like this after all. I think it's wrong.' He paused, letting his gaze dwell on Mma Makutsi and Mma Ramotswe. 'It's just wrong to do something like that.'

Fanwell looked uncomfortable. 'I think you may be right, boss.

Maybe I should have another talk with Charlie. I could try to persuade him.'

Mma Ramotswe made up her mind. 'Yes,' she said. 'Speak to him, Fanwell. I'll lend you the van to go round there this evening. Get him to see sense.'

The meeting came to an end. Mma Makutsi collected the mugs from which everybody attending the meeting had been drinking. As she washed them at the sink, she addressed Mma Ramotswe over her shoulder. 'Why is it, Mma,' she asked, 'that the best way of putting off a decision is to have a meeting about it?'

Mma Ramotswe laughed. 'That is a very interesting question, Mma Makutsi,' she said. And then something occurred to her. 'And why is it,' she continued, 'that the best way of not answering a question is to ask it in the first place?'

Mma Makutsi stared at her, adjusting her new glasses at the end of her nose. 'Did Clovis Andersen say that, Mma? It's a very interesting thing to say.'

Mma Ramotswe shook her head. 'No, I said it, Mma Makutsi.' She paused. 'But it is the sort of thing he says, I think.'

They both laughed. Mma Ramotswe watched as Mma Makutsi took off her glasses and polished them with her handkerchief. That was the third time she had done that since the beginning of their extraordinary general meeting. Many people would not remark on that – perhaps not even notice it – but then Mma Ramotswe was a detective, and it was precisely the sort of thing that a detective would notice. And a detective, moreover, might be expected to have a theory as to why people do things more frequently than might normally be expected. *Look for the irregular pattern*, wrote Clovis Andersen . . .

Chapter Ten

They Say She Is Smart, Smart

The following morning Fanwell was waiting for Mma Ramotswe when she arrived at the office. She had travelled into work with Mr J. L. B. Matekoni in his recovery truck, having lent her van to Fanwell. This meant that she had been obliged to occupy the truck's less than comfortable passenger seat and to tolerate, too, a window that rattled loudly, a floor that vibrated beneath her feet, and that curious smell of fuel and grease that was such a recognisable feature of her husband's working space. Her van might not have been the most sophisticated of vehicles – indeed, it was a vehicle of no sophistication at all – but it had her things in it: her work-in-progress teapot cover, a crochet project to keep boredom at bay when she was parked somewhere in the course of an investigation; the small jar of salted peanuts that she kept topped up for dietary emergencies; and the spare pair of dark glasses that served both as protection for the eyes on a particularly sunny day and as an aid – of dubious efficacy, but still – for circumstances in which she felt the need to disguise herself. And, of course, the cab of her van had its own smell, the source of which she had never been able to trace, but that seemed, curiously, to be redolent of freshly baked bread – that enticing smell that drifted out of a bakery when they were taking a batch of loaves out of the oven. It was one of her favourite smells, but she had been unable to work out how it occurred in her van. Had a loaf of bread slipped out of her shopping bag and disappeared down the back of the seat? The back of any seat was a rich source of unexpected and delightful finds – frequently money – but it might also conceal a long-lost brooch, a watch, a pen that still had enough ink in it to write, or occasionally a wrapped and still edible tube of peppermints or some such treat. But a search had revealed no bread, and the smell remained a mystery – overtaken recently by the mystery, now solved, of the elephant smell.

There was the van waiting for her, parked where she always parked it herself, under the acacia tree at the back of the building that housed both Tlokweng Road Speedy Motors and the office of the No. 1 Ladies' Detective Agency. And there were both Fanwell and Charlie standing beside it, Charlie wearing earphones and listening to the radio station that he would listen to constantly if given the chance. It was a particularly noisy station whose tinny outpourings could be heard escaping from the earphones like the chirrup of some tireless electronic cicada somewhere.

Charlie took off his earphones as they approached.

'No problem, Mma Ramotswe,' he said. 'All agreed. No problem, ya!'

Fanwell explained. 'Charlie says that the elephant can go to Mma Potokwani. He has spoken to his friend, and his friend says that is fine with him.'

Charlie grinned broadly. 'He's pleased that you've found that place up north to take him,' he said. 'He says to thank you very much for solving the problem. And me too – I was running out of milk formula stuff. That little creature drinks and drinks. Milk, more milk ... Ow!'

'We haven't arranged a place yet,' Mma Ramotswe pointed out. 'We are going to try. But there will be formalities.'

Charlie sighed in an exaggerated way. 'Formalities, Mma, formalities. There are too many formalities in this country. Soon there will be formalities before you're allowed to breathe.'

Mma Ramotswe took the keys of the van from Fanwell as she answered Charlie. 'Things have to be done a certain way, Charlie. That is just one of these things.'

'A pity,' said Charlie.

It was one of those days when Charlie's time was allocated to the garage rather than the agency, and so Mma Ramotswe spent the next twenty minutes alone in the office before Mma Makutsi arrived for work. Then the kettle was switched on and the first cup of tea of the day was prepared and served – if one did not count the two cups consumed at home before leaving for work. The excitement caused by the elephant had rather overshadowed other demands on Mma Ramotswe's attention, and now it was time to deal with those. That meant the awkward issue of Blessing and her request for help – an issue that Mma Ramotswe wanted to get out of the way. It would have been simple enough to turn Blessing down and leave it at that, but Mma Ramotswe felt uncomfortable about acting in a way that was contrary to the Botswana tradition of helping a relative if it was remotely within one's power to do so. Even Mma Makutsi, who had reached her own view on this case – and decided that Tefo was a fraud and Blessing was one of those people taken advantage of by a stronger, manipulative man – would acknowledge that a request of this nature had to be given due weight and looked into before being robustly rejected.

Mma Ramotswe had, in fact, decided to ask Mma Makutsi to carry out the next stage of the investigation as she had a quite separate matter, a delicate issue of matrimonial property, with which she was required to deal. This involved a divorce in which the wife was convinced that the husband was concealing assets from the court so as to minimise the divorce settlement. It was an old and familiar issue: men were always trying to hide their business assets; in this case the husband was thought to be hiding an expensive Mercedes-Benz, a substantial number of cattle, and, of all things, a house. The Mercedes-Benz was believed to be parked at his girlfriend's place – but when Mma Ramotswe had gone there it was nowhere to be seen. There were, however, tyre tracks that, when measured, were the exact width of the wheelbase of the model of car he was alleged to be hiding. The cattle proved to be more difficult to track down, but Mma Ramotswe had managed to find a livestock agent who had handled some of them and arranged a transfer from one cattle post to another. The herdsman who had been in charge of that move had been underpaid by the owner and was only too happy to confirm ownership of the cattle. So that left only the house to be located, and she had a plan for that. She would phone the husband and offer to sell him property insurance at a markedly reduced rate. If he rose to the bait and took up her offer of a free insurance survey, then she might expect to be given the address of the missing property. It was a standard trick of the trade, but she believed that it might work. A man who was prepared to hide property on that scale in order to defeat the legitimate claim of a wife of fifteen years who was still looking after three of his young children, might also be expected to be a man who would be interested in the prospect of saving money on insurance. But first she had to find his telephone number: he had recently changed it and had refused to notify his wife of the new number. That was her task that morning – to track down his known associates and see whether she might get the number from them.

She explained to Mma Makutsi what was required. 'I know you don't trust that man, Tefo,' she began.

'I certainly don't, Mma. I don't trust him even that much.' Mma Makutsi indicated a sliver of distance between her thumb and fore-finger. 'Not even that, Mma.'

'You may be right,' said Mma Ramotswe. 'But I'd feel more comfortable having some evidence.'

Mma Makutsi took a more robust view of the need for evidence when something was as obvious as she thought Tefo's dishon-esty was. 'If you're pretending your leg's sore, you should at least remember which leg it is,' she said dismissively.

'Possibly,' said Mma Ramotswe.

'No, Mma, not possibly – definitely. I *know* that man's lying. I knew it straight away. And that Blessing, too. She's a number one big liar, Mma.'

'Even so, Mma Makutsi, I'd like you to check on his story.' Mma Ramotswe paused, and looked at her colleague. Mma Makutsi had come a long way since those early days when she had joined the agency as a secretary, but she still had her impetuosity to conquer. 'Now, Mma, do you remember my old friend, Mma Phiri? Remember her? She was a magistrate, but then she became ill and they gave her early retirement. She was only forty-eight, but the government was very good to her. She lost a lung. One whole lung, Mma.'

Mma Makutsi frowned. There had been a Phiri at the college – a very quiet girl who was a prominent Seventh-Day Adventist. She recalled she had refused to drink tea for some reason, but she did not remember much else about her. It was a common enough name, but it was possible they were the same family, even if she did not remember a Phiri who was a magistrate.

'She came to see me once in the office – after she had retired,' Mma Ramotswe continued. 'Perhaps you were out at the time.'

Mma Makutsi waited.

'She retired out near Tlokweng,' said Mma Ramotswe. 'Not far from Mma Potokwani, as it happens. I think she sees her from time to time. You know how she ropes people in to do things for the Orphan Farm. She used to get her to help her with the books – she has a very good memory, Mma. She remembers everything.'

'She is very lucky,' said Mma Makutsi. 'If you remember everything, then you'll forget nothing.'

Mma Ramotswe thought about this. It was undoubtedly true, although she was not sure that it really needed to be said. 'I'd like you to go and see her,' she said. 'See if she knows anything about Tefo. We've been told that he was convicted of stock theft. If that's true, then she will know something about it. She knew exactly what everybody was up to. She saw them in court if they did anything illegal. She knew everything – she still does, I think.'

Mma Makutsi nodded. 'I'll ask her about that man. We'll see what she says. Mind you, I don't really need any confirmation of what I already know, Mma Ramotswe.'

Mma Ramotswe thought about what Clovis Andersen said about keeping an open mind, but she could not remember his precise words and she decided that this was not the time to extemporise.

Mma Makutsi drove slowly down the dirt road that ran past the clinic at Tlokweng. The clinic was the reference point, Mma Ramotswe had told her: the third turning after the clinic, she had said, was the Phiri turning. The former magistrate's house was one of several at the end of a track, the others being occupied by the families of her two brothers, both of whom were successful cattle traders.

She slowed down as she drove past the clinic, noticing the handful of people seated on the waiting benches. They were lined up outside, shielded from the sun by an expanse of thick shade netting strung across supporting wooden posts; five of them, including a woman with a baby wrapped in a folded shawl across her back. Mma Makutsi stared at the woman from her car, and for a moment their eyes met, across yards of dusty foreground; and Mma Makutsi thought: my sister, my sister ... She had no idea who the woman was, but she felt a sudden surge of feeling for her – a feeling of sympathy so intense that it surprised her. She was just a stranger – a woman whom she had never seen before and would never see again. All she had to do was to continue with her journey, to turn the corner ahead, and it would be as if the other woman had ceased to exist. That was what you could do with most people you encountered in this life: you just continued to do what you were already doing and you passed them by, because you simply could not stop at every moment and think: this is the only time I'm going to see this person on this earth and ... You could not do that because you did not have enough time. There was not enough time, and you were only one person, one small person – because every person, even the largest of us, is still just a small thing when you come to think of it – and there is only so much that one person can do about anything. So there she was, Mma Makutsi, who could have been where that other woman was, and instead was there in her car, with a fine house to return to, and a husband with cattle – and a furniture store – and a job that made her someone when previously she had been nobody in particular; and it had all started in Bobonong and there were plenty of people who were still stuck back there and would never be able to leave; never be able to go off to the Botswana Secretarial College and end up with ninety-seven per cent. For most of the world got nowhere near ninety-seven per cent in their examinations, they simply did not, and ... That poor woman with her child – whatever number of children it was – whose life would be a constant battle, as likely as not. A battle against poverty, a battle to get enough food for her other children, a battle to wash the children's clothes and keep the baby clean, and ...

She stopped her car. She was level with the clinic gate, and by reversing a few yards she was able to turn directly into the short drive that led up to the clinic. She parked the car next to another car that was already there – the doctor's or the nurse's, perhaps – and then she got out and walked up to the waiting patients. They watched her carefully – as if judging her. They would have seen the car, she realised – a new model, belonging to Phuti – and they would have made up their minds about her. These were not well-off people, and they would have decided that there was a wide gulf between them and her.

She greeted them in the old-fashioned way, and they responded politely. She sat down on the bench, next to the woman with the baby.

'I saw you from the car, my sister. I saw you waiting here.'

The woman looked at her over the baby's head. She did not at first respond to Mma Makutsi's remark, but seemed to be waiting for something else.

'So, you are waiting for the doctor?' said Mma Makutsi.

The woman shook her head. 'There is a nurse – that is all.' She spoke quietly, as if she were uncomfortable about disturbing the quiet that lay about them; for the others were silent, and were listening as they watched. And all that there was, all that could be heard about them, was the sound of the cicadas screeching away, as they liked to do in the heat, determined that their hidden kind, concealed in the private places of insects, should hear them and take notice.

Mma Makutsi persisted. 'For the baby? You're taking the baby to the nurse? Or is it for yourself?'

The woman sighed – a sigh that came from a hinterland of acceptance: this is the way the world is. This is what it is like. 'It is for the baby,' she said. 'She is crying, crying, crying after I feed her. She never stops – except when I come here. Then she is silent.'

Mma Makutsi clicked her tongue almost inaudibly – the sound, in Botswana, of a sympathy that may be felt, even if it is hard to put into words. But then she said, 'It is always like that. Children do not do what you want them to do, do they? They do the opposite.' She looked at the baby, at its tiny head in its heavy wool cap – even in this heat, which surely would make the child's head too hot. A lighter, breathable cloth, white muslin and at least cooler-looking, covered the child's face, so that only the eyes and forehead were showing. 'That sounds like *kgadikêgo*, Mma. That is what babies get sometimes – and it makes them cry a lot.' She used the Setswana word, *kgadikêgo* – stomach ache.

The woman patted her baby through the cloth of the sling. 'You're right, Mma,' she said. 'They call it colic these days. It is probably that. Of course, the children themselves don't understand.'

'No, they don't.' Mma Makutsi reached out to touch the baby lightly, against the cheek. The child's small eyes watched her.

'You want to see the nurse too?' asked the woman. 'She is very good at her job, this nurse.'

Mma Makutsi shook her head. 'No, I do not need to see the nurse. I was just driving past and I saw you and your baby and thought ...' She stopped. What had she thought? She was not sure; it was difficult to give sympathy a specific shape. And then it came to her: 'I wondered whether you lived close by, or whether you had to walk here.'

The woman pointed. 'I live that way, Mma. About four miles – maybe five. I had to walk here.'

'That is not easy,' said Mma Makutsi. 'It is not easy in the heat – especially if you're carrying a baby.'

'I am used to it,' said the woman. 'If you're used to something, then it is not so hard.'

Mma Makutsi looked over her shoulder at her car. 'That car has lots of room, Mma. There will be room for you and your baby. I can take you home after you've seen the nurse.'

The woman stared at her in apparent disbelief. 'But Mma, but ...'

Mma Makutsi touched her lightly on the forearm to stem her protestations. 'My mind is made up, Mma.'

The sunlight caught her glasses, and they flashed a warning that she was determined and would not welcome an attempt at dissuasion. Surprised, but nonetheless understanding this, the woman lowered her head and said, 'You are very kind, Mma.'

Mma Makutsi seated herself on the bench next to the woman. The other people waiting had listened to every word of her conversation with the woman, and one of them, an elderly man, now said, 'That lady can go in first, when the nurse is ready. Then she will not hold you up too much, Mma.'

Another nodded, and said, 'It is very hot.'

A third said, 'Yes, it is always hot. Always.'

A few minutes later, the nurse arrived, parking her car next to Mma Makutsi's. She nodded at the waiting patients before unlocking the clinic. Mma Makutsi sat and stared at the sky while the woman went inside; she heard the baby crying, but only briefly, and then the woman re-emerged, clutching a paper bag on which a label had been stuck.

Mma Makutsi rose to her feet. 'Everything is all right, Mma?'

The woman smiled. 'She has given me something to give to the baby. She says it will settle the stomach.'

They walked to Mma Makutsi's car. In the brief period during which it had been parked in the sunlight, the heat within it had built up, even with the windows left open. Mma Makutsi took a newspaper from the passenger seat, unfolded it and spread it over the back seat to protect the woman from the hot upholstery. Then she drove back to the road and followed the woman's directions to her house. In the driver's mirror, she saw the baby resting on her mother's lap. She saw a tiny hand reach out and grasp the woman's fingers. She remembered how her own baby, Itumelang Andersen Radiphuti, had done this when he had first been introduced to his father, and how Phuti had wept with emotion and said, 'He's shaking hands with his daddy – see, that's what he is doing – he's shaking hands.' And she had fought back the tears, too, because only a few years earlier she would never have dreamed that she would have this in her life: a kind husband who loved her – and often told her so – and a healthy baby. And a house. And cattle. And a vegetable garden. And enough dresses to wear a different one every day for three weeks if she wanted to. How had all that happened?

It did not take long to reach the woman's house. Years earlier, when Mma Makutsi had still been in Bobonong, a house of this size and simplicity would not have been unusual – a single room, effectively, with a sloping roof of corrugated tin and walls of distempered daub. Now, with the prosperity that the country had enjoyed, the steady economic progress that the diamond mines, cautious husbandry, and good government had brought to the country, the ranks of those still living in single-room houses – huts, really – had been steadily thinned. People now had at least two or three rooms; they had walls made of breeze blocks; they had running water or at least access to a stand-pipe supplied by a village borehole. And yet there were still those whom this amelioration had bypassed, and who could not afford more than the most cramped living quarters. As the woman in the back seat reached forward to tap her on the shoulder, Mma Makutsi realised that this woman was one of those who had not been invited within the fold of plenty. It was no surprise, really, as she had expected something of this sort, but she found herself drawing in her breath as she took in the meanness of her new friend's home.

'This is my place here, Mma. This is it.'

Mma Makutsi nosed the car over the last few bumps of eroded track. 'To your doorstep, Mma,' she said, trying to sound as cheery as she could.

She stopped the car.

'I would like to make you some tea, Mma,' said the woman. 'There is no milk, but there is some tea.'

Mma Makutsi looked at her watch. 'I would like to say yes, Mma,' she said. 'I would like that very much, but I have to go and see somebody and she will be sitting there thinking: where is this woman who was coming to see me? She will be thinking: this woman is a very rude woman who is always late.'

They both laughed.

'Maybe some other time, Mma,' said the woman.

Mma Makutsi got out of her car to help the woman. She said, 'May I hold your baby? Just for a minute or two?'

'Of course, Mma,' said the woman. 'Here she is.'

She handed the infant to Mma Makutsi, who took her gently, a precious, fragile parcel of humanity. And as she did so, the muslin cloth that had obscured the child's face fell away, and Mma Makutsi saw the cleft lip. Her gaze dwelt on it for a few seconds, and then passed to the woman. She had not intended that her shock should show, but it did; she could not conceal it.

'She is going to have an operation,' said the woman. 'They are going to do it down in Gaborone, at the big hospital there.'

'I see, Mma. That is good. They can fix these things now, can't they?'

The woman inclined her head. 'Yes.' Then she added, 'My sister will take her there.'

Mma Makutsi stroked the baby's cheek. 'She is very beautiful, Mma. Look at her eyes. They are lovely eyes.'

A smile crossed the woman's face. 'They are like the eyes of my late mother.'

'Eyes run in families,' said Mma Makutsi. 'That often happens.' She paused. 'Your sister, Mma? What about you? Wouldn't it be better for you to go with her?'

The woman did not answer.

'How long will she be there?' Mma Makutsi pressed.

'Five days,' said the woman. 'They said five days. My sister is in Gaborone. She works in one of the big hotels, but she will be able to visit her every other day.'

Mma Makutsi drew in her breath. 'But it will be hard for a little baby not to have her mother there, Mma.'

The woman sighed. 'I cannot go, Mma. I am working at that school over there.' She pointed towards the village centre. 'I am one of the cooks. The man who is in charge is very strict. He says that I can go, but I will not be paid for a whole week. And if that happens, then I cannot buy food for my mother, and my brother, too – he is one of those people who cannot work because something went wrong when he was being born and it is very hard for him to walk, Mma.'

Mma Makutsi held the child close to her. She felt its breath against her cheek – a tiny movement of air, like the touch of a feather. There was only one thing for her to do – and she did it.

'I can help you, Mma. I can help you to go to Gaborone.'

'That is kind of you, Mma. But that is not why I cannot go. There are minibuses, but I cannot go because—'

Mma Makutsi handed the baby back. As she did so, she said, 'That's not what I meant, Mma. What I meant is that I will give you the money – the same as your wages for that week. I will give it to you. And you can stay at our place if there is no place for you to stay at the hospital.'

The woman stared at her. 'They have a place for mothers to sleep. You can sleep beside your baby.'

'Then that is what you must do,' said Mma Makutsi.

The woman held the baby with one arm; with the other she reached and gripped Mma Makutsi's blouse. 'Mma, you are the kindest person in this country. That is true, Mma – that is true. You are the kindest person.'

Mma Makutsi turned away, embarrassed by the praise. 'No, Mma,' she said. 'You must not call me that. I am the same as everybody else. No different.'

'But who would help some person they have just met, Mma? That is why I'm saying what I've just said.'

Mma Makutsi became business-like. 'I'm going to write down my telephone number, Mma. And then I shall write down our address too. This is where I work, you see.' She took a piece of paper from her bag and wrote down the details.

The woman said, 'I haven't told you my name, Mma. I am Mma Moyana.'

She took the paper and read what Mma Makutsi had written. She looked up in astonishment.

'You are that detective lady? I have seen the sign often when I have gone into town. It's that place just off the Tlokweng Road, isn't it? Next to that garage? The No. 1 Ladies' Detective Agency? You're that lady they talk about?'

Mma Makutsi hesitated. 'One of them,' she said. 'There is another lady there.' She hesitated. She had to be honest. 'That other lady is called Mma Ramotswe. She is the one who started the business. I am her . . . her associate.'

The woman frowned. 'But I have heard there is another one there, who is a very clever detective. They say she is smart, smart, Mma.'

Mma Makutsi held her breath. Had word got out about her ninety-seven per cent?

'She is called Mma Makutsi,' said the woman. 'That is what I have heard.'

For a few moments Mma Makutsi did not say anything. But the words that the woman had just uttered hung in the air for all to see, like great letters of smoke written across the sky. She savoured the moment, and then said, struggling to keep her voice even, 'Mma, you are the kind one now. Thank you for what you have said. It has made me very happy.'

Chapter Eleven

My Cup Has Too Much Tea in It

'You will find her a very polite lady,' Mma Ramotswe had said of her friend, the retired Mma Phiri. 'Many people are polite, Mma – still – but there are some who are very polite. This lady is very polite.'

Mma Makutsi nodded. She had met some of these very polite people – most of them ladies, she had to admit, although now that she thought of it there were many very polite men too. Her own husband, Phuti, was one who had a natural courtesy about him that was frequently remarked upon by others, and even her baby, Itumelang Andersen Radiphuti, showed every sign of being a very polite baby. There were many babies who grabbed at anything you offered them – snatched it, in fact – but Itumelang never did that. If you offered him his bottle of milk he would look at you first, as if to secure your permission, as if to say, 'Are you sure?' and then he would take it, in both hands, as was the polite thing to do in Botswana. You should never snatch something with a single hand, that was a lesson that parents taught their children at a very early age; but it had not been necessary, it seemed, to give Itumelang that lesson. Presumably that was because manners, although they needed to be taught, could, to a certain extent, be inherited – just as you could inherit a nose or a way of holding your head, or a preference for this food over that food. Mma Makutsi was a strong believer in the inheritance principle: nothing came from nowhere, and most of our ordinary human characteristics were handed down to us from our parents and grandparents, and indeed from the ancestors themselves – those remote, shadowy figures who lived in Botswana so long ago and whose fingerprints, faint and unobtrusive, could be seen upon the land if one cared to look for them.

Of course, inheritance brought bad things as well as good. Violet Sephotho, for instance, was the way she was because earlier Sephothos had been the same, had been interested only in attracting the attentions of men. Mma Makutsi smiled to herself as she imagined Violet's grandmother behaving exactly like her granddaughter, a figure bent with age but still flirting with ancient men, too old to even notice what was going on in the world about them, and certainly immune to the antics of flashy elderly women ...

But even as these delicious thoughts came to her, she found herself at the front gate of the Phiri household and calling out to those within. She could think about the Sephotho clan later on, when she could perhaps imagine what the next generation would be like – worse than Violet, presumably, because they said that in general inherited qualities got worse as the generations went by. That was especially so if there was inbreeding – if one Sephotho married a distant Sephotho cousin, for example – something allowed by the law and by custom but perhaps not the best tactic for the improvement of stock. That was something she could return to later, and perhaps discuss with Mma Ramotswe, although Mma Ramotswe, being as charitable as she was, would be more tolerant of Sephotho failings than she, Mma Makutsi, was inclined to be. Mma Ramotswe, of course, had not been at the Botswana Secretarial College at the same time as Violet, and could therefore be forgiven for not realising the full awfulness of Violet's behaviour. There was a limit to the amount of tolerance one should show, Mma Makutsi thought; if you were excessively tolerant, unacceptable people – like Violet Sephotho – might imagine that they were all right, whereas the message that society should give to such people was an unambiguous 'You are not all right!' That was the problem: not enough people were sending out that signal; not enough people were prepared to shake their heads when they looked at other, unacceptable, people. It was hard work, shaking your head like that, but it had to be done – there was no way round it. And it was hard work, too, having to get up and walk out whenever an unacceptable person entered a room, but that, too, had to be done. There should be far more walking out, Mma Makutsi thought, and as she thought that, from down below, she imagined two thin voices voicing in unison their support for that particular proposition: *too right, boss – count us in on that* . . . Shoes, she thought, know what's what. There is no confusion on the part of shoes when it comes to matters of right and wrong . . .

'Mma Makutsi?' said Mma Phiri, as she opened the door. 'Precious said that you would be coming, Mma. You are very welcome.'

Mma Makutsi followed her hostess inside. She could not help but reflect on the difference between the house she was now entering and the house she had just left – between the world of Mma Phiri and that of Mma Moyana. Mma Phiri's house had a solid feel to it: it was one of those buildings that looked as if it had always been there, as if it emanated from the very ground upon which it stood. There were some houses like that – they seemed to be in the place where they were *meant* to be; whereas there were other houses, constructions with a much flimsier feel to them, that looked as if they had been dropped on the landscape by some great and unseen hand, and sooner or later – probably sooner – the land would shrug them off.

'You have a very fine house, Mma,' said Mma Makutsi.

Mma Phiri gestured for her guest to sit down. Even the sofa at which she pointed, an inviting, cream-coloured three-seater, looked as if it had been there forever, and that the house might have been built around it. There were some sofas that were like that – they had the air, and the confidence, of the thing that had been there first, before walls and roof and other human additions had been built around them. Phuti had a term for that quality in furniture – 'permanent furniture'. That was how he described some of the items that he sold in his Double Comfort Furniture Store, and she had heard him say to prospective purchasers, 'This sofa may be slightly more expensive, but it is what I call *permanent*. It is built to last permanently, you see. This is not a *temporary* sofa. This is a sofa on which your great-grandchildren will be sitting, I think.'

As she sat down, it occurred to her that she might have seen the sofa before, just as she vaguely recognised a small cabinet at the far end of the room. And then it dawned on her: this furniture had all the qualities of Double Comfort Furniture Store furniture. It had that *feel*.

She felt the fabric under her hands. Yes, it certainly had that. It was an indefinable quality – one that would be too difficult to put into words, but it could be picked up by the eye, and indeed by the other senses.

'Mma Phiri,' she ventured, 'do you mind my asking: where did you get this very fine sofa?'

Mma Phiri looked at the sofa with an unmistakable fondness. 'I like that sofa very much, Mma,' she replied. 'There are some sofas that one can take or leave – but that sofa is not one of them. That sofa is very important to me, Mma.'

Mma Makutsi nodded encouragingly. 'I can see that, Mma.'

'There is a big furniture store,' Mma Phiri continued. 'You may know the place. It is near the old bus station. I forget the name of it . . .'

'The Double Comfort Furniture Store,' prompted Mma Makutsi.

'That's it. Yes, that's the name of that place. It belongs to that man with the big nose – you may have seen him.'

Mma Makutsi caught her breath. She was not sure whether she should keep silent or whether she should say something, just in case Mma Phiri might be thinking of digging herself deeper into a hole. She decided to speak, but before she could say anything, Mma Phiri continued, 'Yes, his nose: you should see—'

'That man is my husband, Mma,' said Mma Makutsi.

Mma Phiri froze. 'Your husband, Mma? It's his shop?'

'Yes,' said Mma Makutsi. 'That man is my husband, Mma. He's called Phuti Radiphuti and he is the father of my first-born, Itumelang Andersen Radiphuti.'

Mma Makutsi spoke with quiet dignity. As she did so, she thought of Phuti's nose; it was certainly not a small nose, but it was by no means one of the largest in the country. There were several noses right there in Gaborone that were unquestionably larger than Phuti's. There was that man whose picture was often to be seen in the *Botswana Daily News*, that man who was chairman of that foodstuffs company and who was always handing out prizes for this, that and the next thing. What about his nose? And, anyway,

Phuti could carry off his nose because he was a large-boned man and he was tall enough to have such a large nose. It was different if you were small; in such a case the overall effect would be a bit unbalanced, and one could very easily look like a hornbill, with its overly prominent beak.

Mma Phiri was quick to recover. 'I'm sorry, Mma. I didn't mean to criticise your husband's nose. It was more of a compliment than anything else.'

Mma Makutsi sucked in her cheeks. 'I see, Mma.' She sounded icy; she had not intended to, but she did.

'I've always said that a good nose on a man is a very positive thing,' Mma Phiri continued. 'These men – these modern men – with their small noses don't realise how ineffective it makes them look. Whereas a man with a prominent, distinguished nose – like your husband's – usually has an air of firmness about him.' She paused. 'And women find such noses very attractive, I may say, Mma. They are drawn to such noses as … as moths are drawn to a candle.'

Mma Makutsi frowned. 'Am I to conclude, Mma, that you – you personally, that is – are drawn to my husband's nose?'

Mma Phiri bit her lip. 'No, Mma – not at all. I am certainly not drawn to your husband's nose. I have not given it a second thought.'

'And yet you are the one who brought it up, Mma. We were talking about sofas and suddenly the topic of conversation shifted to noses.'

Mma Phiri laughed nervously. 'It is a handsome nose, Mma. But I'm sure you know that – you married it.' She corrected herself quickly. 'I mean, you married your husband.'

Mma Makutsi waited.

'And anyway, Mma, that shop – yes, that is where we bought this sofa. It was on sale, I think. Ten per cent off, or something like that, although when people say that prices have been reduced I never really believe them.'

Mma Makutsi resumed her icy tone. 'My husband always means what he says, Mma – in business as well as in private.

'Of course, Mma. Of course.' Mma Phiri looked uncomfortable, and Mma Makutsi, realising that this encounter had got off to a bad start, saw that it was up to her to rescue it. After all, she was here, as Mma Ramotswe's representative, to question Mma Phiri, and there was no point at all in antagonising the person from whom you were asking for information.

She made a placatory remark. 'I am very glad that you are pleased with this sofa,' she said. 'My husband is always keen to please his customers. He'll be very happy when I tell him that you're satisfied with the sofa, Mma.'

The tension dispelled, they proceeded to easier subjects. Mma Phiri asked after Mma Ramotswe, and Mma Makutsi told her that Mma Ramotswe was in good health, was very busy, and sent her warmest regards to her old friend. Mma Phiri replied that she hoped Mma Makutsi would pass on her own regards, and assure Mma Ramotswe that she and her entire family were in good health – apart from one grandson, who had broken his arm by falling out of a tree, but had learned his lesson and would undoubtedly be more careful in future.

'It is a pity that some lessons have to be learned in a painful way,' said Mma Makutsi. 'But that is the way the world works, I suppose.'

This sage observation brought a nod of agreement from Mma Phiri, followed by silence.

'Mma Ramotswe has asked me to find out something,' Mma Makutsi said. 'We have an issue, Mma.'

Mma Phiri raised an enquiring eyebrow. 'One of your cases?'

Mma Makutsi shook her head. 'No, it's not exactly a case, Mma.

It's more of a . . . ' She searched for the right term. What was it? A dilemma? That was it. 'It's a dilemma, Mma. We are faced with the issue of whether we do one thing or another. It is that sort of issue.'

'Many issues are like that,' said Mma Phiri. 'My entire professional life, in a way, was just that. Do I do this or that? Do I believe this person or that person? Do I decide this way or another way altogether?'

Mma Makutsi had always been in awe of magistrates and judges, whose job, she thought, was surely one of the most difficult jobs imaginable. When she had been younger – even as recently as a few years ago – she'd been able to make up her mind quickly and then stick to her opinions. She felt that she could sum people up more or less on first meeting, and be reasonably sure that she would not change her mind about them. These days she was not so sure; the world, which in the past had been in sharp enough focus, now seemed rather more blurred. Right and wrong were still there, of course – two gardens side by side, with distinctive flora and fauna – but now the boundary between the two domains was perhaps not quite as distinct as it used to be. During her student days at the Botswana Secretarial College, and indeed when she'd first worked for Mma Ramotswe, there had been no doubt in her mind about many of the issues of the day and their possible solution. In those days she had shown no hesitation in disapproving of people whom she did not like, or those she felt were up to no good. Now it was harder to write people off quite so quickly, with any confidence that one's views would remain stable – with the exception of Violet Sephotho, of course, of whom she held precisely the same opinion as she had done on first acquaintance all those years ago.

She felt emboldened to ask Mma Phiri how she dealt with lies. 'How do you tell if somebody's telling the truth, Mma?' she said. 'If you're sitting there in court on the . . . on the chair . . . '

'We call it the bench,' said Mma Phiri. 'The judge sits on a bench. That word has always been used – for some reason. I think it is historical. They must have sat on benches in the old days, way back – in England, I suppose. Nowadays it is really a chair, but we still call it a bench.'

Mma Makutsi nodded. 'Yes, a bench. You're sitting on the bench and you're listening to a witness, perhaps, and the witness starts to talk. Do you think: is this a truthful person? And how do you answer that, Mma? How can you tell?'

Mma Phiri laughed. 'That's a very difficult question, Mma. They don't teach you how to do that, you know. You go to the University of Botswana and you do a law degree and they teach you all about the law of contract and the law of property and so on. You learn lots and lots of cases and you read and read, Mma, but they never teach you how to look at a witness and work out whether he or she is telling the truth.'

'No?'

'No, they do not. They teach you what the rules are – about what you can ask a witness and what you cannot ask, but they don't teach you about how to tell the difference between an honest person and a liar.'

'Experience, Mma? Is that it?'

Mma Phiri smiled and folded her hands across her lap. 'Yes, experience, Mma. You develop that ability through experience. Most judges and magistrates will tell you that. They know that there are some things you cannot learn by reading a book.'

Mma Makutsi agreed with that. It was the same with detective work. Nobody had taught her how to be a detective ... To begin with, she had fumbled her way into the job, learning by her mistakes, gradually building up a *feeling* for the tasks facing a detective. And the same was true with life in general: you learned

as you went through it, as you got older – that was the only way
to develop judgement, or wisdom, perhaps, because wisdom really
was what we needed if we were to get through life without making
too much of a disaster of it. And yet wisdom, however much people
may speak about it, was a rare quality, and you did not encounter
it every day. Mma Ramotswe had it – Mma Makutsi was sure of
that, and Mma Potokwani too, because she had seen so much of life
looking after the orphans. And then there were some of the elders
who had it – the people who had held office in the government of
Botswana, some of the chiefs, retired principals of schools . . . yes,
there was wisdom about, if you knew where to look for it. And it
was there, she thought – right there in the room with her, in the
shape of this former magistrate who had dispensed justice over so
many years and must have seen the full range of human nature.

A young woman came in with a tea tray. 'This is my daughter,'
said Mma Phiri.

Mma Makutsi and the daughter greeted one another, before the
daughter retreated into the kitchen.

'She has three children,' said Mma Phiri. 'They keep her very
busy because they are still young. But I love having them living with
me. It is my great privilege, Mma.' She reached forward to pour
the tea. 'What do you and Mma Ramotswe need to know, Mma?'

Mma Makutsi took a sip of the tea that had been poured. 'Five
Roses,' she said. 'This is very good tea.'

Mma Phiri smiled. 'That shows you are a detective, Mma.
Nobody else identifies the brand of tea.'

'Am I right, Mma?'

They both laughed. 'As it happens, you are,' Mma Phiri said.
'But you were about to tell me, Mma, what it is that you want to
find out.'

Mma Makutsi began. 'It is about a man who says that he

needs an operation. *Says*, Mma. That's what he says, but we are not so sure.'

Mma Phiri rolled her eyes. 'The usual story, Mma? Money?'

'Yes, but … But we are not sure. I think he's lying, but Mma Ramotswe … Well, you know how kind she is, Mma Phiri.'

'She is very kind, Mma. Everybody knows that. She is a kind lady.' She paused. 'But tell me, Mma Makutsi, do I know this man?'

'You might, Mma. He may have been one of your clients, so to speak. Or you may know about the case – because Mma Ramotswe says that you are a lady with a very good memory.'

Mma Phiri chuckled. 'It used to be rather good, yes, but you know how it is when you're getting on … Well, you probably don't know at your age, but people like me who have had some big birthdays, we're always asking ourselves: where have I put my spectacles? And then you realise they're on your nose, Mma – that sort of thing.'

'Or you remember that you don't wear spectacles in the first place,' said Mma Makutsi.

There was a short silence. Then Mma Phiri said, 'That is very funny, Mma.' And a further pause before, 'It isn't quite that bad, Mma. Try me.'

There was a faint note of reproach in Mma Phiri's voice, and Mma Makutsi tried to sound as respectful as possible as she explained her quest. She had not gone far, though, before Mma Phiri nodded vigorously and raised a hand to stop her.

'I am very familiar with that case, Mma,' she said. 'It was some time ago. Twelve years, probably; just before I retired. But yes, I was the magistrate. I remember stock theft cases very clearly because they always involve a lot of passion. People get very upset about them, and sometimes you have to warn people in court – the public, that is – not to sit there and murmur during the evidence.'

'You remember that man?'

'Yes, as I said, I remember the case very clearly. This man – this Tefo – was a South African Motswana. I felt a bit sorry for him, actually, because those people are very close to us, as you know. They speak our language – we have the same ancestors, way back, but they are citizens of another country and that is what counts these days. So, they don't have all the things that we have.'

Mma Makutsi agreed. It was hard. Botswana was a fortunate country, surrounded by neighbours who were not quite so fortunate. That sort of situation could be as difficult for a country as it could be in ordinary life, where neighbours with a car live next to neighbours without one, or neighbours with curtains live next to neighbours with none. Life was stubbornly unequal, whatever efforts the well-meaning made to reduce the contrast between good fortune and want. One day, perhaps, there would be enough for all, and painful differences of that nature would be no more, or be less obvious, but that day, Mma Makutsi thought, was not one that she would ever see.

'Yes,' continued Mma Phiri. 'That was one of those cases where you sit there . . .'

'On your bench . . .'

'Yes, you sit there on the bench and you see some poor person in front of you. And you have a strong suspicion that he did not do what he is accused of doing, and yet all the evidence is there and you can't just throw the case out because you have a feeling somewhere in your stomach that this is the wrong person. Or you are satisfied that he did it, but there are many good reasons why he did what he did and, worst of all, you think: if I had been there, I would have done exactly the same as he did. You sometimes think that, Mma, and yet you know that the law's the law and people can't take matters into their own hands.'

Mma Phiri poured more tea into their cups. 'I remember, Mma, I had a case once when a man was charged with assaulting another man and he had taken an axe to him, Mma – a big axe used for chopping wood – and chopped one of his fingers off. Yes, actually chopped it off. The police found the finger and there was a photograph of it in court. And the prosecutor said to the witness – the man whose finger had been chopped off – "Is that your finger, Rra?" And the witness looked at the photograph and said, "It is not my finger any longer, sir." I tell you, Mma Makutsi, that was one of those times when I struggled not to laugh, and yet it was a very sad case because the accused had taken the axe to this other man who had kidnapped his teenage daughter and was planning to sell her to some terrible person in the Congo for forced marriage, Mma. Fortunately, the police stopped him in time, before he could take the girl away, but the father came at him with an axe when he found out.' She paused. 'What father would not have felt like doing something like that, Mma? I could understand, but the problem is that we cannot allow people to take an axe to anybody who does some terrible thing to them. That is what the law is for.'

Mma Makutsi asked what happened.

'I had to give him a prison sentence,' said Mma Phiri. 'But I suspended it. That is the great thing about suspended sentences. You can make it quite clear that you disapprove of what somebody has done; you can make it clear that there must be punishment; but then you can allow mercy to do its work. Mercy, Mma. Mercy is a very great thing. We must always remember mercy.'

Mma Makutsi lowered her eyes. This magistrate was not only a wise woman – she was humane as well. And that reminded Mma Makutsi of the fact that she herself was sometimes a little bit unforgiving – just a little bit. She should try harder, perhaps. And then the image of Violet Sephotho came to mind, and her new resolve was immediately tested – to breaking point, in fact.

'But to get back to your stock theft man,' said Mma Phiri. 'The reason why I felt uncomfortable in that case was because I thought he was not guilty. And yet he had lodged a guilty plea and did not withdraw it when I gave him the chance. I said, "Are you sure you don't want to change your plea?" And he said that he did not. But I watched him, Mma, as he spoke, and I saw him looking at a lady sitting in the front row of the public benches. She was a relative of his – I happened to know that – and she had come in with him. She is a woman called Blessing, and I had come across her before.'

Mma Makutsi listened attentively.

'She had been up before me,' said Mma Phiri.

'In court, Mma?'

'Yes. She had been charged with an offence herself. A year or so earlier.'

Mma Makutsi's eyes widened. 'She had, Mma? The lady?'

'Yes. Stock theft, as it happens, Mma. A very minor case. She stole a goat.'

Mma Makutsi was silent as she absorbed the unexpected information. And yet, she asked herself, why should she be surprised? If Tefo had been lying about his operation, then so too was Blessing.

Mma Phiri explained that stealing a goat was a low-value theft, punishable with a fine. And yet, in the eyes of the law, it was technically a stock theft and that meant that if somebody who stole a goat was subsequently convicted of taking a cow, that would make the second offence all that more serious.

Mma Phiri fixed Mma Makutsi with an enquiring look. 'You will see where this is going,' she said.

Mma Makutsi looked blank. She suspected she was missing something, but she was not sure what it was. She felt a certain embarrassment now: she might be the great detective who could identify Five Roses tea, but what use was that if she then missed something rather more important?

Mma Phiri, being too polite to embarrass her guest, immediately reassured her. 'Of course, it's not obvious at all. It's not what any-body would expect, Mma: the real thief was that woman, Blessing. This other man, this Tefo, was her lover, even her husband for all I knew, and she had got him to take the blame. So, he pleaded guilty, and because he did so, it was difficult for me to do anything but convict him. I could have refused to accept his plea, of course, and discharged him, but the Attorney General gets very cross if a magistrate does that sort of thing.'

Mma Makutsi nodded. 'Yes, Mma, I see, I see.'

Mma Phiri continued, 'It was very clear to me, from where I was sitting . . . '

'On your bench . . . '

'On *the* bench, yes, that this was one of those situations where a strong woman has a weak man under her control. She was using him, Mma. You see that sort of thing from time to time: the man is a nothing at all, a useless, and the woman is everything.'

Mma Makutsi noted the term 'a useless'. That was a wonderful description, and she would use it herself, she thought. Every so often one came across 'a useless', and sometimes it was difficult to find just the right words to describe such a person. Now she had them: two short and pithy words – one very short and very pithy: 'a useless'.

She thanked Mma Phiri. 'You have told me everything I need to know, Mma. I shall go back to Mma Ramotswe and tell her what you have said.'

Mma Phiri saw Mma Makutsi out to her car. 'You must pass on a message to your husband,' she said, as fond farewells were exchanged. 'You must tell him that I sit on that sofa every day. I sit there and think how comfortable it is.'

'More comfortable than that bench of yours,' said Mma Makutsi.

The joke was well received. 'Very much so,' said Mma Phiri, laughing. 'Perhaps they should put sofas like that in the High Court for the judges there. They would be more comfortable sitting on them while they listened to the arguments of the lawyers.' She paused. 'Mind you, Mma, the risk is that they would go to sleep.'

'That would not do,' said Mma Makutsi.

'Definitely not.'

As she drove back to the main road, Mma Makutsi reflected with some satisfaction on the afternoon's events. She had met two good women: one with a baby, and a difficult life, and one in much more comfortable circumstances and with a life of achievement behind her. She had found out what she needed to find out. She had enlarged her vocabulary with an excellent term to use, sparingly, when other terms seemed inadequate. And now, after calling in briefly at the office, she was going to go home to a loving husband, a house with a cool veranda, and a young child who meant more to her than anything else in the world. There was a saying that expressed how she felt, but she could not quite remember what it was. It was something to do with cups running over. Cups of tea? Was it about tea? 'My cup has too much tea in it'? No, that was not right, but perhaps it expressed, accurately enough, how she felt.

Chapter Twelve

She's a Useless

Everything had been arranged with Mma Potokwani.

'We shall arrive at about half-past eight,' Mr J. L. B. Matekoni told her on the telephone. 'It will just be me, Charlie and Fanwell.'

'And an elephant,' added Mma Potokwani.

'Yes, and an elephant – but not a very big one, as you know.'

Mr J. L. B. Matekoni asked whether the stockade was ready, and he was assured that it was. 'One of the older boys is a very good little carpenter,' Mma Potokwani said. 'He has built a new gate, and he is fitting that right now. By tonight, everything will be ready.'

They spent some time discussing the baby elephant's requirements. Charlie had been feeding it on infant formula, as recommended by his friend, and a large box of this had been obtained from the supermarket. 'You must have a very large baby, Rra,' said the woman at the checkout when Fanwell had made the purchase. 'Looking at you, I wouldn't have thought . . . '

He had said nothing, tempting though it was to reply. The problem was that he had not been able to think of a suitable riposte.

'That woman is very rude,' said Mma Makutsi, when Fanwell told her what had been said. 'She criticises people's choice of food all the time. She sits there scanning the items and muttering "Unhealthy", or "Junk food", or "Very bad for you". I asked her once not to do this, and she said, "Don't blame me if you die from all this stuff you're eating." Can you imagine that? Those were her very words.

'She's a useless,' Mma Makutsi went on. 'Next time she says anything like that to me, I shall tell her to her face. I shall say, "You're a useless." That will show her.'

Fanwell looked puzzled. 'A useless what?'

'Just a useless,' answered Mma Makutsi. 'Useless in general, you see. There are some people who are like that. You look at them and you know, more or less straight away, that they're a useless.'

Mr J. L. B. Matekoni had offered his truck for the purpose, but Mma Ramotswe had demurred. 'You need that for work,' she said. 'You cannot have clients saying that your work truck smells of elephants.'

'She's right, boss,' said Fanwell. 'Mma Ramotswe's van is different. It's very old and decrepit. Your truck is very smart.'

Mr J. L. B. Matekoni pointed out that he had offered to buy Mma Ramotswe a new van on more than one occasion. 'I have tried to replace that van,' he said, 'but I am always thwarted.'

'There is nothing wrong with it,' said Mma Ramotswe.

'Other than being very old,' said Charlie. 'And having dents in the tailgate. And smelling of elephants. And having great difficulty in getting up hills if they're at all steep. Apart from that, Mma Ramotswe's van is fine.'

Mma Ramotswe chided Charlie, but in a friendly tone. 'It's all very well for you, Charlie. You're young and have no dents ... yet. But you'll learn to appreciate old things when you get a bit older yourself. You'll begin to understand that old is not the same word as bad.'

Charlie laughed. 'I'm going to be a really cool older person,' he said. 'When the time comes – many years from now – then I am going to be a seriously cool older person. They'll say, "Look at him, you'd never know he was forty-two!"'

Fanwell was embarrassed by Charlie's tactlessness. 'There's nothing wrong with being forty-two,' he said, glancing at Mma Ramotswe and then at Mma Makutsi.

'I'm not forty-two,' muttered Mma Makutsi, looking sideways at Mma Ramotswe, and adjusting her glasses as she did so.

Charlie was now staring at Mma Makutsi. 'Where did you get those retro specs from, Mma?'

Mma Makutsi began to answer. 'I sent for them. They came all the way from Cape Town. I had seen ...' She stopped, and in a steely voice said, 'They are *not* retro, Charlie. They are the latest thing. Not retro.'

Charlie disagreed. 'They *are* retro, Mma. Those are exactly the glasses that retro people wore fifty years ago. There are many glasses like that in the museum.' An idea came to him. 'Perhaps it was the Cape Town Museum that sent them up to you.'

Fanwell laughed, but was silenced by a look from Mma Makutsi. 'I'm not going to argue with you, Charlie,' she said. 'These are not retro glasses. They are the latest thing, and I feel sorry for anybody who can't recognise the latest thing when they see it.'

Mma Ramotswe sighed. 'I think we should not be arguing about glasses and such things,' she said. 'Charlie, Mma Makutsi's glasses are very fashionable, and anyway it is very rude to call another person's glasses retro. That is not what we do in this country.'

Fanwell turned to Charlie. 'Say sorry, Charlie. Just say sorry to Mma Makutsi. If she wants to wear old-fashioned glasses, then that is her business.'

Mma Makutsi pursed her lips. 'They are *not* old-fashioned.'

Mma Ramotswe rose to her feet. 'I think we should go and pick some leaves and grass to put in the van for the elephant. We want it to be comfortable while we are taking it to Mma Potokwani's place.'

They went outside. Mma Makutsi had to get home to see Itumelang before he was put to bed, and so she left the rest of them there. 'Be careful,' she called out as she drove away.

Mma Ramotswe waved, and stood for a moment, enjoying the gentle warmth of the evening sun. Soon it would fall below the horizon, a glowing red ball, sinking over the great Kalahari. It was a time of day that never failed to enchant her. In an hour or so, the African night would be upon them, immeasurable, velvet. On such a night might her husband and the two young men drive quietly down a bumpy dirt road, carrying a small elephant, a scrap of elephant-kind, to a secret destination under the starlit sky. She shivered.

Mr J. L. B. Matekoni drove Mma Ramotswe home in his truck before returning to the garage. During his brief absence, Charlie and Fanwell had scoured the neighbouring tract of scrub bush for vegetation with which to line the van. They had managed to find several branches of young acacia plants, twisted off the trunk and lying on the ground; these they purloined for their purposes, and then uprooted tufts of grass to lay beside them. After Mr J. L. B. Matekoni returned, they waited until it was dark before setting off for Charlie's uncle's place, where Charlie's young cousin had been instructed to make sure that all was ready for the next stage of the journey. The baby elephant had been moved, and was now tethered by a foreleg to an iron ring that for some reason was set into a wall of the house. Nobody had ever worked out its purpose, but now, at long last, it was proving its usefulness.

Charlie's uncle was relieved to see that the elephant was being taken away. He had expressed his concerns about its being on his property, pointing out that there were bound to be municipal regulations – somewhere or other – forbidding the keeping of elephants on urban land. 'They're bound to have passed some law on this,' he said. 'Otherwise everybody would be keeping elephants. There must be a law – and I don't want to find myself suddenly put in jail for breaking it.'

Planks had been loaded into the van and these were now taken out to provide a ramp for the elephant to be led up inside. They were stout – the strongest planks that Mr J. L. B. Matekoni could lay his hands on – but even so they sagged under the weight of the little creature. And there was an anxious moment, too, when the baby elephant took his first step onto the van's tailgate; but it bore the burden and was soon fastened in position, with Charlie and the elephant safely ensconced inside.

'We're ready, boss,' Charlie shouted from the back, and Mr J. L. B. Matekoni, with Fanwell beside him in the cab, started the engine. Soon they were out on the road, heading back towards the Tlokweng Road.

'Would we be arrested if the police stopped us?' asked Fanwell nervously.

Mr J. L. B. Matekoni was unsure. 'I suspect we're breaking some law or other,' he said. 'But what else can we do?'

'Nothing,' said Fanwell. 'And it's not against the law, surely, to do something when there ...' He paused to order his thoughts. 'When there's nothing else you can do.'

'I've never broken the law,' Mr J. L. B. Matekoni mused. 'Not once – as far as I'm aware.'

Fanwell whistled. 'I thought everybody had, boss – at some time or another. Not major things, of course, but little offences. Speeding, for instance.'

'Oh, I wasn't counting that sort of thing,' said Mr J. L. B. Matekoni. 'Sometimes you can't help going too fast. You're driving along and suddenly they spring a speed limit on you. And before you know it, the police step out in front of you and say—'

Suddenly Fanwell gripped his forearm. Mr J. L. B. Matekoni remonstrated with him. 'Fanwell, I'm driving. Don't grab my arm—' He broke off, seeing the police car up ahead and the two officers signalling for him to draw in to the side of the road.

'We're finished, boss,' muttered Fanwell. 'Somebody must have warned them to expect us.'

Mr J. L. B. Matekoni brought the van to a halt immediately before the policemen. One shone a light through the windscreen, playing the beam across their faces. Mr J. L. B. Matekoni wound down the driver's window. As one of the policemen approached him, he greeted him politely. The policeman mumbled a response – not discourteously, but almost – and then held out a hand. 'Your driving licence, Rra.'

Mr J. L. B. Matekoni extracted the licence from his wallet, and passed it to the officer.

The policeman examined the licence and then looked at Mr J. L. B. Matekoni. A slight smile played about his lips. 'You're the man from Tlokweng Road Speedy Motors?' he asked.

Mr J. L. B. Matekoni nodded. 'I am that man, Rra.'

The policeman made a signal to his colleague, who had been

shining the beam of his flashlight on the van's registration plate. It was a sign that said 'Don't bother'.

'You have a sister up in Francistown?'

Mr J. L. B. Matekoni hesitated. 'She is a half-sister. Sister by a different father.'

The policeman nodded. 'Yes. She is married to the son of my uncle, who is married to my aunt.'

Fanwell frowned in an effort to work this out, but Mr J. L. B. Matekoni simply said, 'Ah, I see.'

'I have seen her up there, Rra,' the policeman continued. 'When I was last there. She told me about your garage. She said that if I ever needed a car fixed you were the man to do it.'

'That was very kind of her, Rra. We do our best for the cars that people bring us.'

'My aunt will be very pleased to hear that I have met you,' said the policeman. 'Not much happens up there and she is very interested in what is happening elsewhere.'

'That is very good,' said Mr J. L. B. Matekoni. He was being polite, but he was keen to be on his way. It seemed obvious now that this was a random check, and that the policeman was nothing but friendly. 'You must tell her that I was asking after her.'

The policeman smiled. 'You don't think you could step out and we could have a photo together. I could send it up to her through my phone so that she will know that we've met. She'll like that.'

Mr J. L. B. Matekoni opened his door and got out of the van. The policeman handed his phone to his colleague, who then took a photograph of the two of them standing side by side. The policeman had draped an arm around Mr J. L. B. Matekoni's shoulder in a gesture that Mr J. L. B. Matekoni thought perhaps a bit too friendly for so brief an acquaintanceship, but he did not object.

And it was at this point, just after the photograph had been taken, examined, and approved of, that the baby elephant in the back of the van chose to issue a plaintive call. It was a strange sound – an incipient version of the trumpet of a fully grown elephant – and it was not one that could be easily identified.

The policeman raised his head sharply. 'What was that, Rra?' he asked.

Mr J. L. B. Matekoni looked around him. 'What was what, Rra?'

'That sound. There was a sound. It came from your van.'

Mr J. L. B. Matekoni was struggling, but after a moment or two he said, 'Ah yes, that sound.'

The policeman waited. 'Well, Rra: what was it?'

'That was . . . that was a . . . ' He knew he was floundering, and this knowledge made things no easier.

Fanwell now called out from the passenger seat. 'We must hurry, boss. He is feeling worse.'

The policeman peered into the cab. 'Who's feeling worse?'

Fanwell gave a toss of the head in the direction of the closed back of the van. 'In there. Our poor friend with his infectious disease. We're taking him to hospital, but we should hurry. It's infectious vomiting, Rra.'

The policeman drew back sharply. 'Why are you not using an ambulance?' His tone, so friendly before, was now accusing.

'It is too infectious,' shouted Fanwell. 'They do not want the ambulance people to get it too.'

The policeman took a further step back. He hesitated for a moment, evidently torn between duty to investigate and self-protection. Self-protection won. 'You should go,' he said gruffly, and signalled to his colleague to allow the van to pass.

'It was very good to meet you, Rra,' said Mr J. L. B. Matekoni. 'And don't worry. You have not been near him. You will be fine.'

They set off again. As they drew away, Fanwell burst out

laughing, as did Charlie from the back of the van. He had listened to the exchange while struggling to keep the baby elephant from uttering further trumpet calls. This he had achieved by feeding it with its formula from a large bottle and teat.

'That was very funny, Rra,' said Fanwell. 'Did you see his face? When I mentioned infectious vomiting, he looked as if he'd been pricked with a large pin.'

Mr J. L. B. Matekoni looked severe. 'It is not a good thing to lie, Fanwell – especially to the police.' But then the serious look on his face slowly slipped, and he, too, laughed. And they were laughing again, although over something else altogether, when, only a mile or so from the Orphan Farm, the baby elephant decided to shift its weight from one side of the van to the other. It did this so quickly that the van, not known for its robust suspension, swerved sharply to the left. Mr J. L. B. Matekoni struggled to steer it back on course, but the front wheels were now in loose gravel and slid sideways into a wide drainage ditch at the side of the road. Brakes were applied, but the vehicle's momentum was such that it tipped over and travelled the last few yards into the ditch on its side.

It all happened very quickly. Fanwell shouted out, and there was a cry from the back as Charlie, too, yelled out something. Then there was a trumpeting sound and a series of thuds, followed by another shout from Charlie.

Mr J. L. B. Matekoni had toppled over sideways, and found himself lying on top of Fanwell.

'You're squashing me, boss,' muttered Fanwell.

Mr J. L. B. Matekoni struggled to extricate himself. 'Are you all right?' he asked.

Fanwell's response was muffled. 'I'm not hurt. But what about Charlie, boss? What if the elephant has landed on top of him?'

From the back of the van there came a shout. 'I'm all right, boss, but the elephant has gone. Run away, boss. Gone.'

The ditch into which Mma Ramotswe's van had toppled ran alongside a desolate stretch of road. On either side of this road was a broad stretch of scrub bush, heavily wooded with acacia trees. This was criss-crossed with cattle tracks and dotted, here and there, with anthills. It was buffer land between the populated, semi-rural fringes of Tlokweng, and the true bushland beyond. There were some miles of that before the border fence that marked the boundary, the edge of Botswana and the beginning of the country's sprawling neighbour, South Africa. It was a landscape of thorn trees and nondescript shrubs, with grass and rocks and places for snakes to hide, and for birds of prey to circle over. In the dark, it was full of shadows, and shapes for the imagination to worry about.

Once Mr J. L. B. Matekoni and Fanwell had extricated themselves from the front of the van, they immediately went round to the back to join Charlie, who was clambering out over the now more-damaged tailgate.

'What happened?' asked Fanwell.

Charlie dusted himself down. 'He suddenly shifted his weight,' he replied. 'He went over to that side and that did it. Bang. The boss ...' He looked apologetic. 'I'm not blaming you, boss – it must have been hard with this useless old steering ...'

Mr J. L. B. Matekoni brushed this aside. 'But the elephant, Charlie? Where did it go?'

Charlie pointed vaguely into the surrounding darkness. 'Over there, Rra. Or, maybe ...' He pointed in another direction. 'Or maybe over there. It was off like a shot. Bam! Gone, boss.'

Mr J. L. B. Matekoni sighed. 'We're not going to find him in this darkness.'

'No,' said Fanwell. 'And what about us, boss? Are we going to walk now?'

Mr J. L. B. Matekoni looked around him. In the distance, a mile or two away, he could see the lights of the Orphan Farm through the trees. 'It's not too far,' he said. 'But I think we might be able to get the van back on the road. If two of us push on that side, and one pulls, we can get it back the right way. Then we can drive.'

Charlie laughed. 'It's good that I'm so strong, boss.'

'We'll see,' said Mr J. L. B. Matekoni.

'Fanwell's not so strong,' said Charlie.

'I have more brains than you, Charlie,' retorted Fanwell. 'Look at my head, then look at yours. See how small yours is.'

It was good-natured badinage, of the sort that those who have had a shock might resort to for the release of feelings, but Mr J. L. B. Matekoni put an end to it. He took Charlie with him to the side of the van and showed him where to push; Fanwell, on the opposite side, was to try to use his weight to pull the side of the van down. There was a certain amount of grunting and it seemed at first that the van's centre of gravity had shifted in such a way that movement would be impossible.

'You'll have to get your tow truck, boss,' said Charlie, as he pushed unsuccessfully.

'Maybe,' said Mr J. L. B. Matekoni, between exertions. 'Maybe not. You must not be a defeatist, Charlie.'

Charlie was silent for a moment as he shoved at the reluctant van. Then he said, 'This is a big mess, boss. That elephant has gone. We'll never find him in the bush.'

'We can look tomorrow, Charlie. Just push. Ready? One, two, three!'

More effort was expended. The van was not a heavy vehicle – it was, in fact, tiny by the standards of vans, and for a moment or two it teetered on its side, before rocking back into its sideways-on position.

'What if it falls on Fanwell?' asked Charlie, wiping his brow. 'Then we'll have lost an elephant *and* a mechanic.'

'Don't talk like that, Charlie,' Mr J. L. B. Matekoni scolded. 'Fanwell will not let that happen.'

'I won't,' shouted Fanwell, from the other side. 'But I'm going to come round to your side. I'll help you push.'

Fanwell joined them, and it was just the shift in forces that was required. After a further call of 'Heave!' from Mr J. L. B. Matekoni, and a gradually increasing rocking of the van, they reached their objective. With a noise that was rather like a sigh, followed by a convincing crashing sound, the van was righted and was back on all four wheels.

'That will be the end of its suspension,' said Charlie. 'It was always bad, that suspension, with Mma Ramotswe sitting in the van all the time ...'

A stern glance from Mr J. L. B. Matekoni silenced Charlie.

'Now we can get back in and go up to Mma Potokwani's,' said Mr J. L. B. Matekoni. 'She is expecting us.'

'And tell her what, Rra?' asked Charlie. 'That we have no elephant after all?'

'She may have some ideas, Charlie. You never know.'

Fanwell looked miserable. 'This has been a big disaster,' he said. 'When people hear about this, they will laugh. They'll laugh and laugh, boss. They'll say, "So you couldn't take a tiny elephant – not much bigger than a new-born calf – you couldn't take a little creature like that and get it from one place to another. Three of you ... Three! And you end up in a ditch and the elephant runs away ..." Oh, this is a big disaster, boss. Big-time.' He paused; a further unfortunate dimension had arisen. 'And what is Mma

Makutsi going to say, Rra? What will she say? You know how she is. Even if she doesn't say anything, she'll look at us. She'll just look, and we'll feel *that* small.' He indicated with his forefinger their diminished size.

'I don't care what Mma Makutsi thinks,' Charlie snorted. 'She is always thinking. I don't care.'

'We must not worry about things that haven't happened yet,' said Mr J. L. B. Matekoni, climbing into the driver's seat. 'First things first. We'll go and speak to Mma Potokwani and see what she says.'

'What if she laughs?' said Charlie, morosely. 'And there's my friend, too. The elephant is his property, boss, and we've lost it. Imagine what he'll say.'

'He had no business landing you with an elephant,' Mr J. L. B. Matekoni retorted. 'You can't go round giving people elephants and then complaining if something happens.'

'That's right,' agreed Fanwell. 'He had no business doing that.'

Charlie did not respond directly, but still muttering, 'Big mess,' he took his place in the cab and they set off. Ahead of them, through the leaves of the acacia trees, the lights of the Orphan Farm beckoned. Above them, the night sky of Botswana, with its white fields of stars, was impassive. The tiny drama was the least of what it witnessed; far greater things went wrong everywhere, all the time; but this, as each of them knew, was not a good thing to have happened. Without its regular bottles of formula, the elephant would not survive long in the bush, but would dehydrate and die. Charlie knew that, just as did Fanwell and Mr J. L. B. Matekoni. Nobody said anything about it, but they knew it.

'Mma Potokwani will think of something,' said Mr J. L. B. Matekoni as they neared the entrance to the Orphan Farm. 'She always does.' He thought about it further. No, he was right. He had known Mma Potokwani for many years and never – not on one single occasion – had she been at a loss for a suggestion or, even more importantly, a decision. A crisis, to her, was a challenge to be tackled with an assessment; a sigh, perhaps, if it was serious enough, and then a firm command. It always worked. Every single time he had seen her faced with a problem, he had seen it work.

She made them tea, and listened as Charlie spilled out the story of the accident and the elephant's escape. As he spoke, a smile played about her lips, and this, after a while, became a broad grin.

'The important thing,' she said when Charlie reached the end of his account, 'is that nobody was hurt. No bruises, no broken bones – nothing. That is what I call a good accident.'

Fanwell looked surprised. 'But the van was over on its side, Mma. Like this ...' He indicated with his hands the drunken angle at which the van had ended up.

'But you sorted that out,' said Mma Potokwani cheerfully. 'And Mma Ramotswe's van has probably seen worse. It has all those scratches and dents on it. All over the place.' She gave Mr J. L. B. Matekoni a reproachful glance, as if to suggest that he might be ashamed at the fact that his wife was driving round in such a shabby vehicle.

He was sensitive to that. 'That is another problem, Mma Potokwani. I have always tried to get her to use another van – a newer one. There are many good vans that are looking for a home, but she says ...'

He did not finish. 'I know, I know,' Mma Potokwani said. 'Mma Ramotswe is a loyal woman, Rra. She is loyal to her old van – and I am happy that she is, because that means she is loyal to her old friends like me. I have many dents and scratches too.'

Charlie pointed into the darkness. He looked agitated. 'There's a little elephant out there,' he said. 'What are we going to do?'

Mma Potokwani remained calm. 'Have you been the one feeding that elephant, Charlie?' she asked.

Charlie did not see the point of the question. 'We shouldn't waste time talking about all that, Mma. We have to do something.'

'Then answer my question, Charlie.'

He sighed. 'Yes, I've been feeding him.'

Mma Potokwani nodded. 'In that case, I'm sure we shall be able to find him.'

Charlie pointed at the darkness again. 'Out there, Mma? Look at it. That bush is quite thick. He could be anywhere by now – maybe even halfway up to Maun.'

'Oh, don't talk nonsense, Charlie,' said Mma Potokwani. 'He'll be somewhere close by – you mark my words.' She paused. 'And he'll come back to you, I think.'

Fanwell expressed surprise at this. 'Why, Mma? Why will he come back to Charlie?'

Mma Potokwani smiled with the air of one who knew something nobody else knew. 'There is an elephant lady I know,' she said. 'She visited me here last year.'

They waited.

Eventually Fanwell broke the silence. 'Who is this elephant lady, Mma?'

'She is called Mma Stevens,' said Mma Potokwani. 'She does the same job as I do.'

Mr J. L. B. Matekoni looked puzzled. 'At one of the other orphanages?' he asked. 'The one up at Francistown?'

Mma Potokwani laughed. 'Her orphans are different.'

They were not sure what to make of that.

'And this lady,' Mma Potokwani continued, 'told me that when you feed one of these little elephants, it thinks you are its mother.'

'The elephant thinks that?' asked Fanwell. He turned to point at Charlie. 'He thinks you're his mother. You said that before. Remember?'

Charlie grinned. 'Yes. You see? I told you that, didn't I? When you came round to my uncle's place. I told you that the elephant thinks that.'

'So,' said Mma Potokwani. 'I think he'll come to you, Charlie. If you go out there.'

Charlie frowned. 'There?' he asked, pointing to the darkness that was the bush.

'You're not frightened, are you?' Mma Potokwani asked.

Charlie hesitated. 'Me? Of course not.'

Fanwell gave him a searching look. 'Are you sure, Charlie?'

'I am definitely not frightened,' said Charlie.

'What about snakes?' asked Fanwell. 'That is a good place for cobras out there. They like to walk about at night.'

'They do not walk,' snapped Charlie.

'No, they do not walk,' Fanwell retorted. 'But some of them can stand up. Or the front half of them can stand up. Cobras can. And mambas, too. They go up and hiss. That is a bad sign. If a snake like that hisses at you, it is a very bad sign.'

Mma Potokwani put an end to the alarmist talk. 'Snakes keep well away from people if they can,' she said. 'Isn't that so, Mr J. L. B. Matekoni?'

Mr J. L. B. Matekoni was thinking of something else. 'I think Fanwell should go with Charlie,' he said. 'It will be better if Charlie has somebody to keep him company.'

Mma Potokwani thought this a good idea. 'Go out there,' she said. 'Go out there and wait. These elephants have a way of knowing that people are there. Mma Stevens told me about that.'

'Who is this lady?' asked Mr J. L. B. Matekoni. 'And how does she know so much about elephants?'

'She is the one who will be taking this baby elephant,' Mma Potokwani replied. 'When we get it back. She has an elephant orphanage up north. They take very small elephants whose mothers have been shot by poachers. They look after them at a place they have just outside Maun.'

'So that is where you are going to send my elephant?' asked Charlie.

'Yes,' said Mma Potokwani. 'It's all planned. They are expecting it in the next few days.'

Charlie sounded gloomy. '*If* we get it back,' he said, his voice heavy with doubt.

'We will,' said Mma Potokwani. 'I am confident we will.'

Charlie and Fanwell were dispatched into the darkness. 'I am not sure about this,' muttered Charlie.

'I am,' said Mma Potokwani.

Chapter Thirteen

Nice Things About Your Skin

Mma Ramotswe was completely on her own – and it felt very strange. Mr J. L. B. Matekoni had gone off in her van with Charlie and Fanwell to deal with the baby elephant, and the children, Motholeli and Puso, were both spending the night on separate sleepovers with friends, it being a Friday evening, with no school the following morning. She had agreed to their request, although she knew that sleepovers would mean a late night for both of them – in Motholeli's case because of the teenage conversation that would go on past midnight; in Puso's case the friend who had invited him was proposing to make a fire and they would be cooking sausages in the open until well past Puso's normal bedtime. But it did not matter if Saturday was a write-off; the children often did nothing in particular on a Saturday morning and a long lie-in would probably suit everybody.

Mr J. L. B. Matekoni had told her that he might not be back until nine, or even later, and that she should have her dinner rather than wait for him: he would be happy enough with a bowl of soup or a sandwich when he eventually returned. She already had soup in a pot in the fridge and she would leave that on the stove for him, she decided, along with two thick-cut slices of bread between which she would place a thick slice of roast Botswana beef. That was exactly the sort of sandwich that Mr J. L. B. Matekoni – or indeed any man – liked. In Mma Ramotswe's experience, men did not like thin sandwiches, and they certainly did not like sandwiches that had vegetables in them. Lettuce or cucumber, or any other greens for that matter, were all very well, but most men did not like to discover these things in their sandwiches. Meat was what men liked in sandwiches – and if the man was sophisticated, then he might like a bit of mustard as well.

It was a strange feeling being dropped off at the house by Mma Makutsi, who asked her, as she stepped out of the car, 'What are you going to do, Mma?'

'Now, Mma?'

'Yes. You said that the children were off with friends. And with no husband until later tonight – you are a free lady, Mma!'

Mma Ramotswe laughed. 'That is what it's like for us women, Mma. There is always somebody else to worry about, and then suddenly there is nobody and we think ... '

Mma Makutsi took over. 'We think: what are we going to do with our time?'

'Exactly.'

'You could put your feet up,' suggested Mma Makutsi. 'You could treat yourself to a very long bath, with bath salts, Mma. You could close your eyes and imagine what it must be like to be able to do that every day – just lie in the bath with bath salts.'

Mma Ramotswe laughed. 'I don't have any bath salts, Mma.' An idea came to her. 'Would redbush tea do, Mma? I have read that it is very good for the skin. It soothes outside, as well as inside.'

Mma Makutsi had heard that too, but she had not been convinced. People said all sorts of things were good for this, that and the next thing, but she was sceptical – just as she would imagine Clovis Andersen would be about many of these claims. One of the cardinal principles of private detection, he reminded his readers, was the importance of evidence. *Don't believe something because you want it to be true,* he wrote. *Nor should you believe everything you read or are told by other people. Ask them for the evidence, and if they cannot produce it, then politely say 'I am unconvinced' and leave it at that.*

So now she said to Mma Ramotswe, 'I am unconvinced, Mma.' And then she added, for good measure, 'Where is the evidence, Mma? That is what I would like to know: where is the evidence?'

Mma Ramotswe met Mma Makutsi's unbelieving gaze. Her eyes drifted to a patch of slightly angry skin below her colleague's chin. Mma Makutsi had always had skin trouble – nothing too serious, of course, but it would be wrong to describe her complexion as completely untroubled. She used some sort of cream that was meant to keep irritation under control, but Mma Ramotswe was suspicious of creams and emollients. They might be active in the way their makers claimed, but there could be no doubt but that they clogged the pores, and that, as everybody surely knew, was bad for your skin. Skin needed to breathe, and if there was a layer of oily cream preventing it from doing that, then it was no wonder that it flared up.

Bathing the skin in redbush tea cleansed it and opened the pores, and if only Mma Makutsi were to try it, she might find it would help. And now, faced with this hard-nosed scepticism, she felt tempted to point out that she, Mma Ramotswe, who used a lot of redbush tea – principally internally – had very clear skin, when compared with Mma Makutsi's. But that, she realised, would be unkind, and unkindness was never the way to convert others to a truth of any sort. You did not change anybody, she had always believed, by shouting at them or by making them feel bad about themselves. On the contrary, it was kindness and concern that changed people within, that could soften the hardest of hearts, that could turn harsh words into words of love. That had been proved time and time again, and she had seen it herself; she had seen the power of a kind word to change a scowling or suspicious countenance.

So now she said to Mma Makutsi, 'Well, Mma, you're right – as you usually are.' Was that going too far, she wondered. Perhaps not, because Mma Makutsi smiled in response and inclined her head slightly, as if to express agreement. 'Yes, you're right, Mma. It's important to have evidence for anything. But, even so, I was thinking that your complexion is really very nice, Mma – you have beautiful skin. I have heard many people say that.'

Mma Makutsi's eyes widened. 'You've heard people say that, Mma?'

Mma Ramotswe swallowed. She always told the truth – if at all possible – but now here she was being drawn into a lie. So she retrieved the situation by saying, 'I have not exactly heard them, Mma, but I can well believe that is what they are saying.' She paused, noting the fall in Mma Makutsi's face. 'Mind you, Mma, I have heard people talk about how fashionable you are. I have heard people say that they like your clothes and your shoes. They certainly say that.'

She did not say who it was who had said that. It was Charlie, in fact, who had been talking to Fanwell and who had been overheard by Mma Ramotswe. He had said, 'That Mma Makutsi, Fanwell, I'd rate her for her clothes, you know. She has expensive gear, ever since she married that Phuti Radiphuti. That furniture store of his ... I think at her wedding she was standing there, and on her right was the furniture store. And the minister said to her, "Do you take this furniture store?" And she said, "Yes, definitely. The whole lot please." Charlie laughed. 'That's what marriage is, Fanwell. Cattle and furniture stores. Don't tell yourself it's about anything else.'

Mma Makutsi was interested. 'Who was it?' she asked.

'Oh, just somebody,' said Mma Ramotswe. 'They said very nice things.'

'I'm pleased,' said Mma Makutsi. 'I do my best in that department, you know.'

And that provided Mma Ramotswe with her opportunity. 'You do, Mma – you certainly do. That is very well known. But even your very nice skin might be made even nicer if you tried a bit of redbush tea. No harm in trying, Mma. They say that you pour the redbush tea onto a cloth so that it's soaked through. Then you put the cloth on the skin and let it lie there for a few minutes. They say that this makes good skin even better.'

She decided that was enough. The seed had been planted, and any further mention of it might be counterproductive. So she looked at her watch and said to Mma Makutsi through the open window of her car, 'No, I think I shall just cook myself a tasty meal and then sit on the veranda until it's time to go to bed.'

Mma Makutsi had driven off and Mma Ramotswe had lingered at her gate, watching her friend's car disappear. There was almost an hour of light left before night fell, and she would use that time, she thought, to do a bit of work in her garden. She had put a lot of effort into her bed of beans, and the plants were doing well. Then there were her tomatoes, too, they were a new venture, and a melon patch that could probably do with a bit of weeding. If she made herself a large mug of redbush tea she could take that with her and drink it as she attended to these gardening tasks. And then, when dusk came, she could go inside, have a bath – even without bath salts – and then cook the chicken that she had bought the day before and placed in the fridge. That, served with pumpkin, would be her dinner – and she need not show too much restraint in tackling it by herself. She could have both drumsticks if she wanted them, and all the skin, which she particularly prized. Crisp chicken skin, dusted with salt – oh, that would be a very fine dish for one unworried by too much guilt over what she ate. There might come a time when she would eat less chicken skin, but that time was not yet. For the time being she was Mma Ramotswe, a lady of trad-itional build, who needed the occasional evening of comfort food when nobody else was watching. And after the chicken, she might have a fat cake, dusted with sugar, to round off the meal. There was one in the fridge and it would be a terrible waste if it were to be allowed to go stale.

The house seemed so quiet. Children were like traffic noise: they made a constant background hum. It was something you got used to, as people who live near airports get used to the sound of jets landing and taking off. There was a difference, of course, between the background noise made by boys and that made by girls. Girls made a more peaceful noise, rather like running water, in a way, while their brothers made a sort of low-level clattering noise – the sound of things being shoved about and occasionally broken. Husbands, too, made a noise, now that she came to think about it. Their noise was a sort of shuffling noise, interrupted by the occasional cough or clearing of the throat and ... and here she smiled at the thought ... and the sound a beer bottle makes when its cap is taken off with a bottle-opener. Yes, that was a sound that accompanied many husbands when they came home from work. And why not? They had to have something in their lives, and the occasional bottle of cold beer was a reward that many men could justifiably claim as deserved. Poor men: they spent so much of their time working and often got little thanks for it. Yet all that many men wanted was to be loved, which was what everybody wanted, really, at the end of the day. And love did not cost anything; it could be given freely and the wells from which it was drawn could be easily filled again. There was no shortage of love in the world; it was as plentiful as oxygen – and as necessary.

She thought all this on the threshold of the kitchen, while looking at the sink and the fridge and the chopping board. You could think these big things, she told herself, while looking at very small things.

She turned on the radio, partly to break the unnerving silence, partly to hear the news broadcast that went out at that time of day. Nothing special seemed to have happened, and even the newsreader herself sounded bored with what she had to report. The Minister of Water Affairs had visited a dam and made a speech about the government's plans to improve the water supply in certain remote villages. 'If there is more rain,' the minister was quoted as saying, 'then we will have more water.' This had brought applause, the newsreader said.

Mma Ramotswe smiled. She was glad she did not have to make speeches about nothing and be reduced to saying that more rain meant more water. Really! But then she checked herself; the minister was doing his best. It could not be an easy job to be Minister of Water Affairs in a dry country like Botswana. Governments could do many things, but the one thing they could not do was to bring rain in a parched time. Perhaps people needed reminding of this, and needed to be told where water came from. It did not come from the government . . .

She opened the fridge and took out the chicken. It was wrapped in butcher's brown paper, and tied about with string. The butcher at the supermarket meat counter was an old admirer of Mma Ramotswe's, and always took particular care with any meat she ordered, sometimes securing her parcels with coloured ribbon that no other customer seemed to merit. She was vaguely embarrassed by this – there had never been anything between them, although she had always been aware of his appreciative glances before she and Mr J. L. B. Matekoni had married. Thereafter, the butcher had behaved with utter probity, and had sent no glances her way, even if he did use special ribbon for her orders and insisted on serving her himself, elbowing his assistants out of the way when she appeared at the counter.

This chicken, retrieved from a special shelf in the cold room, had come with a particular recommendation from him. 'This is no ordinary chicken, Mma Ramotswe,' he said. 'Most of those chickens over there . . . ' And here he gestured towards the poultry section. 'Most of them come from those big chicken farms. You know the ones. They have thousands and thousands of chickens all crowded together. And then they bring the chickens up from over the border in those big refrigerated trucks. No wonder those chickens taste of nothing, Mma.'

She had thanked him. 'I'm looking forward to cooking this one, Rra.'

'It will be very tasty,' he said. 'That is one of our free-range chickens. We do not have many. They are just for special customers.'

'You're very kind, Rra.'

'That chicken will have eaten a lot of different things, you see, Mma. They wander around and peck at grubs. They are always pecking.'

'That's good, Rra.'

'And they get a bit of exercise that way. That makes a difference.'

And now she took the chicken from its plate and put it on the chopping board to be jointed. She would boil the chicken, as her father's cousin had taught her to do in Mochudi all those years ago. Had her mother lived, then it would have been she who would have taught Mma Ramotswe the right way to cook chicken in Botswana, but the cousin had done that instead, and she had been a good teacher.

She put the pieces of chicken into a pot, saving the carcass for the making of stock. She added carrots and onions and, as a special treat, since she alone would be eating this, a generous pinch of peri-peri chili, to give the whole thing a kick. Then, with the pot heating up on the stove, she prepared the pumpkin, cutting the thick yellow flesh into generously sized squares before immersing them in salted water for boiling. That was all that you had to do to a pumpkin, other than to put butter on it when it was soft enough. And salt and pepper, of course, just before you ate it.

Her feast could now be left to itself for an hour and a half before it could be enjoyed. That gave her time to change out of her office clothes, prepare a mug of tea, and then go out into her garden to tackle the tasks she had planned. She turned off the radio; the newsreader was cut off mid-sentence and silence returned to the house. She went through to their bedroom, where the silence seemed even greater, almost tangible, like something hanging in the air. The evening sun, streaming through the bedroom window, made a square of butter yellow on the polished cement floor. She stood in the doorway for a few moments, taking in the familiar objects of her bedroom: the dresser with its bits and pieces – the half-empty bottle of scent that Motholeli had given her for her last birthday; the pile of three men's handkerchiefs that she had ironed for Mr J. L. B. Matekoni and that he had forgotten to take to work with him; the picture of her father, the late Obed Ramotswe, in its frame of black Bakelite; her bedroom radio, inherited from an aunt, an old Supersonic that still worked in spite of the world's having changed completely since its manufacture at the factory up in Bulawayo, sixty years previously. It was a miracle that the radio still received broadcasts with complete clarity – a miracle, indeed; and she thought for a moment that if there were any saints around these days – and nobody seemed to suggest there were – then they might perform modern miracles to impress the sceptical. So, a modern saint might make a radio that was dumb speak once again; or work a miracle at the supermarket fish counter . . . She stopped herself. It was wrong to think such thoughts, she told herself. The things that people believed were important to them, and it was wrong to make fun of them. And she believed, too. She believed in God, because she wanted to believe in him and because a world without God would simply be too painful for us to bear. Without God the wicked could do what they wanted to, and none of us would be able to do anything about it. At least if there were a God, then she and others could point to him and face up to the wicked and the selfish and warn them that they would not get away with it. She was not sure where or who God was, but she was sure that he was probably not far from Botswana. Beyond some cloud, perhaps, that kept us from seeing him; some place where there was no weeping and no separation from those we loved; where there would be none without a friend to hold their hand, or a brother or a sister; a place of sweet-smelling cattle and gentle, life-giving rain. That was her theology, and it was enough; it had sustained her this far, and it would see her out. That was all that anybody needed, surely.

She changed into her garden clothes and returned to the kitchen to make herself some redbush tea. Then, mug of tea in hand, she went out by the back door into the garden behind the house. It was just that stage of the early evening when the rays of the sun, occluded in part by the acacia trees in her neighbour's garden, no longer fell on her vegetable beds, which were now in shadow. The weeding of the melon patch would be a comfortable task, then, without the sun making one feel too warm.

She knelt down beside the ripening melons and tugged at the weeds that seemed to have run riot since her last spell in the garden. They came up easily; few plants put down deep roots in the sandy soil of this part of Botswana. Trees did, of course, but for the rest, the grip of roots was confined to the brittle surface of the land. She tugged at the weeds, some of which had that sharp smell that weeds sometimes have. They made a growing pile that she would put on her compost heap at the back of the garden.

She felt the sides of the melons, which had prospered in her garden. She thought of them as lazy plants; while other plants reached upwards towards the sky, melons did not bother, but extended themselves along the ground, finding what purchase they could in the horizontal. They did not ask for much, and could survive in just about the driest of conditions. They grew in the Kalahari, where few plants could cope with the lack of rain. And yet somehow their fruit was so moist, so full of water. Another miracle, she thought: the miracle of the melons.

She was examining the frames up which she had trained her bean plants when she became aware that somebody was watching her. It had always puzzled her that people could be aware of the fact that they were being watched before they saw the watcher. It was an odd feeling – a prickling in the back of the neck; a slight current of electricity that told you that there were eyes upon you. And as often as not, when you looked about you, you saw them and realised that those mute senses that had alerted you had not been wrong.

She had been bending down to look at the roots of one of the bean plants, and now she straightened up. It crossed her mind at first that perhaps Mr J. L. B. Matekoni had come back earlier than anticipated – that he had changed his plans and was not going out to Mma Potokwani's place after all. She looked over her shoulder, half expecting to see her van parked outside the house in its normal place, but the front gate was closed and there was no sign of either her van or his truck.

She wiped her brow, as she felt a bead of perspiration on the bridge of her nose, one of those awkward, tickly places. She looked about her.

'Well, Mma, good evening.'

The voice was disembodied. It was a woman's voice, and what it said was clear enough, but she could not see where it came from. For a few moments she remained nonplussed. What should you do if you suddenly heard somebody say 'Good evening' to you but you had no idea who it was or where they were. The voice could even come from the sky, and for a brief moment Mma Ramotswe looked up, before lowering her eyes again because it was absurd to imagine that anybody should address you from that quarter. Talk of heavenly voices was all very well, but they were usually figments of people's imagination.

But you could hardly remain silent: you had to say something. And so Mma Ramotswe, still looking about her in puzzlement, replied, as loudly as she could, 'Good evening, Mma.' And then she added, 'Wherever you are.'

For a few moments there was silence. A bird flew overhead, one of the Cape doves who had taken up residence in the tree by her gate. There was a brief flutter of beating wings, and then nothing – except the noise of the sky, of course, because there was a sound of the sky if you listened hard enough, a sound like wind in the trees, but softer.

Then there came a laugh – a chuckle, really.

'I'm sorry,' said the voice, 'you cannot see me. I am being very rude. One moment.'

On the other side of the fence that separated Mma Ramotswe's garden from the next-door yard, the foliage of a large shrub parted and a woman appeared. She was a woman of about Mma Ramotswe's age, of her general build, but perhaps not quite as traditional in her girth, and wearing gardening clothes – jeans and loose-fitting blouse – and a battered blue sun hat. It was her neighbour.

'Oh, Mma!' exclaimed Mma Ramotswe. 'I did not see you. I was looking everywhere and beginning to wonder whether I was hearing things.'

The woman laughed again. 'I was pruning that bush. I was on the other side, actually, when a pen fell out of my pocket. I had to go into the bush to find it.'

'And have you found it?' Mma Ramotswe asked. 'I am always losing pens. One a day, my husband says, but that is not true, I think.'

The woman advanced towards the fence. 'My name is Margaret,' she said. 'I am Margaret Matlapeng.'

Mma Ramotswe introduced herself. 'I am Precious Ramotswe.'

Mma Matlapeng smiled. 'Oh, I know who you are, Mma. Everybody knows who you are. You're that lady who has the detective agency. What do you call it? The Women's Detective . . .'

'The No. 1 Ladies' Detective Agency. Yes, that is me, Mma. I'm that lady.' She brushed her hands against the side of her skirt. 'It is a messy business, gardening.'

'And being a detective, too, I imagine,' said Mma Matlapeng.

Mma Ramotswe had not been prepared for the quick retort. She looked at Mma Matlapeng. She was a well-educated woman, obviously.

'Yes, you're right, Mma. Being a detective can be a bit demanding sometimes. There are times I think: is this really what I want to do?'

Mma Matlapeng nodded. 'We all think that, Mma, wouldn't you say? If you don't say that, then you must have your eyes closed – that's what I believe, anyway.'

Again, the comment was a thought-provoking one. Was this what one should expect from people who suddenly stepped out of a bush? The thought made Mma Ramotswe smile.

She said, 'I've been meaning to come over and say hello, Mma. I'm sorry. I have been very busy and I wasn't sure when you moved in. I saw your furniture arrive, of course, the other day, but I was not sure whether you were there too.' It was not strictly true; there had been those raised voices, but she did not want to mention that. By saying that she was not sure whether they had arrived, she was allowing her neighbour to believe that she had not heard the row.

Mma Matlapeng made a gesture to reassure her that there had been no breach of comity. 'No, Mma, you need not apologise. We only came a couple of days ago. And I should have come over to see you, but ... but ... ' She shrugged. 'There is so much to do when you move house. Everything is in the wrong place.'

Mma Ramotswe asked her if she had everything she needed. 'If I can help you at all, Mma, while you are settling in, just let me know.' She paused. 'And there is always tea, you know. Even at this time of day, there is always tea.'

Mma Matlapeng clapped her hands together. 'That was exactly

what I was thinking, Mma. It has been a long day and there is a lot of gardening to do, but that is no excuse for not having a cup of tea.'

'Exactly,' agreed Mma Ramotswe. 'Will you come over to my house, Mma? I have plenty of tea.'

Seated on Mma Ramotswe's veranda, nursing a mug of tea – two spoons of sugar, well stirred – Mma Matlapeng began the conversation. 'This is our second move in four years, Mma. Two moves in four years. We are very popular with the removal company.'

'They do not like people to stay where they are,' agreed Mma Ramotswe. 'I have seen their advertisements. They say, "Isn't it time you moved?" I don't think that's helpful, Mma. It makes people who would otherwise be quite happy where they are think: oh dear, I'm not moving enough. That's the danger, Mma.'

'Rental property,' said Mma Matlapeng. 'We rent, you see. We have a house down in Lobatse, but we rent that out now that our work brings us up to Gaborone.'

'Oh yes?'

'Yes. And if you rent, they often won't give you a lease for more than a year or two because the owner wants to get back into the house, or wants to sell it, or something else. That's why we moved from the last place. We were on the edge of the village, back there near the old Gaborone Club – you know that place. And the people who owned the house wanted it for their daughter, who had just got married. She was a very self-satisfied young woman, Mma. Entitlement is what they call it. She was entitled.'

'Spoiled?' said Mma Ramotswe.

'Definitely, oh definitely. One hundred per cent spoiled. Doting parents.' Mma Matlapeng sighed. 'I have met many of those, Mma. I'm a teacher, you see.'

Mma Ramotswe was not surprised. There was something about Mma Matlapeng's manner that pointed in that direction; and her voice, too: she spoke beautifully, with a clear diction that stood out in a time when so many people rushed their words. Mma Ramotswe could not understand that: there was plenty of time in the world for us to say everything we wanted to say. We did not need to hurry to get it out.

'Yes,' continued Mma Matlapeng. 'I'm teaching at that school just round the corner. You know the place?'

'I have two children there,' said Mma Ramotswe. 'They are foster children, but they have been with us for a long time. They are my children now.'

Mma Matlapeng nodded. 'That is kind of you, Mma. I have taught some foster children before, and they were very happy with their homes.'

'And do you ...' Mma Ramotswe began.

'I have two daughters,' said Mma Matlapeng. 'They are twins. They are twenty-three now. The years, Mma ...'

'The years go very quickly. Close your eyes, and a year has gone. Just like that.'

'My daughters are both nurses, Mma Ramotswe. They are working out at the hospital at Molepolole. They trained together and now they are working on the same ward. They are inseparable.'

'You must be proud of them, Mma. Two nurses. That is a very fine job.'

'Oh, I am very proud of them,' said Mma Matlapeng. 'Not everybody can be a nurse. It requires a very special sort of character. You have to be patient. You have to be kind. You have not to mind too much if people are difficult because they're feeling ill or frightened. You have to be able to take all of that.'

'And your girls can?'

Mma Matlapeng nodded. 'They don't mind. They have always been like that.'

Mma Ramotswe noticed that Mma Matlapeng had finished her tea. She topped up her cup. 'And you, Mma?' she enquired. 'What do you teach?'

'Mathematics,' replied Mma Matlapeng. 'I teach mathematics to the older children.' She paused. 'Yes, that is what I do, Mma.'

'And your husband, Mma?'

'He is an accountant,' said Mma Matlapeng.

Mma Ramotswe noticed a change in her tone. You could always tell how somebody felt about somebody else by the way they spoke. There was warmth or coldness according to the state of the heart.

Now Mma Matlapeng continued, in the same, suddenly flat tone, 'He is a big bankruptcy man. If you are going to go bankrupt, you go to see him. He takes over. He fires all the staff and sells the stock and, *bang*, you're bankrupt.'

Mma Ramotswe was silent. The No. 1 Ladies' Detective Agency did not make much profit. In fact, at the end of some months, when she steeled herself to look at the books, it seemed that her business had made no profit at all. Rra Matlapeng no doubt would confirm that if he came round and took a look, then, as his wife had just said, it would be a case of 'Bang, you're bankrupt!'

Mma Matlapeng sipped at her tea. 'He is away on business now. He is up in Francistown. Somebody up there is going bankrupt. *Bang.*'

Mma Ramotswe clicked her tongue sympathetically. 'So many businesses spend all their time on the edge of bankruptcy,' she said. 'My own little agency ...' She sighed. 'We stay afloat, but sometimes I think we are sinking.'

Mma Matlapeng's reply took her by surprise. 'We're all sinking, Mma. Even those of us who are floating, are sinking.'

Mma Ramotswe was not sure how to respond. To a certain extent, she thought, what Mma Matlapeng said was true: nobody was getting any younger, and that meant that most of us were slowing down, even if imperceptibly. And there was also gravity to be considered: as you went through life, the effects of gravity seemed to get more and more and more pronounced: you felt that, you really did. But even if this were all true, there was no cause to dwell on it, and certainly no reason to say that we were all sinking.

She smiled at her guest. 'I don't know about that, Mma,' she said. 'If we stopped swimming we would certainly sink – but we're not going to stop swimming, are we?'

Mma Matlapeng had been about to say something more, but this remark brought her up short. 'That's an interesting way of putting it, Mma,' she said. 'If we stopped swimming . . .' Her voice trailed off. 'Stopped swimming . . .'

Mma Ramotswe felt emboldened. Mma Matlapeng was better educated than she was. She had left school at sixteen, whereas Mma Matlapeng must be a university graduate, with a degree in mathematics, of all subjects. That was impressive by any standards: there were people with degrees that did not involve all that much work, but mathematics . . . So, with the respect that Batswana people feel for education, Mma Ramotswe stood in some awe of a mathematics teacher, but when it came to knowing how to cope with life, then she had no reason to defer to anybody. And now she had said something that had clearly impressed Mma Matlapeng, for all that she had a degree in mathematics. So she said, 'Yes, life is like . . .' She paused. The swimming metaphor had come without much thought, but its further development was not proving easy.

'Like swimming?' Mma Matlapeng suggested.

Mma Ramotswe hesitated. That was not what she had been going to say. She had never learned to swim, and she was not sure now why she should say that life was like swimming. It was possible that it was, but on the other hand there were probably many other things that life was like – once you started to think about it.

'Life is like a river,' she said at last.

Mma Matlapeng nodded. 'I suppose it is. Yes, it is a river, I suppose.' She looked at Mma Ramotswe, as if waiting for more, but nothing was said.

Mma Ramotswe looked down at her hands. She stole a glance at Mma Matlapeng. She had learned in life not to make too many snap judgements of people – that, she thought, was one of the main lessons we learned as we got older – but she still found that her initial instincts were often correct. People revealed their characters to you without too much encouragement; you simply had to listen. Or they might do so even without saying very much: in the expression on their face; in the look in their eyes. Eyes, in particular, were revealing. A malevolent disposition always showed in the eyes, in the way in which the light shone out of them. If that light was gentle, if it reassured you, then you could be confident that the person within was of that temper. But if it was hard, if it was hostile, then you could count on there being a character to match within.

For a second or two she watched Mma Matlapeng as her neighbour reached forward to pick up her mug of tea. Their eyes met, very briefly, and the light that she saw in the other woman's was unmistakable.

Mma Ramotswe said, 'My husband is away too. Not away away – not in Francistown or anywhere like that – but out in Tlokweng. I am going to have dinner by myself, Mma. I have a chicken in the pot.'

Mma Matlapeng smiled. 'I smelled it, Mma. I sat here thinking: Mma Ramotswe is going to have chicken for her dinner. She is very lucky.' She took a sip of her tea. 'Perhaps I should be a detective – like you, Mma.'

They laughed.

'Anybody can be a detective,' said Mma Ramotswe. 'I had no training. But not everybody can be a teacher of mathematics, I think. Certainly not me.'

Mma Matlapeng was modest. 'It is not all that difficult, Mma. Numbers always behave according to some simple rules. Learn those rules and – *bang!* – you are doing mathematics.'

Mma Ramotswe noticed the *bang*. It was the second time Mma Matlapeng had used the word. There had been bankruptcy *bang*, and now there was mathematics *bang*.

Mma Matlapeng referred back to what had been said about training. 'Somebody must have taught you something, Mma,' she said. 'Nobody does a job without at least some training.'

'I had a book,' said Mma Ramotswe. 'There is a very good book on the subject by somebody called Clovis Andersen. He is an American. I know him, actually. He came to Botswana once and my assistant and I met him. Mma Makutsi. She works with me. We both met Mr Andersen.'

'And this book tells you everything you need to know?'

Mma Ramotswe nodded. 'Yes. He sets out a lot of rules.'

'Propositions?'

'Yes, you can call them propositions. They are all about what you should do when investigating a matter for your client. Often they are simply rules of common sense – about how to draw a conclusion, that sort of thing.'

'Logic?' suggested Mma Matlapeng.

'Yes. He talks about that, Mma. About not judging people before you have evidence. About not believing what you want to believe rather than paying attention to what your eyes or ears tell you.'

Mma Matlapeng said that this all sounded very sensible to her. Then she sniffed at the air and said, 'Chicken is one of my favourites. My grandmother used to make us chicken on Sundays. We went to her house and she had a big pot of chicken and she always gave me and my brother the feet.'

They both knew what that meant. Chicken feet were the favourite part of the chicken in Botswana.

'You must have been happy,' said Mma Ramotswe.

Mma Matlapeng turned to her. 'Happy?'

'Yes, you must have been happy at your grandmother's house. With the chicken for lunch, and your grandmother. What else do we need to be happy?'

Mma Matlapeng smiled, and Mma Ramotswe saw that the smile was rueful. She made her decision. 'Mma,' she said, 'I have a whole chicken in the pot, but there is only one of me. My husband will not be back until, oh, ten o'clock – maybe even later. I have made him a beef sandwich. Will you help me eat my chicken?'

'But, Mma, that is very kind of you. I did not mean to ask you . . . When I said that chicken was my favourite dish, I was just thinking. You know how you do, when you smell something, you think about it and may say something? You do not mean to say, "Can I have some of your food?" I would not say that, Mma.'

Mma Ramotswe assured her that she had not thought that – not for a moment. 'One chicken is too much for one person,' she said. 'You should not eat a whole chicken.' It was what she had planned to do, but you should always be prepared to change your plans, she told herself. And if the plans had been slightly greedy plans, then you would always feel better after you had changed them.

'Then I will help you, Mma.'

'That is very kind of you, Mma.'

Mma Matlapeng looked at her watch. 'I will go home and get

out of these gardening clothes. They are very dusty. Then I will come back.'

'We will eat in the kitchen,' said Mma Ramotswe. 'It is easier that way.'

'The best place to eat,' said Mma Matlapeng, as she rose to her feet.

They sat at the kitchen table, the pot of chicken between them. The conversation had flowed easily, and Mma Ramotswe had found that her initial impression of Mma Matlapeng was confirmed. She liked her, and found herself wondering whether this was the same woman whom she had heard shouting at her husband. Was this courteous and engaging woman the same person who had been hurling insults, including that colourful comparison with an anteater? It was hard to imagine that, and yet, as she had found time and time again in the course of her professional duties, one should never be surprised by anything one found out to be going on in a marriage.

Mma Matlapeng told her more about her background. Her father, she said, had been a school inspector. He was a graduate, in history, of Fort Hare, and could have had a career in politics but had had no stomach for arguments.

'He could never see why people couldn't co-operate,' she said. 'He said that he could see good points in all the different parties, and yet they were always running one another down.'

Mma Ramotswe agreed with that. She thought it ridiculous that party leaders refused to recognise that their opponents could get at least some things right. 'And they are so quick to insult one another,' she said. 'I can't stand hearing people insult one another, Mma ...' She stopped herself. She had not intended to stray onto that ground.

Fortunately, Mma Matlapeng did not appear to notice.

'He knew Seretse Khama,' she said. 'He could have been minister of education in his government, I think, but he wanted to stay in the civil service. He was a civil service man at heart.'

'I would not like to be in the government,' said Mma Ramotswe. 'You would have no peace, I think. Problems, problems, problems – every day. That is what it's like being in the government. You have all these problems and then there are all those people waiting to find fault with what you're doing. You get no thanks.'

Mma Matlapeng was of the same view. 'If they came to me tomorrow and asked me to be minister of something or other, I would say no. I wouldn't hesitate – I would just say no.'

'That would be best,' said Mma Ramotswe. Then she asked, 'Are you happy in your job, Mma? Do you like teaching mathematics?'

Mma Matlapeng shrugged. 'I like most of it. Most people like some bits of their jobs and not others. I like it when I get through to some of the kids. Maybe a child who has not been doing well – who has a confidence problem, maybe – and then you show them that they can actually do mathematics rather well, and then you see their face light up and you know that you've got through to them. That is a very special moment.'

'It must be,' said Mma Ramotswe.

'I had a boy, fourteen, maybe fifteen; he was not doing very well in my mathematics class, and so I gave him some extra time in the afternoon. And I managed to get out of him what was bothering him – what was holding him back. You know what it was, Mma? It was his own father. His own father was telling him that he was stupid and would never be any good.'

Mma Ramotswe shook her head. 'There are some very unkind parents,' she said. 'I don't know why they bother to have children.' She paused. 'What did you do, Mma?'

'I let him talk to me. Sometimes half the problem with these children is that nobody ever listens to what they want to say. So I sat there and let him tell me. I heard the lot, Mma. All about his father making him feel small. And the father sounded like a thoroughly nasty piece of work – one of these people who step all over other people. You know the sort.'

'I do,' said Mma Ramotswe, and thought, inevitably, of Violet Sephotho.

'And then a very strange thing happened, Mma,' continued Mma Matlapeng. 'This arrogant father had a big fall. *Bang!* He went bankrupt. My husband told me that he had been appointed to wind up his affairs. I felt sorry for the family, but I was able to talk to the son about it. I did not want to turn him against his father, but I was able to point out to him that his father had shown that he was human, like everybody else. I think it made all the difference, Mma. He had been in awe of his father for a long time; now he could stand up to him – inside.'

'And his mathematics?'

'He started to do very well, Mma. He has gone off now to do a degree in mathematics. He wants to be an actuary. Do you know about actuaries, Mma?'

'They are the people who tell you when you're going to die?'

Mma Matlapeng laughed. 'Well, not you personally – but you as a lady of such and such an age, living in such and such a place, and smoking twenty cigarettes a day, or whatever dangerous things you're doing. Not that you smoke, Mma, I'm not accusing you of that, but some people do. Then *bang*, their arteries get clogged up and they become late. The actuaries can say to these people: you are going to last so many more years because that's what the actuarial tables say about somebody like you.' She paused. 'I'm not sure that it would make me any happier to know when I was going to die, Mma.'

Mma Ramotswe agreed with her on that. That was not knowledge that she wanted to have. She said, almost without thinking about it, 'Are you happy now, Mma? You said that would not make you any happier ...'

Mma Matlapeng frowned. 'Am I happy now?'

'Yes.'

Mma Matlapeng looked away. For some time, she said nothing, and the silence in the kitchen became noticeable. Then, 'You know, Mma, the other day – did you hear something?'

Mma Ramotswe hesitated, but then made her decision. 'I suppose I did, Mma. I heard ...'

She was not sure how to put it. A loud discussion? A little disagreement? There were tactful ways of describing it, but before she could choose which expression to use, Mma Matlapeng continued, 'I am very ashamed, Mma. I have only just moved to this place, and then people hear me shouting.' She paused; she looked shamefaced now. 'And everybody will be thinking: who is this woman who shouts and shouts like that? That's what they'll be thinking, Mma.'

Mma Ramotswe tried to reassure her. 'I hardly heard you, Mma. It was very faint. I really don't think people will be talking.'

Mma Matlapeng reached out and touched Mma Ramotswe's arm briefly. 'You are far too kind, Mma. I'm afraid I lost control. I shouted.'

'We all shout,' said Mma Ramotswe. 'From time to time, that is. Is there anybody – anybody, Mma – who hasn't shouted at one time or another?'

'In private, maybe, Mma. You can shout a little in private, but you have to keep your voice down. I didn't, and now I'm very embarrassed, Mma, because you must be wondering what sort of people have moved in beside you. I wouldn't be surprised, Mma, if you have been thinking that we are a very low sort of person.'

Mma Ramotswe made a dismissive gesture. 'Certainly not, Mma. I have not been thinking that. Although . . . ' She stopped. She had not intended to say anything about her misgivings, and indeed it would be quite inappropriate to mention the single beds.

'Although what, Mma?'

'Although I did wonder if you and your husband were happy together . . . You seemed very cross with him.'

Mma Matlapeng sighed. 'I was. I have been very cross with my husband for ten months now.'

Mma Ramotswe raised an eyebrow. With her experience of matrimonial investigations, there could be only one reason for that: an errant husband. It was a familiar story.

She looked at Mma Matlapeng, who nodded, as if to confirm the suspicions that she imagined were in Mma Ramotswe's mind. Then she said, 'Yes. The usual, Mma.'

'Oh.'

Mma Matlapeng continued, 'I think that one woman does not have to explain these things to another woman. We are all sisters, Mma. We all know how men behave.'

Mma Ramotswe was silent for a few moments. Mma Matlapeng was right, of course; all women knew how men behaved. And although she was not one to consign all men to the crowded ranks of philanderers, many men freely and by their own actions enrolled themselves therein. It was something to do with the way men were *inside*. They had to do these things when common sense and caution, not to say loyalty and simple decency, pointed in the other direction. It was not only tragic – it was puzzling.

She lowered her voice. 'I take it that your husband has . . . has wandered, Mma. I take it that is what you're saying to me?'

Mma Matlapeng inclined her head. Then she raised it, and

gravity of manner was replaced by outrage. 'Yes, he has wandered, Mma.'

Mma Ramotswe made a clicking sound with her tongue. It was a noise that so many women, all over the world, made when they thought of the behaviour of men. It was a universal gesture. 'Men can be very foolish,' she said. 'I believe it is something to do with their brains.'

'I don't think it's their brains,' said Mma Matlapeng. 'The brain often says stop, but the rest of the man is not listening at that point.'

'No, it is in the brain,' insisted Mma Ramotswe. 'Everything we do, Mma, comes from the brain. The brain says, "Do this," and we do it. That is the latest view, Mma.'

'Hormones,' said Mma Matlapeng. 'It is to do with hormones. Hormones are very bad news for men.'

'That is true,' said Mma Ramotswe. 'But the point I'm making, Mma, is that your story must be the commonest story in the country. Up and down the land, there are men being affected by hormones, and doing stupid things.' She sighed once more. 'We women have to live with it, I'm afraid.'

Mma Matlapeng frowned. 'Do we? Do we have to put up with this sort of thing? Why, Mma?'

'Because I don't see men changing,' said Mma Ramotswe. 'We can tell them that we expect better – and that will have some effect – but we are not going to change some things about men. We are not going to be able to change their nature.'

'So, we tolerate it?' asked Mma Matlapeng. And then she continued, 'So, I have to accept that my husband can go off for a weekend with another woman, Mma? Are you suggesting that?'

'Is that what happened?' asked Mma Ramotswe.

Mma Matlapeng did not answer immediately, and Mma Ramotswe wondered whether her question had been too intrusive.

She was about to change the subject when her neighbour suddenly answered, 'Yes. It started about a year ago. I found out quite quickly. A wife can always tell.'

Mma Ramotswe knew what she meant. Over the years she had listened to any number of women in her office saying exactly that. 'You can always tell, Mma,' they would say. 'A wife is never wrong about that sort of thing. Wives have an instinct for such things.' And, by and large, these women who said that were right. Wives could tell, no matter how much their husbands tried to hide what was going on. Women could tell.

'She is another of these bankruptcy people,' Mma Matlapeng continued. 'She works in a different firm, but she does the same sort of thing as he does. They met when a mine went bankrupt.' She gave Mma Ramotswe a sceptical look. 'How can a mine go bankrupt, Mma? All you have to do is dig.'

'I suppose there are wage bills, Mma,' said Mma Ramotswe. 'And then perhaps they dig in the wrong place and they have to start again, and that costs money, and so on. Running a business is not easy. At any moment you can discover that you have no money to pay the bills and none of your clients is replying to your reminder that they should pay the invoice you sent them a month ago. And you don't know where to turn . . . '

Mma Matlapeng thought about this. 'I suppose you're right, Mma, but anyway, he met this woman and she must have encouraged him. You know how there are some women who *encourage* men, Mma. You know about those women?'

Mma Ramotswe indicated that she did. 'There is a well-known woman like that,' she said. 'There is a certain lady in this town called Violet. She is famous for that sort of thing.'

'I have never heard of her,' said Mma Matlapeng. 'This woman is called Rose.'

'They are both names of flowers,' mused Mma Ramotswe. 'Not that there can be any connection, but it's interesting that they should both have flower names.'

Mma Matlapeng tackled a piece of chicken on the side of her plate. 'This chicken is very delicious, Mma,' she said. 'But to get back to this woman. How could she? She knew that he was married. She knew that, and yet she allowed this affair to develop.'

'That is what happens, Mma,' said Mma Ramotswe. 'It is to do with male weakness. Men are weak when it comes to that department, Mma. That is what they are like.'

Mma Matlapeng was having none of that. 'Well, women should tell them that it is not going to happen. If women said "I am not going to have anything to do with a married man" then the man would just go home and behave himself.' She paused. 'I confronted him, Mma. I sat him down in a chair and told him that I knew all about it. He closed his eyes and sank his head in his hands. He said that he would bring it to an end. He said that he did not know what had come over him.'

Mma Ramotswe listened. This was not what usually happened. 'You were lucky, Mma. Often men just say nothing. Or they deny it all and then the next day they disappear with the other woman. There have been many cases like that.'

'I believe that he did as he said he would do,' said Mma Matlapeng. 'She turned up at the house the following day and tried to claim him. Right in front of my nose, Mma. She didn't seem to mind that I knew. She came and tried to drag him away.'

Mma Ramotswe's eyes widened. 'That must have been very awkward, Mma.'

Mma Matlapeng laughed. 'I saw her off,' she said. 'I was in the kitchen when this happened. He was in the garden – he had been washing his car – when she came and grabbed him. I went outside. We had a hosepipe at the side of the house, and he had been using that. I took it and sprayed her with water. She was completely soaked. She was shouting and swearing, Mma – very bad language – but I just turned up the pressure on the tap and tried to get the water into her mouth. She eventually went away, dripping.'

Mma Ramotswe was smiling. She did not approve of violence, but there were times when a bit of gentle force seemed to be justified: people who used bad language should not be surprised if other people came and washed their mouth out with a hosepipe.

'And then I sprayed him too,' continued Mma Matlapeng. 'Just for good measure. I felt very cross, Mma – I hope you can understand why. I soaked him too, and he just stood there because he was in the wrong and could not do anything about it. If you are in the wrong and somebody sprays you with water, you have to accept it.'

Mma Ramotswe was not sure what to say. She could understand how Mma Matlapeng had felt, but she was not certain that this was the way to repair a marriage. So she asked, 'And then, Mma?'

'And then?' echoed Mma Matlapeng. 'And then I told him what he could expect, Mma. I told him that he could stay in the house if he wanted, but that I would not forget what he had done. And that is where we are now, Mma. He is in disgrace. He is like a dog that has stolen the mince and is in disgrace.'

Mma Ramotswe's doubts about the wisdom of this were unassuaged. There was a limit to the extent to which a husband might be punished before it might occur to him to leave. It seemed to her that Mma Matlapeng had embarked on a dangerous strategy. 'You have to be careful with husbands,' she said. 'They might go away if things are too uncomfortable for them. I have seen that happen, Mma.'

'I don't think he will go away,' said Mma Matlapeng. 'I own the farm, you see.'

Mma Ramotswe waited.

'We have a big farm down near Lobatse,' Mma Matlapeng explained, a note of triumph in her voice. 'We have a house in the town, but we also have a farm. It is probably one of the best farms in that part of the country.' She paused, and then, with a smile, continued, 'And it's mine, Mma. It belonged to my parents, who are late, and it is now mine.'

Mma Ramotswe said nothing, but, having first offered the pot to Mma Matlapeng, she helped herself to a chicken drumstick and a spoonful of sauce. There was more pumpkin and a bowl of rice from which she ladled several spoonfuls onto her plate. Then she topped up their water glasses before she tackled her second helping. She needed to think about what Mma Matlapeng had just said: it was the piece of information that made sense of what she had just heard. It was an old, familiar story of a relationship that had gone wrong but that was limping along because of some outside factor – children or property. And both of these, when one thought about them, amounted to the same thing: dependence.

This situation, she thought, was slightly different from the usual case. It was so often the woman who was obliged to remain in an unhappy marriage or partnership because the man held all the financial cards. Here, it was different – she was well off and even if he, as a bankruptcy accountant, was no doubt comfortably placed, the really important asset was hers. And about time, thought Mma Ramotswe – it was about time that men stopped hoarding all the property and allowed women to have their fair share. It would take years – centuries, perhaps – before there was a just division, but at least things were moving in the right direction.

They ate in silence for a while. Mma Ramotswe noticed that

Mma Matlapeng was smiling, as if she were relishing the satisfaction of having an errant husband exactly where she wanted him. Then Mma Ramotswe said, 'And what about the future, Mma?'

Mma Matlapeng laid her knife and fork aside. 'Very good,' she said, and then added, 'I mean the chicken is very good, Mma Ramotswe – not the future. Although I don't see anything wrong with the future.'

Mma Ramotswe considered this. 'The future ... Well, the future, Mma, is ... I mean, what about him, Mma?'

'My husband? He'd better watch out, Mma. If he wants a future – *any* future – he'd better watch out.'

Mma Ramotswe took a deep breath. There was a question that she wanted to ask, but she was not sure whether this was the time to ask it. Perhaps it was.

'Are you going to forgive him, Mma?'

Mma Matlapeng looked astonished. 'Forgive?'

'Yes. Sometimes we do things that we regret. All of us, Mma. We do things and then we think, Oh, goodness, look what I've done. And then we feel very bad about ourselves, and we hope that—'

'That nobody notices?'

Mma Ramotswe shook her head. 'That was not what I was going to say, Mma. I was going to say, "And then we hope that people will forgive us." I think that is what we sometimes hope – often, in fact.'

Mma Matlapeng was concentrating on what Mma Ramotswe said. She was listening. And this encouraged Mma Ramotswe to continue, 'Forgiveness is very powerful, Mma. It can change things completely. It's like the rain that we long for. Everything is dry, dust everywhere, and then the rain comes. You smell it coming and suddenly it is there and it changes everything. You know what that is like, Mma – the first rains.'

Mma Matlapeng was clearly struggling. 'I don't see what the

rain has to do with it, Mma,' she said. 'People still behave badly when it rains.'

Mma Ramotswe shook her head. 'That's not the point, Mma. I'm saying that forgiveness is *like* the rain. That's all I'm saying. It makes things better. Rain does that too. Things grow ...'

Mma Matlapeng went off on another tack. 'But if you forgive people, Mma Ramotswe, then you know what happens?' She did not let Mma Ramotswe respond, but went on to answer her own question. 'If you forgive them, they say, "Good, now I can go and do it again." I'm telling you, Mma – that's how people think. It's just like that in the classroom: you have an unruly pupil and you let him off. The next moment, when you turn your back, he does the same thing again. That's the way it is, Mma.'

Mma Ramotswe looked at her plate, now wiped clean. They had finished the chicken, the two of them, and it was time for a fat cake, dusted in sugar, and a cup of tea perhaps. She offered these to Mma Matlapeng, who accepted with enthusiasm. 'This has been a wonderful dinner, Mma Ramotswe. You are a very good cook, I think.'

Mma Ramotswe took the fat cakes out of the fridge and set them out on two plates. She took a bite, watched by Mma Matlapeng, who was removing excess sugar off the first of her cakes.

'No,' said Mma Matlapeng, as she licked the tip of a finger. 'If you go round forgiving people, then they will be very pleased and will do it again.'

She looked at Mma Ramotswe challengingly as she said this, and Mma Ramotswe almost gave up. But then she thought of Bishop Mwamba, and of what he had said about forgiveness. His words had never left her; she had heard them in the cathedral opposite the hospital, on a warm Sunday morning, with the great ceiling fans above their heads turning slowly. He had said, 'It is our duty to forgive because if we do not, then we sentence ourselves to the repetition of the very things we want to avoid.' And she had thought at the time, yes, that is right: if you forgive somebody, then normal life can resume. You start again.

So she said to Mma Matlapeng, 'We have to forgive, Mma, because it is wrong to hold something against somebody forever.'

Mma Matlapeng was studying her fat cake, poised before her lips. She hesitated.

'We have to, Mma,' Mma Ramotswe continued. 'Because it's cruel to make somebody suffer more than they deserve. Forgiveness stops that.'

Mma Matlapeng continued to study the fat cake. She opened her mouth and took a bite.

'Is that what you really think, Mma?' she said.

'Yes,' said Mma Ramotswe.

She picked up a fat cake and popped it into her mouth. She could no longer talk now, nor could Mma Matlapeng, and so they finished the fat cakes, their mouths full of pleasure.

'Look at the time,' said Mma Matlapeng at last. 'I must go home, Mma. I've enjoyed myself very much, thank you.'

Mma Ramotswe saw her guest out as far as the gate. Then she turned and walked back to the house, through the cool of the evening. Above her, high above her, the constellations of the African sky dipped and swung against the darkness of the night.

Chapter Fourteen

This Is a Big Mess

Mma Makutsi could not contain herself. She arrived early at the office the following morning – a good half an hour before Mma Ramotswe – and had tidied the desks, opened the windows and switched on the kettle by the time Mma Ramotswe's white van swung off the road and was securely parked in its place under the acacia tree.

'You are very early today,' Mma Ramotswe remarked as she entered the office and hung her scarf on the back of her chair. 'A lot of the birds are still in their beds in the trees, and yet the office is already up and running!' She heard the asthmatic hissing of the kettle, and she smiled. 'And I see that the kettle is already heating up. That is all very good, Mma.'

Mma Makutsi waved a hand airily. 'Phuti made an early start today too,' she said. 'He's expecting a big consignment of furniture from over the border and he likes to be there when they unpack it. He says some of the men are very careless.'

Mma Ramotswe shook her head. 'It's a shame, isn't it, Mma Makutsi, that people treat other people's property like that. I think that if something doesn't belong to you, you should be—'

She did not finish. Mma Makutsi waved her hand again. 'Yes, yes, Mma. You're right about that. We should all be careful.' She paused, and then added, 'All the time. We should be careful all the time. But tell me, Mma: what happened? I'm very keen to hear.'

'I shall tell you, Mma,' said Mma Ramotswe. She looked at the kettle. 'That kettle is very old. It takes more and more time to boil. I think that soon we'll have to switch it on when we leave the office the day before so that the water is boiling by the time we arrive in the morning.'

Mma Makutsi sucked in her cheeks. 'Maybe. Maybe. But I was wondering, Mma . . . '

Mma Ramotswe was not deliberately dragging her feet, but she had noticed something different about Mma Makutsi and now realised what it was. 'Your new glasses, Mma,' she exclaimed. 'You've abandoned your new glasses.'

Mma Makutsi's hand shot up to adjust her old, familiar glasses. 'I've decided that this pair is still useful, Mma,' she said. 'I'll keep the other pair for special occasions – when it's important to be fashionable. These will do for everything else.'

Mma Ramotswe suppressed a smile. It was always satisfying to her when functionality won over fashion. In her mind, all the fuss over designer labels was a distraction from the main issue, which was comfort. Things should be comfortable. Shoes should not pinch your feet; glasses should not sit awkwardly on the nose; blouses should not bunch up at the armpits; dresses should not cling to your skin but allow air to circulate freely on a hot day.

Mma Makutsi had good dress sense – even if she tended to prefer colours that were rather too bright, and occasionally clashing – but she was far too easily swayed by the cajolery of commerce. If something was said to be 'the latest thing' then you could be sure that Mma Makutsi would take such a claim seriously, whereas Mma Ramotswe would simply laugh and point out that latest things did not seem to last very long and that many of them, anyway, were instantly recognisable as 'the latest thing' of some years previously, and were now being recycled to a gullible public.

'I like those glasses,' she said. 'I mean, these old ... or, rather, these traditional glasses of yours. I like them a bit more than those new, fashionable ones.'

Mma Makutsi got up from her desk to attend to the kettle, which was now emitting cloudlets of steam from its spout. 'This is a very stupid kettle,' she said. 'But, Mma, let's not talk about kettles and glasses and things. What I am very keen to hear is what happened last night out at Mma Potokwani's place. That is what I want to hear.' She paused. 'And where is Mr J. L. B. Matekoni? And Charlie and Fanwell? Where are all the men?'

Mma Ramotswe laughed. 'That would be a good title for a song, Mma, don't you think? "Where Are All the Men?" It would be a song that many ladies would sing, I think. *Where are all the men, la, la, la? Where are all the men?*'

Mma Makutsi had no time for such frippery. 'Mma, you must tell me. I'm bursting now. I'm bursting with curiosity. Did they move that little elephant?'

Mma Ramotswe sat back in her chair. 'They did, Mma. It all went very well – or rather, it went very well after it went badly. At first it went very badly and then ... well, then, things got better and it went well. Now, I think, it is all going very well again.'

Mma Makutsi poured the hot water into the two teapots – one

containing redbush tea for Mma Ramotswe, and the other containing Five Roses tea for herself.

'Mr J. L. B. Matekoni will be in shortly,' said Mma Ramotswe. 'But I think that Charlie and Fanwell are not expected in until ten o'clock. They were all very late last night, and Mr J. L. B. Matekoni told them they did not need to come in until later. They will be having a long sleep. It was two o'clock, you see, by the time Mr J. L. B. Matekoni got home.'

Mma Makutsi registered her surprise. 'Two o'clock, Mma! What happened? You must tell me.'

She poured them each a mug of tea and then settled in the client's chair, facing Mma Ramotswe across her desk.

Mma Ramotswe took her first sip of redbush tea. 'He was very tired when he got home. I was asleep, but I always wake up if somebody comes into the room. He said that I should go back to sleep as everything was all right and I did not need to worry. But I was awake by then, and so I got him to tell me exactly what had happened.'

'Which was what, Mma?'

'Which was that they had an accident on the way to Mma Potokwani's. My poor van, Mma, it has more scrapes down the side from toppling into a ditch. The elephant moved, you see, and that disturbed the van's balance.'

'Oh, Mma!' exclaimed Mma Makutsi. 'I'm so sorry to hear that. Your poor van is being trampled by elephants and then driven into a ditch. And then there are its suspension troubles . . . How much more can it bear?'

'It is very strong,' said Mma Ramotswe. 'That van has a very strong heart inside it. It will be all right.'

'So what happened then, Mma?'

Mma Ramotswe explained how the accident had occurred very

near the Orphan Farm and how they had managed to complete the trip after righting the van. 'Without the baby elephant, of course. It had run off into the bush and it was very dark. They could not see where it had gone and so they went to tell Mma Potokwani about what had happened.'

'And she said?'

'She said that Charlie should go out into the bush to wait for the elephant to come to him. She said that these little elephants think that the person looking after them is their mother. She said that this would bring him back to Charlie.'

Mma Makutsi listened in fascination. 'They are very strange creatures,' she said. 'They think just like us. They have very large brains, I believe.'

Mma Ramotswe continued her account. 'Mr J. L. B. Matekoni eventually went out with the two boys. Young men, of course – they are no longer boys.'

'Sometimes,' said Mma Makutsi.

'Anyway, he did not want them to get lost or get into some sort of trouble, and so he went with them in the end. And they wandered about through the bush – rather them than me, Mma.'

'Me too,' agreed Mma Makutsi, with a shiver.

'And then, after hours and hours, the little elephant suddenly appeared from behind some trees and rushed up to Charlie. They had its bottle with them and they gave it the formula they've been feeding it. It was very thirsty, and they used the bottle to make sure it stayed with them on the way back to the Orphan Farm. Then they put it in the cattle stockade that Mma Potokwani had fixed up for them, and that's where it is right now.'

Mma Makutsi, who had been on the edge of her seat during this story, sat back. 'Well, well,' she said. 'That is a very good ending, Mma.' She hesitated. 'But what now?'

'Mma Potokwani has been in touch with her friend up north. There is an American lady who has a place up near Maun. They look after elephants that have lost their mothers. She is sending a truck. They'll take it up there. They'll give it a home.'

Mma Makutsi picked up her mug. 'I'm pleased, Mma.'

'So am I,' said Mma Ramotswe.

She looked out of the window, at the patch of sky it revealed. Had it darkened? She thought perhaps it had, and she stood up to get a better view.

'Take a look up there,' she said to Mma Makutsi. 'Do you think those are rain clouds, Mma – or do you think it's just the heat?'

Mma Makutsi stood up. She adjusted her glasses, her large, round glasses, and for a moment Mma Ramotswe saw herself reflected in the lenses. So that, she thought, is what Mma Makutsi sees when she looks at me.

'I think that might be rain,' said Mma Makutsi. 'Yes, I think so. I hope so.'

They finished their tea.

'We have some difficult business today,' said Mma Ramotswe, as she drained her cup. 'I've been trying not to think about it, but I'll have to do something, I'm afraid. And I was hoping that you would come and help me, Mma.'

Mma Makutsi knew immediately what it was. 'Blessing?' she asked.

'Yes,' said Mma Ramotswe. 'I'm going to have to go and see her.'

Mma Makutsi waited, but then she prompted, 'And sort it out, Mma?'

Mma Ramotswe bit her lip. 'I have to. I can't ignore her. She's a cousin – even if a very remote one.'

Mma Makutsi sighed. 'They're trying to trick you, Mma. That man is acting.'

228

'But you heard from the magistrate. She told you. He really was convicted.'

'Yes, but ... But even if that part of the story is true, this business about the operation is obviously a lie. It's a trick to get you to make you give them money. That's all it is, Mma.' She looked at Mma Ramotswe. This good woman, this generous woman, was obviously a tempting target for a couple of confidence tricksters. But such people always were: good people were the ideal victims.

Mma Ramotswe was decisive. 'We need to go down there,' she said.

Mma Makutsi glanced out of the window. 'What if it rains? That road down there will be difficult.'

Mma Ramotswe was confident. 'My van has had worse things happen to it,' she said, with a grin. 'And so have we, Mma Makutsi.'

Mma Makutsi was largely silent on the way down to Blessing's village. Mma Ramotswe knew the reason for this: when her colleague had misgivings about something, she usually expressed these through silence. This, in a way, was a far more eloquent way of expressing opposition than by saying directly why she felt as she did. And now, as the tiny white van bumped its way along the rough track to the village, the silence was a pointed one.

The sky had darkened behind them as they set off on the Lobatse Road; large purple clouds, heavy with rain, had stacked up in the north-west and were moving slowly south. The intentions of these clouds were clear enough: within a short time, a few hours at the most, they would discharge their liquid burden in a heavy deluge. The sky would become white with rain, falling in great curtain sweeps across the land, blown into lashing, cleansing showers. And when that happened, the very earth would seem to leap up into the embrace of the longed-for rain, with dust and soil being confused in a brown blur. Tracks like the one they were on would become seas of mud, with puddles like minor lakes stretching across fields, bordered by ditches that had become narrow fast-flowing rivers. But that had not yet happened as Mma Ramotswe drew up in front of Blessing's house and suggested to Mma Makutsi that they should watch the time. 'Twenty minutes at the most, Mma,' she said, glancing over her shoulder at the storm clouds.

'If that,' muttered Mma Makutsi.

They had been spotted, and as they made their way up the front path, Blessing appeared in the doorway.

She appeared to be surprised. 'Mma Ramotswe!' she exclaimed. 'And Mma Makutsi too. You are bringing us rain. *Pula! Pula! Pula!*' The Setswana word for rain was also the word for good luck – and repeated thus was an invocation of good fortune. It also meant 'money', of course, but in these circumstances, Mma Ramotswe thought, that was a bit unfortunate.

They went inside, where Blessing offered them tea. From the room off the living room, a cough was heard.

'That is my mother,' said Blessing. 'She is sleeping today, but she still coughs in her sleep. She does not wake up so much these days.'

'I thought that I should come to see you, Mma,' said Mma Ramotswe. 'I needed to talk to you in person.'

'You are always welcome, Mma,' said Blessing, her gaze shifting anxiously from Mma Ramotswe to Mma Makutsi, and then back again.

Mma Ramotswe clasped her hands together. She knew what she had to do, but she was not finding it easy.

'You came to see me about Tefo,' she said.

'Yes,' said Blessing. 'The cousin.'

Mma Makutsi exchanged glances with Mma Ramotswe.

'Yes,' said Mma Ramotswe. 'But he is also your friend, isn't he? Your husband, maybe.'

Blessing lowered her gaze. 'He is not a close cousin, Mma.'

'That is not my business,' said Mma Ramotswe.

'You can marry somebody who is not a very close cousin,' said Blessing, her voice rising.

'I know that, Mma,' said Mma Ramotswe calmly. 'But I didn't come to talk about that. I came to tell you why I can't help. I think I must tell you that, rather than ignore your cry for help. You are my cousin and I must speak to you directly.'

Blessing was tight-lipped.

'We do not think that Tefo really needs an operation, Mma. We think that you are trying to get money from me for some other reason.'

She sat back. She had said it.

Blessing's hands shot up to her face. 'Oh, Mma,' she wailed. 'You are accusing me.'

Mma Makutsi had been silent until then, but now she said, 'We are, Mma. We're accusing you – and him too. We're accusing you both of lying.'

Blessing wailed again. 'You are sitting there, in my own house, and telling me that I'm a liar. You are doing that, Mma Ramotswe. I cannot believe it.'

Mma Ramotswe winced. 'We've found out something about the past,' she said, trying to keep her voice even. 'We found out that you had been convicted of stock theft and that Tefo's conviction was really for something that you had done, Mma. If you had been convicted a second time, you would have received a very severe sentence. You didn't want that, and so you made him take the blame. You knew that would have bad consequences for him, but you thought it better than your going to jail.'

It took Blessing a few moments to respond. When she did so, it was through tears. 'How can you say such a thing, Mma? How can you?'

'Because it's what happened,' Mma Makutsi said.

Blessing turned to her. 'You keep quiet, you stupid woman. Who do you think you are?'

'I am a detective,' said Mma Makutsi through clenched teeth. 'And I can spot a thief when I see one.'

Mma Ramotswe tried to stop Mma Makutsi, but failed. Inwardly she groaned; the situation, she thought, was now irretrievable, and it might be best if they were to leave.

Blessing rose to her feet in indignation. 'I am *not* a thief! I am *not*!' She paused. She was shaking, and her fists were clenched tight. Mma Ramotswe spotted that, and the sight disturbed her. She had always believed that clenched fists were a sign of innocence. There was nothing about that in Clovis Andersen's *The Principles of Private Detection*, but she was convinced that it was true, and now, seeing Blessing's fists closed in this way she began to have her doubts. 'Please, Mma, I only wanted to say—'

She was cut off by Blessing. 'He did it once, Mma. I know that. And I protected him. The second time was not him at all, Mma. I was the victim of a man who had become very envious of me. He framed me, Mma, and there was nothing we could do. The evidence was planted by this other man who is now late.'

Mma Ramotswe drew in her breath. 'What are you saying, Mma?' she asked. 'Are you saying that you took the blame for him the first time? That you were wrongly convicted?'

'Yes!' shouted Blessing. 'That's exactly what I *am* saying, Mma. Tefo did take something on that first occasion. I had to take the blame then, because if he had been convicted they would have deported him. I told him that he was never to do it again and that

I would throw him out if he did. But he did not. He was genuinely sorry, Mma.' She wiped the tears off her cheek. She was calmer now, her voice more level.

Mma Ramotswe waited for her to continue.

'And then, much later, I was found in possession of an animal that they said I had stolen. I did not steal it, Mma – it was planted in my herd by a disgruntled herdboy. But it looked very bad for me, because the herdboy had put my brand on it – over the real owner's brand.'

Mma Ramotswe nodded her head. She understood: it would be easy to frame somebody in that way – if you had access to the other person's brand.

'If I had been convicted,' Blessing went on, 'I could have been sent to prison because it would be a second conviction for me. So Tefo had to confess and say that it was him rather than me. They charged him. We were lucky that they did not deport him, but at that stage he had children here and we were told that he would probably not be made to leave the country. So he confessed to something that neither of us had done.'

Mma Ramotswe looked at Mma Makutsi, who seemed nonplussed by this disclosure. But after a few moments, Mma Makutsi said, 'I am very sorry, Mma. I should not have called you a thief.'

Mma Ramotswe sighed. 'This is a big mess,' she said.

'A very big mess,' echoed Mma Makutsi.

'Where is Tefo now?' asked Mma Ramotswe.

Blessing sniffed, and Mma Ramotswe wondered whether her question would inadvertently trigger a further bout of sobbing.

'He is in hospital. He is having the operation.'

The silence was profound.

Then Mma Makutsi said, 'Operation, Mma? What operation?'

Blessing turned to her. 'For his hip. He is having a new hip put in.'

Mma Makutsi looked at Mma Ramotswe.

'Where?' asked Mma Ramotswe.

Blessing pointed to her own hip. 'Here.'

'No, I mean, which hospital, Mma?'

'There is a missionary doctor,' said Blessing. 'He comes from New York. He is a very good man, Mma – he was a very famous doctor over there and now he is spending a year here with us. He is doing free operations for people who cannot get them from the government. They pay the government hospital to use their theatre. He is doing it for Tefo.' Then she continued, 'Both his hips hurt, Mma, but only one needs to be replaced at this point. The other one is not ready.'

Mma Ramotswe exchanged a glance with Mma Makutsi, who dropped her eyes with guilt. That was the explanation for what they had seen as acting, and not very good acting at that.

Mma Ramotswe reached out. She took Blessing's hand. 'I am so sorry, Mma. I was wrong. I was completely wrong.'

Blessing clasped her hand. 'I don't mind, Mma. We can forget it.'

'I would like to give you some money,' said Ma Ramotswe. 'It cannot be much. But it might help for when he gets back.'

Blessing hesitated. 'I don't need it, Mma. You are very kind – but I don't need it.'

Mma Ramotswe insisted. 'We all need money, Mma. And it will help to buy him some good meat for when he comes home.'

'Good Botswana beef,' said Mma Makutsi. 'That is very good for men when they have had an operation and need to recover their strength.'

Blessing agreed, although she was still clearly reluctant to take the money. And then, after an envelope had been slipped into her hand, Mma Ramotswe and Mma Makutsi left, just as the first drops of rain were beginning to fall. 'At last,' said Mma Ramotswe. 'At last, the rain.'

They had negotiated their way back up the track before the storm made a sea of mud of it. Then, back on the tarmac road that led into town, with the rain drumming on the roof of the cab and the wipers swishing back and forwards, Mma Ramotswe said, 'It is very easy to be wrong, Mma. That is what I am thinking at the moment: it is very easy to be entirely wrong.'

And Mma Makutsi, gazing out through the sheets of falling rain, said, 'You're right, Mma. You're right about being wrong.'

Chapter Fifteen

Is It Hard to Raise an Elephant?

It was Mma Potokwani who suggested that the three of them – herself, Mma Makutsi and Mma Ramotswe – should travel north to Maun two weeks later. The rains had set in now – that first storm, through which Mma Ramotswe and Mma Makutsi had driven back to Gaborone – had been the herald of a good season, and throughout the country the reports were of good, soaking downpours. The dams had filled, as dams do, almost miraculously, from the voluminous run-off from the parched earth; the rivers, most of which had for months been no more than dry arteries of sand, were now broad ribbons of muddy water; and everywhere the grass had appeared, springing up through newly softened ground, covering the land with a mantle of green. It was a time of joy, as people saw their cattle become fatter and sleeker before their eyes, and as the air about them that had been so hot and dry became cooler and moister.

Mma Potokwani's suggestion had tickled Mma Makutsi. 'It has never occurred to me, Mma,' she said to Mma Ramotswe, 'to go off on a girls' trip.'

Mma Ramotswe smiled at the thought of being considered one of the girls. Mma Makutsi was young enough, and slender enough, to be so described, but she thought it a bit unrealistic for herself and Mma Potokwani, both of traditional build and matronly status in other respects. But she knew that there were women who treated themselves to trips with their female friends, just as men went off together to fish or to watch soccer or do any of the other things that men liked to do. Why should men have all the fun and leave women behind at home, cooking for the children, and generally keeping the home going?

'Her friends up north invited her,' said Mma Ramotswe. 'They are the people who have taken Charlie's little elephant. They say he is settling in well.'

'And she'd like us to go with her?' asked Mma Makutsi.

'She needs somebody to share the driving. With three of us it would be easier.'

Mma Makutsi was tempted. 'I'm not sure what Phuti would say. He's not very good at looking after himself.'

Mma Ramotswe wagged a finger in mock admonition. 'He needs to learn, Mma. I'm all for looking after men, but they do need to be encouraged to cope by themselves from time to time. It's good for them, I think.'

'Perhaps . . .'

'And there's another thing,' Mma Ramotswe continued. 'If men have a bit of experience looking after themselves, then they will appreciate us all the more when we come back. They will be very relieved that we have returned.'

Mma Makutsi saw the wisdom of that, and she agreed to ask Phuti that evening.

'Don't *ask* him,' said Mma Ramotswe. 'I think you should *tell* him, Mma. Say that we have decided to go off for a few days and you have accepted because you know that he will be able to look after himself. And you have the nanny for Itumelang, anyway. He will not be lonely.'

This gave Mma Makutsi an idea. 'That might be a good business,' she mused. 'There could be an agency that provided husband-sitters for women who needed to go off on business – or on holiday with their friends. They could hire a lady who would come and cook and tidy up and make sure that the husband changed his socks and such things.'

Mma Ramotswe thought that might be dangerous. 'Would there not be a risk that these ladies might move in, so to speak, Mma? They might turn the husbands' heads and then when the wives came back they would discover there is another lady who has taken her place.'

'There might be a slight risk of that,' said Mma Makutsi. 'But the agency would be very careful about the sort of lady they employed. She would have to be a church lady, perhaps, or a lady who is a retired school principal, or a lady police officer – something of that sort. Such ladies would not try anything with the husbands they were sitting.'

But nothing of that sort proved to be necessary. Phuti readily agreed that it would be an enjoyable experience for Mma Makutsi, and Mr J. L. B. Matekoni was also encouraging. He could look after Puso and Motholeli, he said, and he would not mind cooking. He had one or two ideas about what he could make, Mma Ramotswe reported, and even if these were conventional rather than innovative, any expansion of his culinary skills was to be welcomed.

Charlie was disappointed that he would not be included in the party going north; it was his elephant, he claimed, and if anybody deserved to visit it then it should be him. But his air of grievance soon disappeared when Mma Ramotswe pointed out to him that during the four days when they would be away, he would be in sole charge of the agency. 'You will be Acting Manager,' Mma Ramotswe told him. 'You can use my desk, Charlie, and I shall leave some money in the petty cash for you to cover your expenses – your *reasonable* expenses – while Mma Makutsi and I are away.'

There was some discussion as to which vehicle they would use. Mma Potokwani had initially suggested that it should be her car, as the trip was her idea, but had then withdrawn the offer when her husband had pointed out that he might need it for work. That left a choice between Mma Makutsi's car, which was reliable and comparatively new, and Mma Ramotswe's van, which was far from new but could be trusted to do its best. Eventually the van was chosen, as Mma Makutsi had expressed reservations about taking her car on a trip that might involve using rough tracks. 'The main road to Maun itself is fine,' she said, 'but we don't know about the road to this elephant place, do we? My car is heavier than your van, Mma, and it is very sandy up there. What if we get stuck in the sand? Your van can be pulled out easily enough, but my car . . .'

Mma Ramotswe had not argued, and when they set off from Gaborone at six in the morning, the three of them were seated in the front of the van, with Mma Ramotswe at the wheel and Mr J. L. B. Matekoni and the children, Phuti, and Mma Potokwani's husband waving them on their way at the gate. As they headed up Zebra Drive the van gave a slight lurch, as if a fuel line were objecting to some blockage, but Mma Ramotswe was unfazed. 'It often does that early in the morning,' she reassured her friends. 'It is something to do with the cold. Once the sun comes up, it will go very smoothly.'

And the sun rose not long after that – a great fiery ball floating up over the bushland to the east. By the time they reached the Mochudi turn-off, it was ten degrees up, bathing with gold the distant shape of Mochudi hill and the sprawling village about its skirts; then Mosomane, Dibete, Mahalapye, Palapye – a roll call of the towns that punctuated the long, straight road north. Shortly after noon, they were in Francistown, and stopped for fuel and tea before setting off on the second leg of the journey. This they planned to break in Nata, a small town on the edge of the Makgadikgadi Pans, where Mma Potokwani had an old friend who had offered to put them up for the night. That there should be such a conveniently placed friend of Mma Potokwani's did not surprise Mma Ramotswe at all, as Mma Potokwani was known for her contacts in every sphere of activity and in every corner of the country. This friend was the chairman of the local council, the owner of a fleet of bulldozers that were used for road maintenance and dam-building all across the northern part of the country. 'He is a big man for digging things,' said Mma Potokwani. 'He has dug many things up there – Francistown, Maun, everywhere. Dams, drainage, roads: that is all his department.'

They were tired by the journey but while Mma Potokwani caught up with her friends, Mma Ramotswe and Mma Makutsi went for a walk before dinner, to stretch their legs. It was different there: the sky, the light, the smell of the land – all of these were of a different nature, as if they belonged to another country altogether. As in the south, the horizons were flat, and far away, but here there was a shimmering line of heat haze just above them, a dancing in the air that came with the burning-off of water from the flooded salt pans. Until the rains had arrived, those had been dry, caked expanses of brittle white; now the salt had become grey-blue with water, reflecting the colour of the sky above.

They enjoyed dinner together with their hosts, Mma Potokwani entertaining them all with her stories. They explained the nature of their trip, and the background of Charlie's elephant. The contractor said, 'It is very sad what is happening to elephants. They are being driven out of their other places – up there,' and he waved in the direction of the Zimbabwean border not far away. 'Poachers, you see. They'll take any risk to get the ivory – any risk at all. They're desperate.'

They were silent. It was not easy to see a solution to the problem of human need. It was easy to condemn those who stole, who poached wildlife, until you were asked what would you do if your only other option was starvation? That made it harder.

'So the elephants are migrating,' said Mma Potokwani. 'That is very sad. They come to Botswana because ...'

Their host smiled. 'Because everyone wants to come here. Elephants. People. Everyone.'

Mma Makutsi looked away. 'But we can't take everyone, Rra.'

'I didn't say we could, Mma. I was just pointing out that they want to come. All over the world, I think, it is much the same. People want to escape places where there is war and poverty, and not enough water even. Or too much water. And they look at places where there is peace and good government and they think: why can't I go there? They just want to work and have a roof over their heads and not wake up to the sound of bombs and gunfire. That's all they want.'

'But,' began Mma Makutsi, and stopped. They all knew the arguments. They all knew the hard facts, and yet each knew in their hearts that if they were in the shoes of the unfortunates they would think exactly the same as they did. Of course we would, thought Mma Ramotswe.

There were other things to talk about, and most of these things were not sad, and they were able to laugh at what was said. They heard about a man in Nata who had written a song that everybody was singing – a love song – but then had found himself in trouble with his girlfriend because the words seemed to refer to somebody else and not to her. They heard about a young woman who had recently had triplets and who was going round the village saying that each child had a different father. Mma Potokwani expressed doubt about that, but Mma Makutsi thought that it could be biologically possible – who knows? And as she said this, she and Mma Ramotswe exchanged glances, and they both knew that they were both thinking of Violet Sephotho and her multiple boyfriends during her less-than-distinguished career at the Botswana Secretarial College. Then they listened as their host told them about a dam he had built recently and about how a crocodile had appeared in it shortly after it had filled, and nobody knew where it had come from. 'They can walk very long distances,' said Mma Potokwani. 'They have very short legs, but they can walk a long way. And that proves, I think, what I have always said: be very careful around any river or dam because you never know.'

They did not stay up too late, as they had an early start from Nata the following morning. By seven o'clock they were on the road, and five hours later they arrived at the Elephant Havens camp outside Maun, where they met Mma Potokwani's friends and the small elephant that had briefly been in Charlie's care and was now one of seven orphans being looked after at the camp.

'Look at him,' said Mma Ramotswe, as they were introduced to the tiny waif. 'You can tell that he is happy.'

They took photographs to show Charlie, and then they drank tea with the staff under a sheltering tree. The two founders, Boago Poloko and Debra Stevens, were joined by their manager, Ipeleng Chabata. They told the story of the sanctuary and of other pro-grammes to rescue the orphans left by poaching. 'They shoot the mother,' said Boago. 'And the herd runs off. But the baby stays by the mother because it doesn't know what to do. It's vulner-able then.'

'To?' asked Mma Potokwani.

'Hyenas,' said Boago. 'Lions, too. Any large meat-eater will like a very small elephant that can't defend itself.'

He pointed to a small elephant in an enclosure nearby. It was being fed from a giant suckling bottle, eagerly draining the mixture prepared for it. 'That little one,' he said, 'was very ill when we got her. She had an infection. She was dehydrated too, and that can be very serious. Debra and Ipeleng stayed up with her all night two days in a row.'

'I shall never forget it,' said Debra. 'We thought we'd lose her.'

'And then,' said Ipeleng, 'suddenly, just like that, they can get better. And you see it in their eyes. They tell you: I'm feeling better now. They can say so much to us.'

After their tea, they went to see the pens where the elephants slept. Each one had its own place, with hay and leaves for bed-ding. In the corner, on a raised platform, was a bed for the elephant's keeper.

'Each of them has one person,' Boago explained. 'That is the person who feeds them. They think that he or she is their mother. You know that, I think.' He paused, and pointed to one of the beds. 'But you know what? The keepers usually end up sleeping on the ground, right next to the elephant. Come in here in the morning and you'll see them together. The baby may have its trunk wound across the keeper's shoulder – like a child in bed with its mother. It is a very moving sight, Mma Ramotswe.'

Mma Ramotswe opened her mouth to say something, but she could not think of anything to say. Nor could Mma Makutsi. Only Mma Potokwani, who had seen the same things with human orphans, was able to say, 'I can imagine how it is, Rra. I can just imagine it.'

'Tomorrow morning,' said Boago. 'Get up early enough and you will see it.'

There was more talk of elephants and their ways over dinner that night. Boago explained how an elephant orphan project would try to create a new herd and then gradually release its members back into the wild. That was what they were doing there, he said. It had been done before, he told them, in other schemes. And when the elephants were released they came back – frequently at first, but then less often as they created their own lives. 'But there's an amazing thing,' he continued. 'They will bring their children back to introduce them to their old keepers. They bring them back to the camp shortly after they are born. Elephants are very proud of their children.'

Dinner was served under the same tree whose branches were the umbrella for all social meetings in the camp. As they sat around the fire on which their dinner had been cooked, there was darkness all about them. Above them the night sky, there on the edge of the Okavango Delta, as pure and unsullied as any sky could be. The absence of a moon that night made the heavens white with stars, including, down towards the horizon, the angled constellation of the Southern Cross. Mma Ramotswe pointed it out and said, 'When I was a little girl, I thought that was suspended in the sky by wires. I thought that.'

'Children believe so many things,' said Mma Makutsi. 'I thought

Santa Claus lived in Francistown and came down to Gaborone by train.'

'We have to believe in something,' said Mma Potokwani, adding, 'Don't we? Because if we don't, then why bother ...' She pointed towards the elephant pens. 'Why bother with this, or anything really?'

Mma Makutsi thought about this – she broadly agreed – as did Mma Ramotswe, who had always thought it a great pity that some people went through life without seeming to believe in any-thing – even kindness, or happiness, or the importance of cooking pumpkin the right way. You did not necessarily have to believe in big things – small things would do. But you had to believe in them and you had to do what you could to make them come about. That was important.

Debra asked them about Charlie. 'This young man who looked after the elephant down in Gaborone – could you tell me about him?'

It was Mma Makutsi who answered. 'He is our assistant. Very junior.'

'But doing very well,' Mma Ramotswe interjected.

'He is certainly trying,' conceded Mma Makutsi. 'One day he will be better at everything – I hope.' She thought for a moment. 'He was good at this, though, Mma. He was very kind to the little elephant and I think he will be happy when we show him the photographs we have taken of it up here. He will be pleased to see it with its friends.'

Debra smiled. 'Do you think we might be able to bring him up here to see it in its new surroundings?'

Mma Ramotswe hesitated, but then thought: why not? Charlie had never had a paid holiday and he deserved one, she thought. And Mma Makutsi was thinking exactly the same thing, as she now said, 'Phuti and I could stand him to the trip, I think. We'll get his bus fare.'

'That will be wonderful,' said Debra. 'That little elephant will remember him, you know.'

And then, just before they all went off to bed, and the last logs of the fire were crackling into embers, Mma Ramostwe asked, 'Is it hard to raise an elephant?'

It was some minutes before anybody answered. But then Debra said, 'I don't think so, Mma. It's not hard to do anything if you do it with love.'

Mma Ramotswe nodded. It was just the right answer – of course it was.

They returned home two days later, having retraced their steps back past the Makgadikgadi Pans and down the long arrow of the Francistown to Gaborone road. Mma Ramotswe did most of the driving at this stage of the trip, as she found that Mma Potokwani drove too slowly and Mma Makutsi drove too fast: she drove at just the right speed, which, although she would never have said so her-self – nor even have entertained a thought to this effect – was how she did everything. Just right. Mr J. L. B. Matekoni would certainly have said that, as would all those who knew her: the world was not always an easy place, and people could so easily get it all wrong – except for Mma Ramotswe, who somehow simply seemed to *know*. And how did that happen? Mr J. L. B. Matekoni sometimes asked himself. Was it to do with the example of her father, the late Obed Ramotswe, of whom people said very much the same sort of thing? Possibly; but then that explanation – the explanation of heredity – did not always work: there were plenty of people who were quite unlike their parents one way or another. There were plenty of good people who had flawed parents, and flawed people who had good parents. So was it to do with the place you were born in – your village – and the people who taught you the things that you needed to learn: your first teacher at school, perhaps, or those who came later? Or was it to do with your friends, with the people you spent your time with and with whom you shared your secrets? Often that was a matter of luck as to who happened to be around at the time when you were ready to send out the first, tentative messages of friendship and of love. So luck could play a large role in it, and it was luck, he thought, that had brought him and Mma Ramotswe together. They might easily have not met; she might so easily have gone to another garage to have her van repaired and quite another mechanic might have been blessed with the fine marriage that he had been vouchsafed. Yes, luck was there, lurking in the shadows, ready to play its role, for better or worse; although one hoped, of course, that it would be for the former.

They dropped Mma Makutsi off first, at her house, where Phuti Radiphuti was waiting, holding Itumelang Andersen Radiphuti, who was waving frantic, childish greetings of delight to his mother. Then Mma Ramotswe drove out to Tlokweng to drop off Mma Potokwani at the Orphan Farm, where a small child suddenly appeared from behind her office and ran to embrace her legs and bury his head in her skirts. And Mma Potokwani looked at Mma Ramotswe and smiled, and Mma Ramotswe's heart gave a lurch, because somehow she felt this whole trip had been about that, about the thing that she was now seeing before her.

And then, at last, she returned to Zebra Drive, and to her own house just as the sun was setting, where she found the children doing their homework, supervised by Mr J. L. B. Matekoni. They all hugged her and gave her a kiss, and she hugged them, and kissed them back. 'I have made dinner for all of us,' said Mr J. L. B. Matekoni. 'It is scrambled eggs, Mma, and fried sausages too. It is in the warming oven – all made in advance.' He spoke so proudly that she did her best to suppress her smile – but it was hard.

After the children had gone to bed, Mma Ramotswe sat on the veranda with Mr J. L. B. Matekoni, and they talked, as they liked to do, while sipping a mug of tea – the last tea of the day, the finale.

He said, 'There was more rain today. People are very happy. And your beans are doing really well, Mma. They are growing and growing. It is all very good.'

Yes, it was all very good, she thought.

Then he said, lowering his voice, although there was no need to do so, 'The neighbours – I have seen them.'

'Oh yes?'

'Yes, I saw them last night, over the fence. I was sitting here, on the veranda, but with no light on. I don't think they would have been able to see me. They were on their veranda and they were playing music. They were dancing, Mma.'

Mma Ramotswe smiled. 'I see.'

'Dancing like teenagers in love, Mma. That sort of dancing.'

Mma Ramotswe's smile broadened. 'Like that? Well, well.' She paused. She was thinking. Then she said, 'You know something, Mr J. L. B. Matekoni? There are times when things work out well. You don't think they will, but they do.'

He laughed. 'Yes, I think you're right, Mma.'

They lapsed into silence. A wind had arisen – and it touched them now, gently, reminding them; and it had rain on its breath, a token of that which heals the things that need to be healed.

Read the next in the series ...

Precious and Grace do not always agree on important issues – one being the complex male psyche. Grace believes that food is the source of men's happiness, while Precious believes that men are not so different from women – they want to be loved and needed, too. It is pride that is so often their undoing.

Mma Ramotswe is reminded of this when her husband is offered a daunting business opportunity; one which, if it fails, threatens their existing livelihood, including the detective agency. Meanwhile, a wealthy client's elderly father has changed his will, making his devoted live-in nurse a significant beneficiary, and the ladies are tasked with uncovering the woman as a fraud.

Professional and moral duty battles with female instinct and Mma Ramotswe is determined not to jump to conclusions until she has all the facts. She knows only too well how cunning people can be. After all, she herself is not beyond a little trickery.

The Joy and Light Bus Company

Coming soon from Little, Brown

Alexander McCall Smith is the author of over one hundred books on a wide array of subjects, including the award-winning The No.1 Ladies' Detective Agency series. He is also the author of the Isabel Dalhousie novels, the Detective Varg novels and the world's longest-running serial novel, *44 Scotland Street*. His books have been translated into forty-six languages. Alexander McCall Smith is Professor Emeritus of Medical Law at the University of Edinburgh and holds honorary doctorates from thirteen universities.